# This is London

by Simon McCleave

A DC Ruth Hunter Murder Case

Book 4

First published by Stamford Publishing in 2021
Copyright © Simon McCleave, 2021

For Eirlys and Dave

# PROLOGUE

It was almost midnight by the time Private Ashley Campbell prepared himself to leave the rec room in Central Block A of Cranleigh Barracks in the heart of Surrey. It was virtually empty. The television blared in the far corner, reporting on an incident that had happened the previous day at Sheffield Wednesday's football ground, Hillsborough. It had been the FA Cup semi-final between Liverpool and Nottingham Forest. News reports said there had been a crush on the terraces and over 90 people had been killed. He couldn't help but be shocked by the footage he had seen on the television. Liverpool fans using advertising boards as make-shift stretchers to ferry the injured over to ambulances. They had created a makeshift morgue in the ground's gymnasium. No-one deserved that.

Ashley glanced at his watch. He was due to take over armed guard duty and would be on until 4am. While on duty, he would be responsible for controlling entry and exit to the barracks. He knew it was unlikely there would be any visitors in the early hours of the morning. He would need to patrol the perimeter of the site, looking out for anything suspicious. The barracks were on high alert ever since MI5 found intelligence that the IRA was planning to attack British Army barracks on the UK mainland. In October 1988, two IRA members used forged British Army identity cards to gain access to the Thiepval Barracks in Lisburn in Northern Ireland. They drove two cars onto the base containing 800 pound bombs. The first car bomb detonated close to the barracks' travel centre, injuring dozens. A second bomb detonated a few minutes later beside the medical centre, which was reduced to rubble. The barracks' warrant officer was killed and thirty-one soldiers seriously injured.

As Ashley headed outside, the base was silent. Recruits were all fast asleep in the accommodation block after a hard day. The afternoon had been taken up with gruelling fire and movement training. With a 30kg backpack and rifle in hand, recruits had to crawl fifteen metres, then sprint fifteen metres, across the muddy Surrey countryside. It was exhausting.

Coming out of the Mess building, Ashley strolled across the gravelled courtyard, heading past the military hospital and St Stephen's Church. His boots crunched noisily in the stillness. As the wind picked up, the air smelt of silage from a nearby farm.

*So much for fresh country air,* he thought dryly to himself.

Up ahead was the wooden guard building, close to the red and white barriers that marked the entrance to the barracks. The high, mesh perimeter fence loomed over him. Although it was only early spring, the night air was warm, and he got a waft of cigarette smoke from somewhere. He guessed that whoever was inside the guard hut was smoking. He'd forgotten which recruit he was replacing.

*I just hope the kettle's boiled so I can get a cuppa,* he thought to himself.

As he got to the door, he peered in through the small glass panel and saw that Private Jackie Rosen was sitting with her boots up on the desk, smoking a cigarette.

'Ash!' she said with a smile, taking her feet down and sitting up.

'All quiet on the Western Front?' he asked, smiling back at her. He liked Jackie. She was a *proper* South Londoner and came from Streatham, which was only a stone's throw from where Ashley hailed from in Peckham.

'Dead as a fucking doornail,' she replied.

'Better quiet than some IRA paddies trying to get in here with a bomb,' Ashley pointed out.

Jackie patted her standard issue L85 rifle. 'At least I'd get to use this bloody thing.'

Ashley grinned. 'Yeah, easy there Rambo.'

With jet black hair and a rounded face, Jackie was a laugh. She gave as good as she got most of the time, although he'd seen the toll that the brutal regime at Cranleigh was having on her. The female recruits were definitely treated worse than the male ones. But then again, the black recruits were also singled out too.

'Guard duty is fucking boring, mate, end of,' she groaned.

'You didn't actually believe those adverts on television, did you?' Ash joked. 'Helicopters, skiing, a quick game of beach volleyball before running around firing a machine gun.'

Jackie snorted. 'Not really. My house was a bloody nightmare, so anything was better than staying there.' She reached down and pulled out a half bottle of rum that she had tucked into the top of her boot. It still had about a third left. 'You want me to leave you this? Makes sitting here a bit more bearable, if you know what I mean?'

'No, ta,' Ashley replied. He wasn't much of a drinker, unlike most of the recruits.

Jackie raised an eyebrow. 'I thought your lot liked a bit of rum?'

*Here we go!*

'My lot?' Ashley asked with a shake of his head. 'Do you mean black people?'

'Yeah, of course,' Jackie shrugged. '*Black* people. Can't say anything else these days can you? My dad still says *coloured* but I know that's not right, is it?'

'No, it's not,' Ashley said, rolling his eyes.

'Why's that then? Why can't I call you my *coloured* friend?'

'If you say I'm *coloured*, it sounds like white people have normal skin but ours is coloured – you know, like it's been coloured in,' Ashley explained to her as best he could.

'My nanna says *darkies,* but I told her off,' Jackie laughed. 'Yeah, I thought black people like rum?'

'My dad does. But then again, he drinks two bottles a day so...'

'Alchy is he?' Jackie asked as she stubbed out her cigarette and got up from the chair.

'Something like that,' Ashley shrugged.

Taking the clipboard, she handed it to him. 'Can I have your autograph, Ash?'

As he signed it, he was aware that Jackie was looking him up and down.

'I don't usually like black fellas,' Jackie admitted. 'But you're really fit. I think it's because your skin's lighter.'

Ashley forced a smile. He wasn't going to explain that he was actually *mixed race* and his mother was white and his father black. 'Is that your attempt to flirt with me?'

'Yeah.' Jackie laughed. 'Not very good is it?'

'No,' Ashley snorted. 'That was about as subtle as that prick Hurst.'

He was referring to Captain Dennis Hurst, one of the officers and instructors. Hurst was unpleasant, volatile and sometimes cruel. Hurst was also a racist and highly inappropriate with the female recruits.

'He squeezed my tits yesterday to make sure I was wearing a bra before we did our 4km run,' Jackie groaned. 'I'd quite happily shoot him, given half a chance.'

Ashley frowned. 'Did you say anything?'

'Like what?' Jackie shrugged. 'I just don't want to get on the wrong side of him. He's a psycho!'

'Neither do I,' Ash agreed. It was a frightening thought.

'And you know what they're like here. They don't give a shit about us or how we're treated.'

Suddenly, there was a noise from outside.

They exchanged a look.

*What the hell was that?*

A figure loomed in the doorway and Ashley felt his stomach tighten.

It was Hurst.

*The Yard Nightclub*
*Rye Lane, Peckham SE15*
*February 1998*

*Wow! She's got incredible, big brown eyes.*

Ashley had been watching the young woman, Alma, DJ'ing for the past hour. He'd managed to get her name earlier at the crowded Peckham bar. He then scanned the packed club. It was a mixed crowd. A group of moody-looking black kids sat in the corner. They were here for the two-step UK garage – Kelly G's remix of *Never Gonna Let You Go* by Tina Moore. The older crowd, who sat at the back, smoking and drinking at tables, were there for the reggae or RnB. And there was a sprinkling of white kids who liked black music and were there for the deep vocal house – Rosie Gaines' *Deeper Than Deep*. Given the club's postcode, SE15, the atmosphere inside was surprisingly calm. Maybe that's because half the crowd had taken pills or MDMA.

Most people's vision of Peckham as *a bit rough around the edges* stemmed from the popular BBC sitcom *Only Fools and Horses*. The postcode was, except for Brixton and Notting Hill, the most ethnically diverse in London. Rye Lane Market sold cheap fruit and vegetables from across the globe, most of which your average Londoner would never have heard of. Plantain, Mamey Sapote, Tamarind or Chayote Squash.

Rye Lane had an abundance of chicken shops and the ever popular *Canavan's Pool Club*. The iconic Bussey building was named after the manufacturer George Bussey and ironically, the building was originally a gun factory and shooting range in the 19th century. Now, a hundred years later, in the 1990s, the building was used to host club nights, exhibitions, screenings and events.

Rye Lane ran half a mile from Peckham High Street, down to the corner of Copeland Road where The Nags Head Pub sat.

'Thought you were gonna buy me a drink?' said a voice.

Ashley turned. Alma was now by his side, giving him a cheeky grin.

As she put a flirtatious arm on his, he smiled back at her. She was black, high cheekbones, with long dark cornrows held back by a thick orange scarf.

*She is definitely a honey,* he thought to himself.

He gestured to the bar. 'What d'you want?'

Nodding towards the doors, she moved closer to talk into his ear. 'Too late. I've got to DJ somewhere else later. Sorry. I'll see you around.'

Ashley shook his head and laughed. 'What? Nah, you can't go just like that.'

She frowned, recalling his name. 'Ashley, right?'

'Yeah,' he nodded. 'Come on. You've got to be giving your number, girl.'

'*Girl?*' she pulled a face. 'I ain't no *girl*.' She kissed her teeth and turned to go. He'd really pissed her off now.

Putting his hand on her shoulder, he shrugged. 'Sorry.'

'Are you actually touching me?' she growled, but he could see there was a little sparkle of something in her eye.

*Is she playing with me? She definitely fancies me.*

'Sorry.' He took his hand away as if he'd just touched molten lava. He then pointed to the box of records that she had carried over from the DJ decks. 'Tell you what. I'll carry your records. Where we going?'

'Where *we* going?'

'Yeah,' Ashley shrugged, giving her his best cheeky grin.

She raised an eyebrow and then laughed. 'Are you for real?'

'They look heavy,' he said with a playful smirk.

She snorted, 'Oh, really. Do they? You're gonna carry my records and now you're coming with me to King's Cross?'

'Why not?' Ashley shrugged. He was certain she fancied him. 'I'll be your bodyguard for the night.'

'Bodyguard?' She laughed and then beckoned him with her finger. 'Come on then, what you waiting for, Mr Bodyguard?'

Grabbing the crate of records, he followed her out of the doors and into the sharp, icy relief of the wintry air. She went over to an old blue Renault 5, popped the boot and pointed. 'Chuck them in there, would you?'

Ashley peered into the messy boot that was filled with empty cans, crisp packets, and general rubbish.

'Bloody hell, looks like someone's emptied a skip in there,' he joked.

'Shut up and put my records in there, *Ashley*.'

'There you go, my lady,' Ashley said with a grin.

'Yeah, and you can stop with all that *my lady* shit! I've gotta get my money,' Alma explained as she turned back towards to the doors into the club. 'I'll only be five minutes.'

'Take your time,' he said with a grin as he leant casually against the car. 'I ain't going nowhere.'

As Alma disappeared, Ashley smiled to himself as he thrust his hands deep into his pockets. He imagined how the rest of the evening was going to go. Off to a club in King's Cross. Maybe get hold of some ecstasy. Convince Alma to come back to his place. Smoke a spliff, few drinks and listen to chilled soul music – and then progress into the bedroom. She seemed pretty feisty, and he found that attractive. He had dated girls before who were timid. Even though it allowed him to run rings around them, he soon lost respect and moved on. If he was ever going to settle down, then he knew deep down he needed a girl like Alma. Someone who could give as good as she got and wouldn't put up with any of his shit.

His attention was drawn to a small group of teenage boys on their bikes. They were on their phones as they slipped drugs hand to hand to punters at the end of the road. It's what he and his brother had been doing ten years earlier, but there weren't any phones in those days. Instead, they used lookouts and runners. And that was why his mother, Beverly, had made him join the army and get away. Ruben had done a decent job of getting out of Peckham and had made a good life for himself.

A shout from across the road startled him. Further down, a vanilla coloured streetlight was flashing intermittently, throwing strobed radiance over the pavement. He couldn't see where the shout had come from. The old recreation ground that ran across the back of the street was in total darkness. He and Ruben used to play football there. Ruben always wanted to be Ian Wright, whereas Ashley pretended to have the silky skills of Laurie Cunningham.

He squinted into the darkness, waiting for his irises to adjust. The only thing that was visible was a shifting in the shadows. He thought he could make out two teenage boys standing with their backs to the fence, virtually motionless.

Out of the shadows, about ten yards away, came a figure. A teenage boy, dark hoodie, dark trackies, orange Nike high-top trainers. Unremarkable. He looked like every other kid from the estate. As he got closer, he glared at Ashley, whose eyes had adjusted to the light. He had a thin mouth, quick eyes, and a mandatory line shaved into his right eyebrow. Ashley braced himself. He'd been in far more dangerous situations than this. Although, he had normally been armed with a Heckler & Koch SA80 L85 assault rifle, to be fair.

The boy walked by and they locked eyes for a few seconds. It was the standard kind of bravado that teens in that area exhibited all the time. The only problem was that a surly '*What you lookin' at, blud?'* sometimes escalated into a fatal knife fight.

The boy walked away, heading for Peckham High Street.

Then everything went quiet for a few seconds.

The wind picked up and an empty coke can came skittering down the pavement, rolled noisily out into the road and stopped.

Taking his hands out of his pockets, he felt a little uneasy. He put his hands on the roof of the car and drummed his fingers.

*What's taking her so long?* he wondered.

In the distance, he heard a police siren. It wasn't a big surprise in South London. It was a familiar piece of the audio tapestry of SE15.

The only noise now was the thudding bass from the club.

Suddenly, Ashley felt a piercing cold pain in his lower back, just below his rib cage.

*Jesus! What the hell is that?*

It took his breath away.

Spinning around, he saw a figure in a hoodie and mask. The figure stabbed him again, this time in his lower stomach. The figure then turned, broke into a run and headed towards the estate.

*What the hell is just happened?*

Clutching at his back, Ashley could see his hand was covered with warm blood. His t-shirt was already sticky from the stomach wound. He winced at the pain as the energy drained out of him and he slowly sunk to the pavement.

*Come on, Ashley. You got this! Stay calm, mate, stay nice and calm.*

'Help!' he yelled, but his voice was weaker than he thought it would be.

*Shit! If I'm not careful, I'm gonna bleed out here!*

He tried not to let the thought of that paralyse him with fear.

'Somebody help me! Please!' he shouted.

He'd been trained not to give up. He was trained to remain calm and think clearly under the most horrendous of circumstances. When two of his platoon had been blown to pieces by an IED in Kuwait. When a suicide bomber attacked a market they were protecting and killed seven children.

'Come on! Help! I need some help here!'

The strength was ebbing from him by the second. He lay down on the cold pavement and stared up at the star speckled sky in despair.

*Come on! I didn't serve my country to die like this on a back-street in Peckham.*

He choked on something in his throat. It was blood.

As his breathing became shallow, he could feel his body shutting down.

Everything went black.

# CHAPTER 1

*3 hours later*

By the time Detective Constable Ruth Hunter and Detective Constable Lucy Henry arrived at a side road off Peckham High Street, the area was awash with blue flashing lights. Uniformed officers were busy taking statements, keeping bystanders back and cordoning off the crime scene. The SOCO team, scene of crime officers, had just arrived and had begun to take photos of the area.

Ruth and Lucy flashed their warrant cards at the young female PC who stood holding the scene log and was taking note of everyone who entered and left the crime scene itself.

'DC Hunter and DC Henry, Peckham CID,' Ruth said, peering over at the body on the pavement. It now had a white linen sheet placed over it by the paramedics once they had verified that the victim had died at the scene.

'What have we got, Constable?' Lucy asked.

'Victim was stabbed,' the PC explained. 'No wallet or phone, so we couldn't ID him.'

'Anything else?' Ruth asked.

The PC took out a small evidence bag. 'He had car and house keys on him.'

Lucy shrugged. 'Sounds like it might have been a mugging.'

'Maybe we can get a fingerprint or DNA off the keys if we're struggling to ID him,' Ruth said, thinking out loud.

'Ma'am, he's got a military tattoo on his forearm,' the PC explained.

'Okay,' Lucy said with a grateful nod.

'Anyone see anything?' Ruth asked.

The PC gestured to the club and then peered down at her notepad. 'A woman in there. An Alma Salihu. She said the victim's name is Ashley. She said she didn't really know him, but he had helped her put her records in her car. By the time she got back, he was unconscious on the pavement. He was dead by the time the paramedics arrived.'

Lucy pulled a face. 'Records?'

'Yeah, she'd been DJ'ing in The Yard club,' the PC explained, pointing to a pair of black double doors on a nearby building. 'She's still in there if you want to have a word?'

'How is she?' Ruth asked.

'Very shaken, ma'am.'

The PC lifted the blue police crime scene tape as they approached the body. The SOCOs were erecting a Forensic Tent and had wheeled two large forensic arc lights over to the scene. Another officer was setting up a portable generator, which would be used to power the lights.

'What do you think?' Lucy asked.

'I dunno. He's standing outside waiting for the DJ. Someone pulls a knife, stabs and mugs him,' Ruth replied with a shrug. 'Maybe it's as simple as that.'

'If he's ex-army, he might have put up a struggle,' Lucy suggested.

As they reached the body, a SOCO pulled back the sheet as one of the halogen arc lights burst into life.

Snapping on her forensic gloves, Ruth crouched down to look at the victim. He was mixed race, probably mid-30s, cropped hair and muscular. His jacket was open and the t-shirt he wore underneath was soaked with blood, as was the pavement underneath.

'Looks like he bled out,' Lucy commented.

Taking a pen from her jacket, Ruth used it to move the jacket back. A dark burgundy slit in the t-shirt's material revealed the location of the victim's stab wound. She glanced at his neck to see if he was wearing any kind of jewellery that might help identify him. Nothing.

'No defensive wounds that I can see,' Ruth said as she inspected the palms of his hands that were outstretched on the blood-stained pavement.

'Maybe he was taken by surprise?' Lucy suggested.

Ruth inspected the tattoos on his forearms. The one on his right forearm was a detailed skull and crossbones design, with a scroll underneath that read *Or Glory*. She assumed the combination meant *Death or Glory*. Underneath that was written *The Queen's Royal Lancers – Desert Storm 1991*.

'He served in the invasion of Iraq in '91,' Ruth said, showing the tattoo to Lucy. 'The Queen's Royal Lancers.'

'That might help us track him down then.'

Giving the SOCO a nod, the sheet was replaced over the victim and Ruth got up. If this was just a simple mugging, then it felt like a terrible waste of a life of a man who had served his country.

Lucy went over to a young male PC. 'Anyone checked for CCTV yet, Constable?'

'Nothing down here, Ma'am,' the PC said in a thick cockney accent. 'Nearest camera is up on Peckham High Street. It'll be run by the council.'

Lucy nodded. 'Thank you.'

Ruth pointed up the road, 'If our killer went up that way and onto the High Street, we might get a sighting of him. We need uniform to do a door to door and visit all the shops both ways.'

'But if he went that way,' Lucy said, gesturing down the road. 'And into the Cossall Estate, we've got no chance.'

'No,' Ruth agreed, and then pointed to the club's double doors. 'Shall we have a chat with the woman he was waiting for?'

Ten minutes later, Ruth and Lucy were sitting at a corner table inside The Yard nightclub. Alma Salihu sat opposite them nursing a drink and looked totally shocked. She had an elegant face and long eyelashes. Her face was streaked from where she had been crying.

Ruth turned another page of her notebook. 'So, he told you his name was Ashley?'

Alma nodded and mumbled, 'Yeah.'

'Did he tell you his surname?' Lucy asked.

Alma shook his head. 'No.'

'And had you seen him before?' Ruth asked.

'No, I don't think so. But it's only the third time I've DJ'ed here so ...' Alma explained with a puff of her cheeks. 'I can't believe what happened.'

Ruth gave her an empathetic look. 'You're doing really well. And what you're telling us is going to help us catch whoever did this. So, Ashley talked to you at the bar early in the evening. You saw him looking at you a couple of times while you were

Dj'ing. He then asked to buy you a drink and get your number? And then what happened?'

'I told him I was DJ'ing over in King's Cross,' she said in a virtual whisper. 'He offered to carry my records for me. He was being funny, you know. And he was nice looking. He carried my records to my car outside. I told him to wait while I got my money for Dj'ing. And I came back five minutes later and...' She shook as tears welled in her eyes.

'And you didn't see anyone around when you first went out to the car?' Lucy asked gently. 'Anyone standing outside the club. Anyone lurking around?'

'No, no-one.' Alma shook her head as she took a deep breath.

'What about when you went back to the car?' Ruth asked.

'No, sorry. It was deserted,' she said. 'There were some kids on bikes further down the road. They looked like they were dealing.'

'Did you get a look at any of them?' Ruth enquired.

'No, sorry. It was dark and they all wear hoodies,' she shrugged. 'They all look the same.'

Ruth gave her a kind smile. 'Is there anything else that you can think of that might help us to identify him? It doesn't matter how small or insignificant you think it might be.'

'No, not really,' Alma said, and then she frowned. 'Actually, he told me he lived just round the corner.'

Ruth nodded.

*That's interesting.*

'Did he say where?'

'No. I asked him why he was at the club,' Alma said.

Lucy frowned. 'Why did you ask him that?'

'He just looked a bit out of place, you know?' Alma explained. 'The Yard is very hot and sweaty. It's just jeans, t-shirts, trainers. No-one dresses up to come here. But he had smart, expensive clothes on. He looked like he should have been in a club like Twilights or something. And that's when he said that he lived just round the corner.'

'Thanks. You've been very helpful, Alma,' Ruth said compassionately.

# CHAPTER 2

Ruth and Lucy walked away from The Yard nightclub and down an adjacent residential street. The temperature had dropped and there was a light drizzle in the air.

The car key that had been found on Ashley's body belonged to a Mercedes, and it had a small button that showed it had a central locking system.

'You know what struck me about tonight?' Lucy asked as they walked along.

'Go on.'

'It's a Saturday night, and we were both home alone,' Lucy sighed.

'I was quite enjoying it, until I got the shout to get down here,' Ruth admitted.

'I hate it. I just imagine everyone else my age, out there having a great Saturday night,' Lucy explained. 'And then I feel like a sad loser.'

'I know I'm a sad loser,' Ruth laughed. 'I'm going to be found dead, being eaten by my army of cats. And I'm happy with that.'

'Jesus!' Lucy rolled her eyes and gave her a more meaningful look. 'I heard from Harry.'

It had been six weeks since DCI Harry Brooks, her ex-boss and ex-boyfriend, had transferred from Peckham to the Surrey Police. Although the break-up had been painful, Lucy knew there had been no way forward for them. Harry had finally admitted that he didn't want kids – and Lucy did. And despite loving each other, there was nothing that would solve that problem.

'How is Surrey?' Ruth asked. 'Or is it *Sorry*?' She was mimicking the posh accents of the people that inhabited England's wealthiest county.

'To be honest, he didn't give much away,' Lucy said with a shrug. 'But he said he was fine.'

Looking down a long line of parked cars, they eventually saw a red Mercedes.

'Here we go,' Lucy said, pointing at it.

Ruth pressed the button but the central locking system didn't activate – wrong car.

'Unfortunately, we could be doing this all night,' Ruth groaned.

'Yeah, and unfortunately, neither of us has got anything better to do,' Lucy joked sardonically.

Holding the key up at head height, Ruth pressed the button again.

There was a metallic clunk from the other side of the road.

They turned to see a black Mercedes SLK which was parked opposite.

'Bingo!' Lucy said.

They put their forensic gloves back on, walked across the road, and Ruth took out the key to unlock the car doors. While she went into the front, Lucy moved the passenger seat forward to look at the back seat. The car was immaculate and still had that new smell, as though it had just been picked up from the garage.

'Whoever he is,' Lucy said, '... Ashley must have had a decent job. This is twenty grand's worth of brand new Mercedes.'

Opening the glove box, Ruth pulled out a handful of Estate Agent's details for several houses. She showed them to Lucy. 'Maybe he's an Estate Agent or in property? They make a fortune.'

'Could be,' Lucy said as she then followed Ruth to the back of the car where they opened the boot.

Inside was a designer hold-all. Lucy unzipped and opened it. It was full of sealed packs of £50 notes. Each packet contained £5,000 and by her estimate there were around four packets – so £20,000.

'That's a lot of cash to be carrying around in the boot of your car,' Ruth observed with a raised eyebrow.

Lucy noticed there was a roll of black industrial gaffer tape and some plastic ties inside the holdall too. Something in the far corner of the boot caught her eye. An object wrapped in a dirty cloth. At first, she wondered if it was to do with the spare tyre – a jack or a wheel spanner.

As she pulled it towards her, she felt it was heavy. But she also got the recognisable waft of gun oil. Opening the cloth, she saw a large revolver.

'Bloody hell,' Ruth said.

'Yeah, I'm pretty sure he's not an Estate Agent,' she said dryly as she peered over at Ruth.

# CHAPTER 3

It was nearly 9am the following morning and Ruth had been in CID for an hour and a half, already catching up on some tedious paperwork. She had dropped her daughter Ella, who was now five, at the breakfast club at the local nursery. Being a single mum, especially a single mum who was a copper, was difficult. A significant proportion of her wage went on Ella's childcare. However, Ruth knew that in September, Ella would join St Mark's, a lovely little primary school in the next street, and her education would then be free until Ella was eighteen.

'Apparently there's a new DCI in the building,' a voice said in a hushed tone.

It was Lucy, and she had a twinkle in her eye.

'What's his name?' Ruth asked.

'I dunno. But Yvonne in Traffic reckons he's fit and not married,' Lucy explained, raising an eyebrow.

'Brilliant,' Ruth said sarcastically. 'Those are the two most important qualities I look for in my DCI after all.'

'Don't be such a bore,' Lucy said giving her a playful shove.

'Firstly, I'm gay, which kind of rules him out,' Ruth joked. 'Secondly, maybe you shouldn't jump into bed with the DCI that's taking over from Harry.'

'Hey!' Lucy pulled a face of mock indignation. 'I'm not some kind of slag, thank you very much.'

Ruth raised an eyebrow. 'That's debatable.'

Before they could continue, Detective Sergeant David Gaughran approached with a knowing grin. Ruth had a love / hate relationship with Gaughran. Sometimes she thought he was a good copper and a decent human being. At other times, she was convinced he was a homophobic, misogynistic prick.

'Oi, oi,' Gaughran said quietly. 'New guvnor in the building. DCI Pat Ferguson. He's moved to here from Edinburgh. Wife got a new job in London and we had a DCI vacancy. Not keen on the Scots mind you.'

*Here we go,* Ruth thought.

'That is a big surprise, Tim,' Lucy quipped sarcastically. 'And why's that?'

'Aggressive, drink too much, no sense of humour,' Gaughran explained, with no hint of any irony.

Ruth rolled her eyes. 'And that's all people in Scotland, is it Tim?'

'Yes,' he said with a shrug as though this was common knowledge. 'That's just my experience.'

At that moment, the doors to CID opened and Superintendent Phillips, the highest ranking police office in Peckham nick, entered. Beside him was a tall, wiry looking man in his 40s. He wore glasses and a suit.

It was DCI Pat Ferguson.

*He looks more like a geography teacher than a tough Scottish copper*, Ruth thought to herself.

There was a buzz of mumbled conversation around the CID officer. DCI Harry Brooks had been a very popular guvnor at Peckham nick. And there was always a bit of resistance when a new DCI arrived at CID until the natives had checked him out.

'He's not fit,' Lucy whispered to her. 'He looks like a carpet salesman.'

Ruth smiled but didn't respond.

'Morning everyone,' Phillips boomed in his well-educated voice. 'If we can settle down please.'

The officers in CID stopped talking, moved chairs and sat down so Phillips could introduce Ferguson properly.

'I want to introduce to you our new DCI and Chief of CID, Pat Ferguson, who has joined us from the Edinburgh Police Force. I believe that the fantastic work DCI Ferguson did, especially in the Muirhouse area of the city, challenging the gangs and the street drug trade, will be very useful for us and the problems we're seeing in SE15,' Phillips explained. 'And I know you're all going to make him feel very welcome as he settles in here.'

'Yeah, we'll see about that,' Gaughran mumbled.

Ruth shot him a look as if to say *Shut up*.

'Right, I'm going to let you get on,' Phillips said to Ferguson as he pointed to the doors to CID. 'So, good luck and welcome to Peckham.'

As Phillips headed for the doors, Ferguson gave them all a wry smile. 'Good morning everyone. Firstly, I want to say thank you to those of you I've already met for making me feel welcome. I know that DCI Brooks was very popular here and I realise they are big shoes to fill. And it's going to take me some time to get up to speed and get to know you all. Where I come from, I'm called *Boss*, but I understand down here it's *guvnor*, which is fine by me.' He then grinned at them. 'Just not *Jock* or *Taggart*, eh?'

He was referring to a popular Scottish TV cop series, *Taggart*, with a grumpy DCI Taggart as the lead character. There was some muted laughter in the room.

'Right, I'm trying to get up to speed with the murder that took place last night outside The Yard nightclub,' Ferguson said as he wandered over to a scene board. At the moment, it only featured a map of the area and photo of the victim at the scene of the crime. 'How are we getting on identifying him?'

Lucy signalled she wanted to talk.

Ferguson smiled at her. 'If you can introduce yourself when you speak, I can get to know who's who as quickly as possible.'

'Yes, guv. DC Lucy Henry,' she said. 'We've run the plates from what we believe was the victim's car through the PNC and the DVLA. There is no car registered with that plate.'

Ferguson nodded. 'Okay, so false plates. Any signs of where the car was bought? Chassis or VIN number?'

'I've asked Traffic to send those up, so I'll check them today,' Lucy explained.

'Good, thanks Lucy,' Ferguson said enthusiastically. 'What about his prints, anyone?'

DC Syed Hassan indicated he had an update on this. 'Hi, guv. I'm DC Syed Hassan. We've run the prints through the database, but there's nothing. We have his tattoo which shows our victim was in The Queen's Royal Lancers and served with them during Desert Storm in Iraq in 1991. I'm waiting to hear back from someone at Cranleigh Barracks, where the regiment in based.'

'Thanks, Syed,' Ferguson said with an encouraging nod. 'It's really important we get our victim identified asap so we can inform any relatives. His wallet, and phone, if he had one, were taken, is that right?'

'Yes, guv,' Ruth replied.

Ferguson gave her a look.

Ruth shook her head. 'Sorry, I'm DC Ruth Hunter, guv.'

Gaughran grinned and then coughed.

*He's such a twat!*

Ruth continued. 'Our victim was stabbed in the back, which we think is why he didn't manage to fight back. And then in the stomach. He bled out and died at the scene before the paramedics arrived, guv.'

Ferguson frowned. 'Are we thinking that this is just a violent mugging?'

Lucy shook her head. 'Maybe, guv. But we found a handgun and twenty thousand pounds in sealed cash bags in the victim's car. My guess is that the attack is linked to what we found in the boot.'

'Anything to suggest he deals drugs?' Ferguson asked.

'Nothing concrete, guv,' Ruth explained. 'But the flashy, expensive car, false plates, gun and money could suggest drug dealing.'

The phone rang on a nearby desk, and Lucy went to answer it.

'Okay.' Ferguson nodded. 'And no sign of the weapon that was used?'

'No, guv,' Gaughran said with a shake of his head. 'We've got uniform and POLSA team doing a thorough search of the area.'

'CCTV?' Ferguson suggested.

'There are two cameras up on Peckham High Street, but we're still waiting for the council to deliver it to us,' Hassan replied. 'And I've checked and we've had no reports of a missing person overnight.'

'Guv?' Lucy glanced over from where she had answered the phone.

'Lucy?'

'That was MD Evans' Estate Agents,' Lucy explained. 'We found their property details in the victim's car. A Madeleine Taylor thinks our victim was in their office yesterday morning and she's got an address.'

Madeleine Taylor arrived back in her office with a client folder, which she placed down in front of Lucy and Ruth. Madeleine, late 20s, was well spoken, smartly dressed and very confident.

'Here we go,' she said as she sat down opposite them.

Opening the file, Ruth saw the name *Ashley Campbell* and a Peckham address and phone number. 'Can we get a photocopy of this before we leave?'

'Of course,' Madeline replied.

'Flat in Jocelyn Street,' Lucy said. 'That's only two minutes from The Yard nightclub isn't it?'

'Yeah.' Madeleine nodded. 'He rented his flat from our letting department upstairs, which I suppose is why he came to talk to me about buying.'

'We might need access to a spare set of keys for his flat, if it turns out that it is him,' Ruth explained.

'Mike is the manager,' Madeleine said. 'I'm sure he can help you with that.'

Taking out a thin evidence bag, Lucy showed her the MD Evans' property details that they had found in Ashley's car. 'These are the details we found in his car.'

Madeleine took the evidence bag, peered at it and then nodded. 'Yes, it's definitely him. I haven't given the details to that house on Lakewood Road to anyone else as we've only just been instructed.'

'Did you see what car Mr Campbell was driving yesterday?' Ruth asked.

Madeleine raised an eyebrow. 'A brand new Mercedes. Black. He parked it outside. You couldn't miss it as it looked like it had come straight out of the showroom.'

'Can you tell us what you talked about with Mr Campbell?' Lucy asked.

'He told me he was looking to buy a property or two as an investment,' Madeleine explained. 'He said he was going to be letting out the properties and wanted us to handle the letting side of things too.'

Ruth stopped scribbling in her notebook and asked, 'Did he mention if he needed to secure a mortgage?'

Madeleine shook her head. 'No. He said he was a cash buyer, which I told him put him at an advantage when making an offer on a property.'

'And you gave him some details of properties to look at?' Lucy asked.

'Yes,' Madeleine confirmed. 'I told him to have a look and let me know if he wanted to view any of the properties I had given him. And then he left.'

Ruth nodded. 'Is there anything else you can tell us?'

'No, that was it,' Madeleine said with a shrug. 'Is he in some kind of trouble or something?'

There were a few awkward seconds of silence. They couldn't say anything until Ashley's family had been informed.

Ruth looked at her. 'I'm really sorry, but we can't discuss that with you at the moment. But thank you for your help.'

# CHAPTER 4

Gaughran and Hassan walked down the long, cold and windowless corridor in King's College Hospital on Denmark Hill. There had been a hospital on the site since 1840 and it had served as a training base for student doctors ever since.

'Saw your lot lost to the Gooners at the weekend,' Hassan teased. He was referring to the fact that Gaughran's football team Chelsea had lost 2-0 to their London rivals Arsenal.

'Yeah, well, they were lucky, as always. Lucky Arsenal, as the saying goes,' Gaughran growled. He hated Chelsea losing and his mood could be affected for days following a defeat.

'A mate of mine reckons Gullit is gonna get sacked,' Hassan said, meaning Chelsea's charismatic Dutch manager, Ruud Gullit.

'Bollocks!' Gaughran pulled a face and snorted. 'He's just won us our first FA Cup in nearly thirty bloody years. Why would they sack him?'

'Just saying,' Hassan shrugged. 'He told me Gerry Francis was gonna leave Spurs before it happened.'

Hassan pushed open the doors to the mortuary and held them for Gaughran. As they entered the cavernous examination room, the hospital's Chief Pathologist, Professor Sofia Deneuve, came over. She was tall and thin, with angular features and a no-nonsense attitude to her work.

Gaughran found her incredibly intimidating, and he got the feeling that she didn't like him one bit. As he approached, his shoes squeaked on the white-tiled floor.

'This places give me the willies,' Hassan admitted in a whisper.

'Well, don't let Miss Prissy Pants see you're scared or she'll have you for breakfast,' Gaughran joked under his breath.

As they approached, Deneuve glanced over. 'Morning, gentlemen.'

'Professor,' Gaughran replied with a forced smile.

*Why do I feel like I'm back at school every time I come in here?*

The underlying hum of fans and the air conditioning added to the eerie atmosphere. The buzz of the enormous fridges at the other end of the room only reminded Gaughran of their grisly contents.

*Great! Chiller cabinets for bodies,* he thought to himself.

Gaughran got a waft of the sterile smell of clinical disinfectants and other cleaning fluids that masked the underlying stench of death. The lighting was cold and stark. The steel scales used to weigh internal organs were unsettlingly shiny and clean.

A body was lying out on the gurney. It was Ashley Campbell.

As an experienced police officer, Gaughran had become virtually immune to seeing dead bodies. The disassociation became instinctive that by the next day, seeing a dead body would be totally forgotten. He did sometimes wonder if that was good for his mental health.

'What have we got, Professor?' Gaughran asked. He was hoping for some clues as to what had happened to Ashley. He didn't know if he'd been killed in a very violent mugging or he had been targeted.

Dressed in pastel-blue surgical scrubs, Deneuve came over and adjusted her black rubber apron.

'The victim was stabbed in the back first,' Deneuve explained as she turned the body a little and prodded the skin with her finger to show where the knife had entered. 'The knife hit the abdominal aorta, and that's what killed him. Massive internal haemorrhaging.'

Hassan pointed to the wound in his stomach. 'What about this?'

Deneuve shook her head. 'This stab wound missed all the vital organs. It was the wound in the back that did all the damage.'

'Anything you can tell us about the weapon?' Gaughran asked.

'Not really,' Deneuve said. 'Blade was about five inches. Could have been any kind of kitchen knife to be honest.'

'So that doesn't narrow it down,' Gaughran said in a frustrated tone. 'Anything else that might help us?'

'Actually, yes,' Deneuve said as she moved back to the body and pointed to a patch of purple and black bruising around his rib cage. 'This bruising is very fresh. Plus, there's two broken ribs there.' She then went up to the head and pointed to the right side of Ashley's face. 'He also had his jaw fractured around the same time.'

Gaughran raised an eyebrow. 'Sounds like someone gave him one hell of a kicking. Any timescale on those?'

Deneuve nodded. 'I'd suggest that the injuries are no more than a month old. I'm not trying to do your job for you, but if you know your victim was attacked a month ago, you could talk to A&E upstairs and see if anyone remembers him.'

Gaughran exchanged a look with Hassan – it was a good point.

*Maybe the two attacks are linked?*


Having spoken to Mike at the MD Evans' letting agency, Ruth and Lucy had picked up the keys to Ashley Campbell's flat in Jocelyn Street. Technically, they needed a search warrant but Mike had been more than happy to help by handing over a spare set of door keys.

They parked up outside the address, which was a small mansion block that had been built in the 1930s. As they made their way up the staircase, their heels echoed around the cold stairwell. Someone inside the block had been cooking spicy food, and the air was thick with the smell of the exotic seasoning. The dark wooden handrail of the stairs were original to the building. Everything else had been painted rather carelessly a uniform white. The floor outside the door to Ashley's flat had large black-and-white tiles like a giant chess board, that were scuffed and dirty, with flecks of white paint from when the walls had been decorated.

'Here we go.' Ruth turned the lock and opened the door.

The flat was warm and smelt of aftershave or shower gel.

'Heating must be on a timer,' Lucy said under her breath.

As Ruth made a quick sweep of the one-bedroom flat, it was clear that Ashley Campbell wasn't much of a homemaker. It was incredibly sterile.

The living room was sparse. Venetian blinds at the window, an expensive television and VHS player and a dark navy sofa and armchair. There was no clutter of any kind – no books, no records or CDs, no magazines.

'I get the feeling that Ashley didn't spend much time at home,' Ruth said dryly.

'No,' Lucy agreed. 'To say that it could do with *a woman's touch* would be an understatement.'

They moved into the bedroom.

Opening the wardrobe doors, Ruth saw half a dozen designer suits and jackets – Armani, Boss and Paul Smith. Next to them, around ten smart shirts and a handful of ties. There were lace-up shoes and trainers on the floor at the bottom of the wardrobe. She crouched down to move the shoes. There was nothing underneath.

'Jesus!' Ruth sighed in frustration. 'He's not giving much away in here, is he?'

Lucy went into the bathroom. 'Shower gel, deodorant, aftershave.'

Going back into the bedroom, Ruth frowned. Lucy seemed to have vanished. 'Lucy?'

Nothing.

*Where the hell is she?*

'I think we're a bit old to be playing hide and seek,' Ruth joked.

Without warning, Lucy popped up from behind the other side of the bed. She had a black leather attaché case in her hand. 'Bingo! This was under the bed.'

Her appearance startled Ruth. 'Bloody hell, Lucy! You made me jump.'

Laying the attaché case down on the bed, Lucy laughed, 'Sorry.'

She tried to open the case, but it had a combination lock. 'Great. How are we getting this open?'

Marching into the kitchen, Ruth opened a couple of drawers until she found a hefty-looking screwdriver. She returned to the bedroom and pulled the attaché case towards her.

'Let's see if this works,' Ruth said as she wedged the flat-headed screwdriver into the gap behind the locks and twisted.

'You're going to ruin the case,' Lucy muttered.

'Yeah, I'm pretty sure that Ashley isn't going to miss it,' Ruth joked sardonically as the first lock snapped open. 'There you go.'

'You know sarcasm is the lowest form of wit?' Lucy asked her rhetorically.

Ruth raised an eyebrow. 'And you know that the actual saying is *Sarcasm is the lowest form of wit, but the highest form of intelligence*?'

'And which bloody smart arse said that then?'

'Oscar Wilde.'

'Check you out, Miss *I'm going on bloody Mastermind*,' Lucy laughed.

At that moment, the second lock snapped open and Ruth opened the attaché case. It was full of letters, documents, and newspaper clippings.

Pulling out the front page of a tabloid from 1991. Ruth held it up. The headline read *FOURTH RECRUIT DIES AT UK BARRACKS!* There were several photos of young British soldiers. One of them was a woman in her early 20s.

'We know he served in Desert Storm,' Lucy said with a frown as she pointed at the newspaper article. 'Do we think he was caught up in any of this?'

Ruth peered at a letter addressed to Ashley Campbell. It was from the Director of the Service Prosecution Authority dated September 1997.

Her eyes widened as she read the contents of the letter. 'Ashley was due to be giving evidence at an MOD inquiry into allegations of severe bullying and abuse, and the unexplained deaths of four recruits at Cranleigh Barracks in the early 90s.'

'Really?' Lucy asked.

'It says that he had made a preliminary statement to the lead officer in November 1997 and he was due to give a full statement to the board of inquiry.'

'And when was he due to do that?'

Ruth raised an eyebrow. 'Tomorrow.'

# CHAPTER 5

It was now late afternoon and Ferguson had called a meeting of all CID officers who were in the building to get everyone up to speed with developments in the case. As he walked over to the scene boards, Lucy noticed he had a slight limp.

For a moment, she was taken back to the Natasha Weston case that she and Ruth had worked on five weeks earlier. Weston was a young actress who had been murdered by a television writer called Marcus Jankel. Before they had discovered Jankel's guilt, Lucy had started a sexual relationship with him. It had nearly cost her her life. After a car chase, it was believed that Marcus Jankel had perished in a car crash and fire. However, while Lucy was recovering from her ordeal, Jankel had sent her flowers and a note. It had made her feel incredibly uneasy ever since. Ruth was the only person on the planet that knew about the note. No-one else knew about Lucy's affair with Jankel as Ruth and Harry had done a decent job of covering for her to save her job. Yet, at least once a day, her mind was drawn back to Jankel. She had no idea where he was. He had finished the note with an ominous, *I'll be in touch.* So, there was a part of her fully expecting Jankel to appear at some point – she just didn't know where or when.

'Right guys,' Ferguson said, as he turned to the assembled CID team. 'We now have an identity for our victim. Ashley Campbell, aged thirty-two. We've been to his address, a flat in Jocelyn Street, Peckham.' Ferguson stated. 'Have we found his next of kin?'

Lucy looked over. 'Yes, guv. His next of kin is his brother, Ruben. We couldn't find an address but I've just found out that he works in a bar over in Clapham.'

'Okay,' Ferguson said. 'I want you and Ruth to see him straight after this.'

Lucy nodded at Ruth. She would never get used to breaking the news of a death to a family member, even though she had done it dozens of times. Relatives' reactions could range from utter shock, silence or denial, to anger and hysterical crying.

Ferguson glanced over at Gaughran. 'Tim, what happened at the PM?'

'Cause of death was a fatal stab wound to the lower back which severed the abdominal aorta,' Gaughran explained. 'Our victim haemorrhaged and bled out very quickly, guv. The stab wound to his stomach didn't actually do that much damage.'

'Okay, thanks,' Ferguson said. 'Anything else that might help us?'

'Analysis of the entry point of the wound found a trace of Mentha Piperita,' Hassan said, looking at his notebook.

Ferguson shrugged. 'I don't know what that is.'

'It's mint, guv,' Gaughran explained. 'You know, like the herb you get in your garden.'

'Mint?' Ferguson frowned. 'So, the knife had been used to cut mint?'

Gaughran nodded. 'Yes, guv. I'm not sure it helps us much.'

'Ashley had been attacked a few weeks earlier, guv. Two broken ribs and a fractured jaw. We're wondering if the two attacks might be linked,' Hassan explained. 'We've been onto

A&E at King's College Hospital and we're waiting for them to get back to us.'

'Anyone know if he reported the attack to the police?' Ruth asked.

Gaughran shrugged. 'We need a precise date for when it happened.'

'Okay, when you get it, let's find out if anyone went out from this police station to investigate the attack,' Ferguson stated. 'Tim, can you make sure you chase the A&E department?'

Gaughran nodded. 'Guv.'

'Ruth, Lucy,' Ferguson said. 'You went to Ashley's flat. Can you bring us up to speed with what you found.'

Lucy and Ruth had already told Ferguson what they had discovered in the attaché case, but they needed to explain it to the rest of CID.

'We found a locked briefcase under Ashley's bed,' Ruth explained. 'Inside were some letters, documents and newspaper clippings about allegations surrounding a series of unexplained deaths at Cranleigh Barracks in Surrey from 1990 to mid-1996.'

Gaughran nodded. 'Yeah, there was a BBC documentary about it last year.'

Ruth continued. 'Apparently four army recruits died from almost identical gunshot wounds to the head. According to initial investigations, the wounds were self-inflicted.'

'Four army recruits committed suicide by shooting themselves in the head?' Ferguson asked with a dubious frown.

'That's what the initial army coroner's inquest concluded in each case,' Ruth explained. 'However, the family and the media have been pushing for a public inquiry. They claim that there was a culture of abuse and bullying at the barracks. Ashley's testimony was part of the preliminary part of a new MOD inquiry.'

'Do we have any idea about what was going to be in his testimony?' Gaughran asked.

'No, there was nothing detailed in the documents that we found,' Ruth replied. 'But I'm guessing he was a witness to something criminal, otherwise they wouldn't be asking him in to expand on his original statement to the inquiry.'

'And if he was a witness to something criminal,' Ferguson said. '... that could be a motive for him being attacked.'

'Yes, guv,' Ruth agreed. 'Brigadier Stephen Hastings, who is heading the inquiry, has agreed to see us first thing tomorrow. He needs to tell us the level of Ashley's involvement and give us a list of anyone who he might have been about to implicate.'

'Tim and Syed, I'd like you to go and see this Brigadier Hastings in the morning,' Ferguson said.

Ruth pulled a face. 'Any reason you don't want me and Lucy to go, guv?' It had been their search of Ashley's flat that had turned up the evidence and they had made the phone calls to Cranleigh Barracks.

'Listen, if you think the Met police is full of misogynistic pigs, then wait until you start digging around in the British army,' Ferguson explained. 'Don't get me wrong. You and Lucy are more than capable of following this line of inquiry. But I think Tim and Syed have a much better shot at getting the dinosaurs in the army on side.'

Ruth nodded. 'Yes, guv.' What Ferguson said was true. It was just incredibly annoying to be ruled out based on gender.

'Good,' Ferguson said. 'If Ashley felt he was in danger from men he had served with, that might explain why he had a gun in his car and false plates. But it doesn't explain why he had twenty thousand pounds in cash sitting in the boot. Nor why he was looking to buy investment properties. Anyone got hold of his bank details so we can see where or who he was getting all this money from?'

Hassan took a fax from the fax machine and peered at it. 'Guv, this is Ashley Campbell's bank records. He was being paid a thousand pounds a month by some place called *Harvey's*. It's an SW4 postcode.'

'That's Clapham,' Ruth said.

'And his brother, Ruben, works in a bar in Clapham,' Ferguson said with a frown. 'It has to be the same place.'

# CHAPTER 6

*Harvey's* was a swish bar on Venn Street, around the back of Clapham Common tube station. Gentrification was alive and well in SW4, and had been for some time. Property prices had gone through the roof in the last five years and the working-class inhabitants had been driven south. The new well-heeled Generation X inhabitants had been given the label DINKY – dual income, no kids yet. And the tatty bookmakers and hardware stores had been replaced by upmarket coffee shops and expensive gift shops.

Parking outside *Harvey's*, Ruth and Lucy made their way towards the bar that was filling up with a relaxed Sunday evening crowd.

As they went in, Ruth spotted the long gleaming silver bar, red cushioned bar stools, low dark oak tables and leather sofas. The air was full of cigarette smoke, expensive perfume and the chilled Ibiza sounds of *Café del Mar* .

*This is definitely a step up from Peckham, or even Balham,* she thought as she scoured the fashionable 20-something clientele.

They headed for the bar.

'Jesus, it's two quid for a bottle of beer in here,' Ruth observed, looking at a blackboard with drinks written in chalk. 'It's three quid for a glass of bloody wine.'

Lucy grinned. 'Maybe we should arrest them for daylight robbery.'

'Very good,' Ruth laughed.

A young man with cropped hair approached, and they flashed their warrant cards. He had a silver cocktail shaker in his hand. 'Can I help?'

'DC Henry and DC Hunter, Peckham CID,' Lucy explained, raising her voice over the music. 'We're looking for a Ruben Campbell?'

The young man nodded and gestured to a door. 'Yeah, he's upstairs in the office.'

'Thank you,' Lucy said as they turned and headed across the bar.

They went through the door and up the stairs. The interior was newly decorated and the walls were covered in a dark carpet-like material.

As they reached the top of the staircase, they saw a good-looking mixed race man coming the other way. He was dressed in a charcoal grey designer suit and a blue shirt with no tie. From his physique, he looked like he could handle himself.

'Toilets are downstairs, ladies,' he said with a friendly smile and gestured for them to return to the staircase.

They pulled out their warrant cards.

'Ruben Campbell?' Ruth asked.

Ruben nodded, narrowed his eyebrows – he was concerned. 'Yeah. Is ... everything all right?'

'Can we go somewhere for a chat?' Lucy explained in a low voice.

'Yeah, of course,' Ruben said, sounding anxious. 'My office is just up here.'

He led them into a smart, neat office and gestured to a couple of padded chairs.

'Is it Mica?' he asked in a concerned voice as he sat at his desk.

'We're here about your brother,' Lucy said quietly.

'Ashley?' he asked with a baffled look.

'There's no easy way of saying this, Mr Campbell,' Ruth said gently. 'We have some very bad news for you. Your brother, Ashley, was stabbed last night, and he died from his injuries.'

'What?' Ruben's eyes widened as he took in what they had said for a few seconds. 'Are you sure?'

'I'm afraid so,' Lucy said. 'We're really sorry for your loss.'

Ruben swallowed as he let out a breath. His eyes filled with tears. 'I can't believe it ... What happened?'

Ruth gave him a benevolent look. 'Ashley was standing outside The Yard Club in Peckham last night when someone attacked him. I'm afraid he died at the scene before the paramedics arrived.'

'God, I don't ...' Ruben stammered. 'I didn't think The Yard ... was his sort of place.' He puffed out his cheeks as he ran his hand over his face.

'There are a few questions we'd like to ask you about Ashley, if you're up to it, Mr Campbell?' Lucy asked as she took out her notebook.

'Yeah,' Ruben said. 'Of course.' He blinked as the shock of what they'd told him sank in. 'It's Ruben.'

Lucy clicked her pen and peered at him. 'When was the last time you saw Ashley?'

'Friday afternoon,' Ruben replied. 'He popped in for a quick chat.'

'What time was that?'

'About four, I guess.'

'Was there a reason that he came to see you?' Ruth asked.

'He works for us. He looks after all the security for the bar,' Ruben explained. 'And he books DJs and other stuff.'

'When you say *us*, what exactly do you mean?' Lucy asked.

He pulled out a packet of Marlborough Lights. 'Mind if I smoke?'

'No, of course not,' Ruth said, thinking she wouldn't mind one herself, but that wouldn't be very professional.

'Me and my wife Mica run this bar,' Ruben explained.

'Do you own it?' Ruth asked.

Ruben hesitated for a second. 'It was Mica who put up the money for the bar.' Something about the question had made him uncomfortable.

'Can I ask why Ashley wasn't working here last night?'

'Staff get one Saturday night off every couple of months,' Ruben replied. 'It was just Ashley's turn.'

Lucy stopped writing in a notebook and asked, 'Did Ashley say anything about what his plans were for the weekend?'

'No, not really,' Ruben said. 'He said he was going out for a few drinks locally but he didn't say who he was meeting.'

'But you were surprised that he'd been to The Yard in Peckham?' Ruth asked.

'Yeah,' Ruben said as he blew smoke from his nostrils. 'It's a bit moody down there, if you know what I mean?'

Ruth sat forward in her chair. 'Can you think of anyone who might want to harm Ashley? Any arguments on the door about people getting into your bar?'

'No. We don't get many problems on the door here,' Ruben stated. 'The odd drunken dickhead who wants to show off to his girlfriend, but that's about it.'

'What about drugs?' Ruth asked.

'No, no way.' Ruben shook his head emphatically. 'I don't allow drugs or dealers in here. If we think anyone is dealing or taking drugs, they're out or I call the police.'

'What about Ashley?'

Ruben frowned. 'How do you mean?'

'Did he have the same attitude towards drugs?' Lucy asked.

'Yeah. We both agreed that it was zero tolerance for that kind of thing,' Ruben explained.

'Just as a matter of routine, can you tell us where you were last night?' Lucy asked.

Ruben shrugged. 'I was here. It was a Saturday night.'

'And what time did you leave?'

'It was gone three by the time we'd done the tills and bottled up,' he said with a frown. 'You can't think I had something to do with it?'

Ruth gave him an empathetic look. 'Sorry. We have to ask everyone. It's just routine.'

'Can you tell us where your wife was last night?' Lucy asked.

Ruben was getting annoyed. 'She was with me here.'

'All night?' Lucy asked.

'No,' Ruben shook his head. 'She was tired and had a headache, so I sent her home.'

'And what time would that have been?' Lucy asked.

'Seriously, why are you wasting your time asking where me and Mica were last night?' Ruben snapped. 'Why aren't you out there trying to find the scumbag who killed my brother?'

Ruben put his head in his hands for a moment. It was all getting too much for him.

'I understand this is a very difficult time for you, Ruben,' Ruth said quietly. 'We just need to have a clear picture of where everyone in Ashley's life was on Saturday night.'

'Sorry,' Ruben mumbled as he looked up at them. 'Mica left here in a cab around ten, I guess.'

'And she went home?'

'Yes.'

'We found a large amount of cash in Ashley's car and we also discovered that he was looking to buy property as an investment,' Lucy said. At this stage, they weren't prepared to mention the gun they had found. 'He couldn't have earned that much from working here, did he?'

'No. Not enough to invest in property.' Ruben then shrugged. 'But Ashley was into all sorts of things. Fancied himself as a bit of an entrepreneur. He never really talked to me about it but he always seemed to have money.'

Stubbing out the cigarette, Ruben blew out his cheeks again. 'I can't believe he's just gone. It just doesn't feel real.'

'Are your mum and dad still alive?' Ruth asked.

Ruben looked over at them. 'Mum died two years ago. And dad ... well, to be fair, he's a waste of space. A nasty piece of work. He left us when I was five.'

Ruth raised an eyebrow. 'And you haven't seen him since?'

'Oh yeah.' Ruben gave an ironic snort. 'He pops up every few months when he needs money. I don't want anything to do with him. But Ashley was a bit of a soft touch when it comes to our dad.'

'Do you know if he had seen him recently?' Lucy asked.

'Yeah, actually,' Ruben nodded. 'A few weeks ago. Just after New Year.'

'Could we have his name?'

'Dion. Dion Campbell.'

'Any idea where he's living at the moment?' Ruth asked.

'Peckham somewhere,' Ruben shrugged. 'To be honest, I don't care.'

Ruth gave him a sympathetic nod. 'Ashley was in the army, wasn't he?'

'Yeah, he was very proud of that. We all were,' Ruben said. 'He went out to Kuwait when it was invaded.'

'Did he ever talk about his time at Cranleigh Barracks?' Ruth asked.

For a few seconds, Ruben didn't answer. Then he said with a grim expression, 'Yeah, he did.'

'What did he say?'

'He said that the barracks were hell on earth, especially if you were a new recruit. In fact, he said it was better being in a war zone than being at Cranleigh.'

'Did he tell you exactly what he meant by that?'

'When he was a recruit, one of the instructors made him take a banana instead of a gun to the parade ground,' Ruben growled. 'The sergeant thought it was funny. Ashley said he'd seen recruits beaten up, pissed on and even put in hospital. And he said he thought one of the female recruits had committed suicide because she had been raped by an officer.'

Ruth and Lucy exchanged a dark look.

# CHAPTER 7

It was early evening. Ruth was at her flat in Balham with Lucy as they continued to look through evidence for the investigation. As a single mum, Ruth often had to leave CID before other officers. However, Lucy was always happy to head back with her to continue working from home.

Walking down the hallway, Ruth quickly checked on Ella. She was sitting on her bed colouring in and listening to a Disney Princess CD.

'You okay, darling?' she asked.

Without looking up from her Princess colouring book, Ella nodded. 'Uh huh.'

'What are you doing?' she asked.

Ella held up a picture of a princess on a unicorn that she had coloured in almost perfectly. 'Look!' she said proudly.

'Oh wow! That's amazing!' Ruth beamed. 'Come and show me and Auntie Lucy when it's finished.'

'Okay,' Ella said as she went back to colouring with an expression of utter concentration.

*Oh God, she's growing up way too fast.*

Ruth decided she would leave Ella for another half an hour before reading her a bedtime story and tucking her into bed. She sometimes wondered when the bedtime stories stopped. As long as Ella enjoyed them, Ruth would read them to her.

'Is she okay?' Lucy asked.

Ruth nodded. 'Yeah. I know she's my daughter but I don't think she could be any cuter if she tried.'

'She really is adorable,' Lucy agreed.

Ruth pulled a face. 'And I'm going to enjoy her while she's like this, because in ten years the hormones will have kicked in and she'll be an argumentative banshee with a serious attitude problem.'

'Is that what you were like then?' Lucy laughed.

'I was a nightmare,' Ruth admitted. 'Argumentative, bolshy and stubborn.'

Lucy grinned and asked, 'I know that, but what were you like as a teenager?'

'You're hilarious, you know that?' Ruth gave her a sarcastic smile and poured her some more wine. 'Here you go, chuckles.'

Ruth's phone buzzed. It was a text from Kara, an attractive but rather needy woman she had been seeing for the past few weeks.

'Booty call, is it?' Lucy joked.

'A what?' Ruth asked. She didn't know what she was talking about.

'Someone texts you late at night to see if you want to hook up and have sex,' Lucy explained.

'Well, I guess it is a *booty call* then,' Ruth sighed.

Lucy frowned. 'You don't sound very excited? Who is it?'

'Her name's Kara,' Ruth explained.

Lucy shrugged. 'Who the hell is Kara? You've never mentioned her.'

'She's a dispatch controller at the nick. Very needy and a bit naïve,' Ruth said. 'But she's incredibly attractive.'

Lucy looked at her. 'Want my advice?'

Ruth grinned. 'Do I want the advice of someone with the morals of an alleycat? No thanks.'

'Hey, I'm offended!' Lucy protested.

'No, you're not!'

'Well, no I'm not,' Lucy admitted. 'Is the sex good?'

'Yes, it's amazing,' Ruth exclaimed.

'Jesus, Ruth. You're still in your 20s. Life is short,' Lucy said. 'A very attractive woman wants to come round and have great sex with you? Only you could find that problematic.'

Ruth gave her a sarcastic smile – but she had a point.


Marching up the corridor on the first floor of King's College Hospital, Gaughran peered up, looking for the name of the ward that his father had been moved to. The air smelled of hospital food and disinfectant.

As he entered the ward, Gaughran saw his father in a bed on the far right-hand side. His immediate response was hesitant. It was his duty to check that his father was all right. Yet in the past twelve months, Gaughran had unearthed too many dark secrets to feel truly comfortable in his presence.

Arthur Gaughran, in his mid-60s, was a retired South London copper who had worked in the Murder Squad in the 60s and 70s. He was tall and thin, with a long face and curious eyes behind thin-rimmed spectacles.

Beside the bed was his Uncle Les, Arthur's younger brother, who had followed a similar career path in the Met.

'Bloody hell,' Gaughran said with a forced laugh as he approached. 'You two are like Morecambe and Wise. I'm surprised Dad doesn't shift over so you sleep in there with him.'

He was getting used to presenting a façade of good humour and leg-pulling in their presence.

Les rolled his eyes. 'Sit down, nob-head. Your dad and I were in the middle of an important conversation.'

'Yeah, you're talking about who the next Chelsea manager is going to be if they really do sack Gullit. And I've heard a rumour it's going to be Vialli,' Gaughran informed them as he took a seat.

'No chance,' Arthur said, shaking his head. 'I reckon George Graham.'

Les groaned. 'That would be two steps backwards.'

'Where's Mum?' Gaughran asked.

'You just missed her,' Arthur said, and then laughed. 'I think she'd had enough of me talking about my prostate gland.'

'Yeah, well, I'm going if that's what you think we're going to be talking about,' Gaughran joked.

Les got up from the chair with a slight groan. 'Right, old son, I'm going to leave you two to it. I'm off down the driving range for an hour.'

Arthur gave him a mock scowl. 'Oh, yeah, that's it you toss-bag, rub it in while I'm stuck in here.'

'It's an incentive to stop fucking about and get out of here.' Les said with a shrug. 'I'll see you losers later, eh?'

Gaughran smiled over at his dad as Les walked away.

There were a few awkward seconds.

'Where are my bloody grapes?' Arthur asked.

Gaughran frowned. 'You don't like grapes.'

'That's not the point,' Arthur joked. 'I'm in hospital so you bring me grapes.'

Gaughran threw a copy of the *Evening Standard* newspaper onto his bed. 'I got you a copy of the *Standard* instead.'

'Ta,' Arthur said.

'What have they said then?' Gaughran asked, referring to the tests that the hospital had been running since he had arrived two days earlier.

'Not a lot,' Arthur said with a nonchalant shrug.

Gaughran frowned. 'They must have said something, dad? They've done a load of tests, so what's wrong with you?'

Arthur pulled a face and shrugged. 'Bollock cancer.'

'What?'

'Well, it's not actually bollock cancer, it's prostate cancer. But bollock cancer sounds funnier, doesn't it?' Arthur joked.

Gaughran could see there was fear behind his father's attempt at humour.

'Yeah, but it's not funny is it Dad?' he said.

'Oh fuck off. You sound like your mother,' Arthur said. 'Early stages of prostate cancer. They've caught it in time. Might be a bit of radiotherapy but there's no need to worry.'

Gaughran raised his eyebrow. 'And that's what they told you, is it?'

'Well, I'm paraphrasing,' Arthur admitted. 'But yeah, essentially that's it. So, you and your mother don't need to get all hysterical, all right?'

'Yeah, okay. As long as that is what they told you,' Gaughran said seriously.

'Tell you what, son,' Arthur said. 'I'm parched. Could you ask one of those pretty nurses to get me and you a cuppa?'

'Yeah, of course.'

As Gaughran got up and went to search around for a nurse, he spotted a woman sitting on a chair. She was in her early 50s, glamorous-looking in a brassy sort of way, with curled blonde hair. He recognised her from somewhere and searched his memory – was it an investigation he'd worked on?

Then it came to him.

She was the woman he had seen his father embracing at the golf club a few months earlier. The woman he was pretty certain his father had been having an affair with.

*What the fuck is she doing here?* he thought angrily.

Approaching slowly, he waited for her to look up and register his presence. He was fuming.

'You waiting to see Arthur, are you?' Gaughran snapped.

'Eh? Erm, no.' She shook her head as if she had no idea what he was talking about.

'Don't piss me about,' Gaughran growled. 'I know you're here to see my father.'

The woman seemed nervous. 'Yeah. You must be Tim. I'm ...'

'I don't give a fuck what your name is, love,' Gaughran snapped as he interrupted her. 'Tell my dad that I've gone and he can get his own fucking tea!'

# CHAPTER 8

Ruth was busily cleaning her teeth in her bathroom. She checked her make-up and hair.

*Not too bad for 11pm on a school night,* she thought to herself. She just needed to make sure that Kara was up and gone before Ella rose in the morning. She didn't want to have to explain who Kara was or why she had stayed over.

There was a knock on the door and Ruth felt a tingle of excitement.

She walked down the hallway and opened the door.

'Hi, Ruth,' Kara mumbled awkwardly.

'Hi,' Ruth replied and showed her in.

Physically, Kara was gorgeous. She had a great body, big brown eyes and short blonde hair. So, what was the problem? Why did Ruth not find her incredibly attractive as a package? In fact, why did she find Kara irritating?

'Come in, come in,' Ruth said, gesturing to the hallway.

Taking Kara by the hand, Ruth led her down to the living room and kitchen area. 'Do you want a drink?'

'Not on a Monday,' Kara replied.

Slumping down on the sofa, Ruth grabbed her half-drunk glass of Sauvignon Blanc and swigged it. 'I can't even think about switching off until I have alcohol in my system.'

Kara pulled a face. 'That doesn't sound healthy.'

'I can make us some food,' Ruth suggested with a smile.

'I'm not really hungry, but thanks,' Kara said as she sat forward on the armchair.

'How was your day?' Ruth asked.

'It was okay,' Kara said with a shrug.

*Jesus, this is hard work,* Ruth thought. *We really don't have very much in common.*

She remembered some advice an old colleague had once told her. If you can find someone that you want to spend the night with, and then get up the next morning and you want to spend the day with them, keep hold of them. Unfortunately, the latter wasn't true for Kara.

*Right, I'm done trying to make conversation,* Ruth thought. She got up and took Kara by the hand.

'Come on, I'm taking you to bed.'

Walking up the steps to her front door, Lucy got the distinct impression that someone was watching her. However, that wasn't something new. Since the Marcus Jankel case, she had been hyper-vigilant to the point of paranoia. Every time she came home or left her house, she half-expected to see him.

Glancing around, she wiggled the key into her door. Something in the lock had caught her eye. The metal had deep scratches around the lock itself, as if someone had tried to force something metallic into it.

*Was that there before?* she wondered to herself. She had no idea, and she was finding it increasingly difficult to distinguish between what was a genuine, logical concern and what was just her mind playing tricks.

She opened the door, went in, and slammed it behind her. Pausing for a moment in the darkness, she held her breath and listened. It was now her daily routine. She strained her hearing

for the slightest sound or movement that might indicate someone was inside.

*Nothing. Phew.*

Turning on the hall lights, she went around the downstairs,
pulling curtains and turning on every light she could find.

As she walked into the lounge, she caught something moving in the garden in the corner of her eye.

*Shit! What was that?*

Moving swiftly into the kitchen, she grabbed a large knife
and returned.

Stepping gingerly towards the patio doors and windows
that led out to the garden, she held her breath again. She
squinted, trying to see if there was anything or anyone out
there.

FLASH!

She was blinded by a sudden explosion of light in the garden.

*JESUS CHRIST!*

She flinched and took a step back.

Two weeks earlier, she'd had security lights with motion
sensors fitted around the outside of the house. The next step
was to have an alarm installed, which she hoped to get done
next week.

She squinted outside through the windows into the garden
that was now lit up. Obviously, something had triggered the security lights. The wind, or those bloody cats again - or was it
something else?

Whatever it was, it had made her jump out of her skin.
She'd be glad to get a glass of wine and take the edge off the day.

Just in case, Lucy moved forward towards the glass. She peered cautiously outside.

*It could have been a fox?* She had seen several urban foxes in recent weeks.

The light dropped again as the motion sensor switched off.

The patio was again plunged into darkness.

All she could see now were shadows and the outline of the fence at the end of the garden.

*Well, I can't stand here all bloody night!*

She went to turn to head back to the kitchen.

A split second later, the garden exploded with light again, and where previously was just an empty lawn, a shadowy figure stood.

*Oh, my God!*

Lucy shrieked and jumped away from the window.

The figure was back-lit.

Lucy couldn't see anything but the outline of a person standing there.

Although she couldn't see their eyes, she could feel their stare boring into her. She took another step back from the door, gripping the cold steel of the knife.

*Jesus Christ!*

She was about to turn and run when the figure stepped into the light.

It was the young man she had seen moving into the flat above with his girlfriend the week before.

James and Natalie, wasn't it?

She'd even given them a hand with some boxes and a television before inviting them down for a drink when they got themselves settled.

*For fuck's sake, what are you doing out there, you dick head?*

'You scared the shit out of me!' Lucy shouted through the glass.

'Sorry!' James said and then pointed to her patio door. 'I need to talk to you.'

'Okay?' Lucy said, shaking her head as she went and got the key and slid the doors open. She gripped the knife just in case he turned out to be a serial killer.

'What the hell are you doing out there? Auditioning for a horror movie? You nearly gave me a bloody heart attack!'

'Sorry,' James said, pulling a face. 'I don't want to alarm you, but I saw someone in your garden.'

'What?' Lucy exclaimed. 'Are you sure?'

'Yeah.' James nodded. 'He was peering through these doors from the patio. The lights came on, so I looked down from the balcony and shouted at him. Then he did a runner.'

'Did you get a look at him?' she asked.

'I guess he was about forty. Tall, long hair down to his shoulder,' James explained.

*Shit! Sounds like Marcus Jankel.*

'How did you get into the garden?' she asked.

'I jumped down from the balcony,' he explained.

*Bloody hell, he's brave.*

'I'm surprised you didn't break your legs,' she said.

James shrugged. 'One of the other neighbours told us you were a copper ... sorry, I mean a police officer. So, I guess you're going to tell me off for going after him?'

Lucy smiled at him as she went over and turned on the living room lights. James was very handsome, with cropped blond hair, blue eyes and preppy style glasses.

'Yeah, it's not advisable to go chasing after people,' she said with a smile.

'Are you going to be all right?' James asked. 'I know you're a ...'

'Copper,' Lucy joked.

'Yeah, but I know you live on your own.'

Lucy gestured to the kitchen. 'I've got a nice Malbec I'm going to get stuck into, so I'll be fine.'

James laughed and looked directly at her. His eyes lingered on hers for a second longer than was normal.

*Erm, hello? What was that?*

'I'd invite you to stay for a drink,' Lucy explained, and then pointed to the ceiling. 'But I'm guessing that you need to get back to Natalie and explain to her you're not actually dead.'

James snorted. 'Yes ... Actually she's away for the week on a work trip, so I'll take you up on that drink ... if that's okay?'

*Mmm. Handsome man in my flat sharing a bottle of wine. What's not to like?* she thought.

'Of course. Come through to the kitchen.'

# CHAPTER 9

It was 8am the following morning and Ruth and Lucy were sitting in Interview Room 1 at Peckham nick. Sitting opposite them was Jermaine Daniels aka *Stigs*, a seventeen-year-old black teenager, who had been caught in the early hours trying to use Ashley Campbell's bank card at various cash machines on Brixton High Street. When uniformed officers went to pick him up, they found Ashley's wallet and phone.

Daniels sat with his hood up, legs apart, giving them his best mean and moody look. He had an obligatory line cut into his eyebrow. Next to him sat the female Duty Solicitor, who was in her 40s.

Ruth opened the folder on the table in front of her. She waited for a moment before making eye contact with Jermaine.

'Jermaine, I'm Detective Constable Ruth Hunter, and this is Detective Constable Lucy Henry. We're here to talk to you about what happened earlier today. You have already been read your rights at the time of your arrest, but I need to remind you, you are still under caution. Do you understand what that means?'

Daniels nodded. She couldn't tell if he was nervous or angry. He wasn't giving anything away with his face or his body language, which was unusual.

'We're also going to be recording this interview, as it may be used as evidence. So, I'm going to press this button. You'll hear a long beep and then I'll start off by naming everyone who is in the room. Okay?'

Jermaine peered around at the room casually. 'Yeah.'

Ruth pressed the button to record and a five-second electronic beep began. 'Interview commencing at eight am. For the purposes of the tape, present are Jermaine Daniels, Duty Solicitor Jill Davies, Detective Constable Lucy Henry and Detective Constable Ruth Hunter.'

'Can we just confirm that you are Jermaine Daniels, and that you live at 23a Benmar Drive, Brixton, SW2?' Lucy asked, as she peered down at the paperwork in front of her and clicked her pen open.

'Yeah,' Jermaine mumbled.

Taking the evidence bag in front of her, Ruth held it up. Inside was Ashley Campbell's bloodstained wallet and phone.

'Officers found these in your bedroom, Jermaine,' Ruth said. 'Can you tell us anything about that?'

Jermaine stared at the floor and jigged his foot nervously. 'No.'

'Okay,' Ruth said calmly. 'This wallet and phone belong to a man called Ashley Campbell. Do you know him, Jermaine?'

Jermaine shook his head but didn't look up.

'For the purposes of the tape, the suspect shook their head to indicate that he doesn't know the victim,' Ruth explained.

Lucy sat forward in her seat. 'Can you tell us where you were around midnight on Saturday night, Jermaine?'

For a few seconds, Jermaine didn't answer. Then he looked up and shrugged. 'At home. Ask me mum.'

Ruth frowned. 'Are you sure you were at home?'

Jermaine narrowed his eyes and glared at her. 'Yeah. You saying I'm a liar?' he asked aggressively.

Reaching into the folder, Ruth pulled out a still from the CCTV footage on Peckham High Street. It showed a young man in a hoodie walking past a fast food shop.

'Could you look at this for me please, Jermaine?' she asked, turning the photo for him to look at.

Jermaine rolled his eyes, leant forward for about half a second and then sat back.

'That image is from CCTV footage that was taken just after midnight on Saturday night,' Ruth explained. 'We think that's you, Jermaine ... Is it you?'

Jermaine shook his head.

'For the purposes of the tape, the suspect shook his head,' Ruth stated.

'Are you sure?' Lucy asked as she leaned forward. 'Because it really looks like you. In fact, the person in that photo is wearing the same orange Nike trainers that officers found in your bedroom. And we also found blood on the soles of those trainers. Can you explain that to us?'

Jermaine took a breath. 'No.'

'Jermaine, I need you to look at me,' Lucy said gently. Jermaine blinked as he glanced up. He was definitely rattled. 'A man was stabbed to death about two-minutes' walk from where this photo was taken. And he was stabbed about ten minutes before it was taken. So, the problem we've got is that we also found that man's wallet and phone in your bedroom. Can you see how this looks, Jermaine?'

He didn't say anything.

Ruth moved her chair forward and put her arms on the table as she peered over at him. 'I need you to listen to me Jermaine, because I really want to help you. A man called Ashley Campbell was stabbed to death outside The Yard Club just before midnight on Saturday night. Can you tell us anything about that?'

Jermaine continued to look at the floor and shook his head slowly.

There were several seconds of silence.

'Jermaine?' Ruth said in a virtual whisper. 'Did you stab Ashley Campbell?'

Jermaine screwed up his face and rubbed a tear away from his eyes. The pressure was really getting to him. 'Nah. I never touched him.'

Ruth looked at Lucy. *At last we're getting somewhere.*

'Why have you got his wallet and phone?' Lucy asked.

'I dunno.' His voice broke a little.

'Come on, Jermaine. If you don't tell us, we're going to assume that you killed this man.'

Jermaine closed his eyes and whispered, 'I took them from him ... after ...'

'You took them from him after he had been attacked?' Ruth asked with no hint of judgement.

Jermaine stared at the floor again, nodded and rubbed his face.

'For the purposes of the tape, the suspect is nodding,' Ruth explained.

'Did you see who attacked Ashley?' Lucy asked.

Jermaine shrugged. 'Not really.'

'Not really?'

'They came out of nowhere, wearing a mask and a hoodie, you know?'

'Can you tell us if they were white or black?' Lucy asked.

Jermaine shook his head. 'Nah, it was too dark. But it wasn't me that stabbed him, I swear.'

'So, you saw Ashley being attacked?' Ruth asked.

'Yeah,' Jermaine mumbled.

'And you saw him fall to the pavement?'

'Yeah.'

'And then what happened?'

'I went over to see if he was all right.' Jermaine's voice was wobbly. 'But there was blood all over him, you know?'

'Why didn't you call for an ambulance, Jermaine?' Ruth asked.

Jermaine shrugged. 'I dunno.'

'So, you took his wallet and phone?'

'Yeah.'

'Did you see where the attacker went afterwards?'

Jermaine blew out his cheeks. His eyes were still wet. 'They ran down the road, got into a car and drove away.'

'Did you see the car?'

'Nah, not really,' Jermaine replied. 'A big car. Range Rover maybe.'

'What colour?'

'I dunno. Dark. Black maybe.'

Lucy peered over at him. 'Where was the car parked? Towards the High Street or the other way?'

'The other way,' he replied. 'They drove into the Cossall Estate.'

Gaughran and Hassan parked in a space marked *Visitors* at Cranleigh Barracks in Surrey. A large green sign read *Army Training Regiment – Training and Recruiting Unit.*

As Gaughran got out of the car, the wind picked up and swirled around. The temperature had dropped, and the air was icy cold. The barracks were laid out across a large swathe of ground and resembled university halls of residence merged with a secondary school.

As they headed over towards reception, a platoon of recruits marched past.

*Christ, they look so young! They've still got bloody acne,* he thought to himself.

'Ever fancy it, Sarge?' Hassan asked, gesturing to the recruits.

'Jesus, me?' Gaughran snorted. 'I hate people telling me what to do at the best of times. Can you imagine me here?'

Hassan gave a knowing laugh. 'No, Sarge, I really can't.'

They made their way to the barracks' reception, explained who they were, and that they had a meeting with Brigadier Stephen Hastings.

Two minutes later, a young soldier led the way down a series of old-fashioned wooden corridors. The walls were lined with photographs of officers who had died in combat, dating back to the First World War. The air was musty and smelled of cigarette smoke, old books and stewed tea.

The young soldier knocked on Brigadier Hastings' door.

'Come in!' a deep, authoritative voice boomed.

Opening the door, a severe-looking man with a thin, craggy face glanced up from his desk.

Gaughran got out his warrant card. 'Brigadier Hastings?'

He narrowed his eyes, 'Yes?' And then the penny dropped. 'Ah, you're the chaps from Peckham police. Why don't you come in and sit down?'

'Thank you,' Gaughran said as he and Hassan sat down on two wooden chairs on the other side of the Brigadier's desk.

'I understand you're looking into what happened to Ashley Campbell?' Brigadier Hastings asked. 'Terrible tragedy.'

'I'm surprised that you know about that already,' Gaughran said suspiciously.

Hastings shrugged with an air of conceit. 'Oh, I've got friends in the Met. And the Queen's Royal Lancers were based here in the early 90s. It wasn't long before someone picked up the phone to tell me what had happened.'

Gaughran had already taken an instant dislike to Brigadier Hastings. He reeked of privilege. He knew the sort. Boarding school, Oxbridge, Sandhurst – a well-worn life path of many of England's upper classes.

'You knew Ashley?' Hassan asked taking out his notebook.

'Not when he was here as a recruit,' Brigadier Hastings explained. 'But I did meet him when he made a preliminary statement to the Board of Inquiry that I am leading for the British Army.'

'Can we see that preliminary statement?' Gaughran asked.

'I'm afraid not,' Brigadier Hastings replied. 'At the moment, this an internal inquiry by the MOD. As you are probably aware, Cranleigh Barracks has received a lot of negative press in recent years. My inquiry is to establish if there were any staff or instructors at Cranleigh who should be facing criminal proceedings.'

'I understand that, Brigadier,' Gaughran said. 'But this is a murder investigation. We need to see if there is a link between what Ashley was going to tell you and his murder.'

'I wish I could help, but my instructions are that you will need a court order before I can release the evidence that I've gathered,' Brigadier Hastings said sternly. 'However, I can tell you that Ashley Campbell spoke to an officer at Surrey Police a few years ago regarding an incident here.'

'What incident was that?' Hassan asked.

'I think that's something you need to discuss with Surrey Police,' Brigadier Hastings said. 'I believe he spoke with a DCI Carter there.'


Lucy rang the buzzer of a dilapidated three-storey house on Wilson Road, which was just around the corner from Camberwell College of Art. She looked down at the weed strewn path, the litter and the old fridge in the front garden.

*At least that's not a health hazard,* she thought sardonically.

Eventually, the door opened and an old Afro-Caribbean man in his 60s peered out at them. 'Hello?' he greeted them meekly.

Ruth and Lucy showed their warrant cards.

'DC Henry and DC Hunter, Peckham CID. We're looking for Dion Campbell?'

'Yes...' The man nodded slowly. 'Is this about Ashley?'

'Yes,' Ruth said. 'Do you mind if we come in?'

'Okay... I suppose so ...,' Dion mumbled as he opened the door. He was wearing a baggy navy cardigan and ill-fitting, slightly stained trousers. He had a worn pair of tartan slippers on his bare feet and smelled strongly of body odour.

They followed Dion down the draughty corridor to the front door of his flat and went inside. It was a cluttered mess of old newspapers, empty beer cans, dirty plates, and mugs.

*Jesus! I've been to messy flats before, but this is right up there,* Lucy thought.

As they went over to a threadbare sofa, Lucy and Ruth exchanged a look as if to say, *Is it actually safe to sit here?*

'My son, Ruben, he called me just now,' Dion said with a slight slur to his words as he sunk into an armchair that was covered in patterned lime green and orange material. 'He told me that Ashley had been killed.'

'Yes, we're very sorry for your loss,' Ruth said gently.

Les shook his head sadly and frowned. 'Ruben said he was stabbed? Is that right?'

*I can't tell if he's in shock or if he's drunk.*

'Yes, I'm afraid so.' Lucy shifted uncomfortably on the sofa and moved an aluminium foil tray, with a mouldy takeaway inside, out of the way with her foot.

'You know who did it?' Dion asked. His eyes were lined, glassy and bloodshot. He reached for a mug and took a long swig. Lucy was pretty sure it wasn't tea in there – she could smell the rum a few seconds later.

Lucy shook her head sympathetically. 'We don't know at the moment, Mr Campbell.'

'It's Dion,' he corrected her as he took out a tin of tobacco. 'Was he mugged?'

'We don't know that either,' Ruth explained. 'But we'd like to ask you a few questions, if that's okay?'

Dion nodded forlornly as he took out a cigarette paper and tried to crumble his tobacco into it. His hands were shaking so that it was virtually impossible.

Ruth gave him a kind smile. 'Do you want me to do that for you?'

'Erm, yeah, yeah,' he said with a wry smile at his own ineptitude. 'If you don't mind, dear.'

Ruth leaned forward and took the tobacco tin and papers from him.

*Florence bloody nightingale,* Lucy thought sardonically to herself, but she knew it was a friendly gesture for an old man who was clearly struggling with life.

'Could you tell us where you were on Saturday night?' Lucy asked as she clicked her pen ready to write.

'Me? Saturday night?' Dion asked with a droll laugh. 'I was in here. It's a long, long time since I went out on a Saturday night, you know?'

Lucy looked over at him. 'Did you speak to anyone or have any visitors?'

Dion shook his head. 'No. No-one.'

Ruth leaned forward and handed him back the tin and a rolled cigarette. 'Here you go.'

'Very kind of you, my dear.' Dion gave an almighty cough and took a box of Swan Vista matches from the arm of his chair.

'When was the last time you saw Ashley?' Ruth asked.

Dion struck the match loudly and then lit his cigarette. His hands were trembling and the tips of his fingers and nails were heavily stained with tobacco. 'A few weeks ago now.'

'How did Ashley seem when you met up?' Lucy asked.

'Fine, he was fine,' Dion said with a smile. 'His life was good, you know?'

'Ruben told us that Ashley would sometimes give you money?' Lucy asked. 'Is that right?'

'Yeah, he helped me out,' Dion said with a shrug. 'Last few times, he told me he had plenty of dough. Proper pompasetting about it.'

Lucy didn't know exactly what that meant. 'You mean he was showing off about having lots of money?'

'Oh yeah,' Dion chortled. 'Showed me that car he'd got himself and everything.'

Lucy turned a page of her notebook and then asked, 'Did he tell you where the money had come from?'

'No,' Dion replied. 'I know that place Ruben got was a big success. And they was workin' there together. Make me proud, they'd done so well.'

'Did Ashley and Ruben get on?' Ruth asked.

'Yeah, man. They was brothers,' Dion said. 'Drove that bitch wife mad sometimes, you know?'

'Mica didn't like Ruben and Ashley being close?' Ruth asked Dion to clarify what he was implying.

'No way,' Dion explained as he kissed his teeth. 'She want Ruben to herself. Her and Ashley sometimes fight like cat and dog.' Les pointed to his face. 'Once she stuck her nails in his face and Ashley ended up with stitches.'

'What were they fighting about?' Ruth asked.

'I dunno. Money stuff. She thought Ashley was taking Ruben for a ride,' Dion explained. 'Last time he was here, he told me Mica warned him to keep out of her and Ruben's affairs.'

Lucy glanced over at Ruth. Was that significant? It sounded like there was no love lost between Mica and Ashley.

'Did he seem scared?' Lucy asked.

'Of Mica?' Dion snorted. 'Nah. Ashley wasn't scared of nobody.'

# CHAPTER 10

Gaughran tapped his biro impatiently on the table and then sat back on his uncomfortable plastic seat. He and Hassan had been sitting in a police interview room in Surrey Police Headquarters in Guildford for over twenty minutes. The building was a large, grey 70s building with ten floors. The room itself was warm – almost too warm, he thought. It was bright and newly painted with decent furniture – it was a far cry from the dingy interview rooms over at Peckham nick.

'Should be the other way around, shouldn't it?' Gaughran observed.

Hassan frowned. 'What's that then Sarge?'

'This nick isn't much to look at from the outside,' he said, 'But inside everything's bloody shiny and new.'

'Yeah, I noticed that,' Hassan agreed.

'Crime rate in Surrey is one of the lowest in the country. No gangs, virtually no drug dealers and a murder about once a year. So, why have they got a shiny comfortable nick when we're at the sharp end in SE15 and we're working out of a dump?'

Hassan shrugged, but before he could answer, the door to the interview room opened and a man in his 50s walked in. He was rotund, balding, and wore a short-sleeved shirt. His stomach strained at the waistband of his trousers.

*Christ, he's no stranger to a fish supper, is he?* Gaughran thought dryly to himself. *And probably washed down with a few pints of lager.*

'You the guys from Peckham CID?' he asked as he approached, hitched up his trousers, and came over.

'DS Tim Gaughran and DC Syed Hassan,' Gaughran explained as they all shook hands. Carter had an old-fashioned signet ring on the pinkie of his left hand.

'DCI Wayne Carter,' he said as he lowered himself into a chair and put some files on the desk. 'You're interested in Ashley Campbell, is that right?'

'Yeah,' Gaughran nodded. 'Someone stabbed and killed him on Saturday night in Peckham. We've got reason to believe that it wasn't a mugging or a robbery. So, we're looking into anything else that might have given someone a motive to kill him.'

'Duty Sergeant told me you've come straight here from Cranleigh Barracks?' Carter asked with a sour, humourless expression.

'Yeah,' Hassan replied. 'We spoke to a Brigadier Hastings.'

Carter snorted and then rubbed his nose. 'Talking to him is like getting blood out of a stone, isn't it? But that's the British Army for you.'

'Yeah, he wasn't very helpful.' Gaughran agreed. 'We understand that Ashley Campbell had recently given an internal MOD inquiry an initial statement about certain events that he had witnessed in 1989 while he was a recruit at Cranleigh. He was meant to go back today to talk to Hastings and the full inquiry panel to go through and expand upon that statement.'

'And you think his murder has something to do with what was in that statement?' Carter asked as he rubbed his nose again.

'Possibly. If he was going to give evidence about a serious criminal act, that could give someone motive to kill him,' Hassan suggested.

'Fair point,' Carter agreed. 'And Hastings sent you over to us?'

'Yeah. He seemed to think you'd spoken to Ashley a few years ago about a specific incident at Cranleigh.'

Carter leaned over, took a file, opened it and turned it for Gaughran and Hassan to see. There was a photograph of a young female soldier and a name – *Private Jackie Rosen*. Wearing her dress uniform and black beret, she had a beaming smile in the photo.

*Pretty girl,* Gaughran thought to himself.

'Private Jackie Rosen,' Carter said, pointing to the photo. 'She committed suicide in April 1989 at Cranleigh Barracks. She had a single gunshot to the head and a rifle beside her. The MOD dealt with it internally. It wasn't until her parents went public with their concerns and a local MP got involved that we were called to take a look in 1991. The SIO at that time had his doubts. I was only a DC then, but I remember thinking that a lot of things didn't quite add up.'

'You didn't think she committed suicide?' Hassan asked.

'We weren't sure. But because the army assumed it was suicide, they dealt with it accordingly. Jackie's body had been buried for two years, the crime scene destroyed and the firearm in question lost by the time we were called in,' Carter explained in a withering tone. He clearly thought Jackie's death hadn't been given the kind of investigation afforded to a civilian. 'There was nothing to go on except for testimonies from those recruits and staff who were at Cranleigh that night. And they refused to talk to us.'

Hassan frowned. 'Do you know why?'

'They'd been told to keep their mouths shut,' Carter said. 'Most of them were still in the army, so I assume they wanted it to stay that way.'

'So, how does Ashley Campbell fit in to all this?' Gaughran asked.

'Ashley was a recruit at Cranleigh at the same time as Jackie Rosen. Apparently, they were friends,' Carter explained. 'He came forward in 1991 when Surrey Police investigated her death. Some of the stuff that was going on at Cranleigh at the time was horrendous.'

'How do you mean?' Gaughran asked.

'Racial abuse. Assault, humiliation and bullying,' Carter explained. 'Allegations that officers demanded or even forced sex from female recruits. Either that, or sex was traded for long weekends on leave. When we did our investigation, a third of the 500 recruits at Cranleigh were women. But there were only two female instructors in the whole place. The place was out of control.'

'And Jackie Rosen?' Gaughran asked.

'Jackie Rosen alleged she was raped while on guard duty in April 1989,' Carter said. 'Those in charge at Cranleigh covered it up. They told other recruits who were around that night not to talk to anyone outside of Cranleigh or talk to the media. It was made clear there would be serious repercussions for anyone who spoke up about what had happened to Jackie.'

Gaughran raised an eyebrow. 'I assume that Ashley Campbell knew something then?'

Carter nodded and sat forward in his seat. 'Ashley had seen what had happened to Jackie as he was due to replace her on guard duty. When we investigated Jackie's death, Ashley came forward and said that he was willing to tell us exactly what he'd seen.'

'But he didn't, so what happened?' Hassan asked.

'Someone got to him,' Carter explained. 'He withdrew his statement a few days later and told us he hadn't seen anything.'

'But something made him come forward eight years later,' Gaughran said, thinking out loud.

Carter shrugged. 'Yeah. Ashley was no longer serving in the army. I assume he thought he wasn't in danger.'

Hassan frowned and asked, 'But why did he talk to an internal MOD investigation? Why not come directly to you?'

'I don't know,' Carter replied with a shrug. 'And I guess we'll never know the answer to that. But we did get the name of an officer that kept cropping up like a bad smell. We suspected that he was involved in what happened to Jackie Rosen that night. We also know that Ashley filed a complaint against him for racism just after he left the army, but like everything else, it was *dealt with internally*.'

Gaughran and Hassan exchanged a look. It was sounding like there was a powerful motive for someone to stop Ashley testifying to what he had seen.

'I'm gonna need the name of that officer,' Gaughran said.

'Of course.' Carter flicked open the file to a photograph of a man in his late 40s with a moustache. 'Captain Dennis Hurst. Ashley wasn't the only recruit who came forward about Captain Hurst. From all accounts, he was a nasty bastard. The army pensioned him off a few years ago to get him out of the way.'

'And he never faced any disciplinary action from the army?' Gaughran asked.

'No. Never.'

'Do you know where he is now?' Hassan asked.

'Not far,' Carter explained. 'I've got an address for him in Crawley.'

Gaughran looked at Hassan. 'I think we probably need to go and have a chat with Captain Hurst.'

# CHAPTER 11

It was midday by the time Lucy and Ruth arrived back at *Harvey's* in Clapham. It was virtually empty as they approached the bar, showed their warrant cards, and explained that they were looking for Mica Campbell. From what Dion had told them, Mica and Ashley didn't get on and she didn't have an alibi. It was something that needed further investigation.

Walking up the stairs, Lucy remembered what had happened the night before and James' account of the man in her garden. Once James had gone back upstairs to his flat, she had found it difficult to get to sleep. She hadn't told Ruth yet, but now needed to get it off her chest.

'I had a prowler last night,' Lucy said.

Ruth stopped and turned to look at her. 'What do you mean?'

'I was going to tell you earlier, but Ferguson waltzed in,' she explained. 'The bloke that's moved in upstairs saw someone in my garden looking in through my patio doors.'

'Bloody hell, Luce!' Ruth exclaimed. 'How did you forget to tell me that? What happened?'

'The bloke from upstairs, James, jumped down from the balcony and chased him away.'

'Christ, that was brave. And idiotic. I didn't know Jason Bourne lived upstairs from you,' Ruth said, raising her eyebrow.

'Yeah, I did tell him it was reckless,' Lucy explained. 'The thing is, he got a look at the prowler. Tall, about 40, with shoulder length hair.'

'You think it's Marcus Jankel, don't you?' Ruth asked.

'Maybe.' Lucy shrugged. 'The description fits, doesn't it?'

'Yeah. Why don't you come and stay at mine for a bit?' Ruth suggested.

'No, it's fine,' Lucy said shaking her head. 'I'm getting an alarm fitted next week. I refuse to be scared out of my own home.'

'Okay. But if anything else happens, you're coming to mine, okay?' Ruth said sternly.

Lucy nodded. 'Yeah. Thanks.'

As they reached the top of the stairs, a tall, elegant Afro-Caribbean woman, late 20s, came out of an office with a mobile phone to her ear. She frowned when she saw them and said, 'Eddie, I'm going to have to call you back.' before hanging up.

'We're looking for Mica Campbell?' Lucy explained as she and Ruth got out their warrant cards. 'We're from Peckham CID.'

'Is this about what happened to Ashley?' the woman asked with a sad expression.

'Are you Mica Campbell?' Ruth asked.

'Yes, sorry,' Mica said shaking her head. 'I'm not really with it after everything that's happened. It's been such a terrible shock.'

'If we could go somewhere quiet, there's just a few routine questions we'd like to ask you,' Lucy explained.

'Of course.' Mica pointed to an open door. 'My husband Ruben is out, so we can use his office.'

'Thanks,' Ruth said. 'We spoke to your husband last night, actually.'

'That's right,' Mica said, nodding her head. 'He told me. As I said, it's been a massive shock.'

Ruth gave her a sympathetic look. 'Of course. Were you close to Ashley?'

'Yes,' Mica confirmed with a sombre look that Ruth thought seemed a little forced. 'He was like a brother to me.'

Ruth didn't believe her. There seemed to be some disconnect between what she was saying and what she actually felt.

'And when was the last time you saw Ashley?' Lucy asked.

'Erm, let me think,' Mica said with a pensive face. 'Friday some time. I think he popped into the bar in the afternoon to talk to Ruben.'

'Do you know what they talked about?' Ruth asked.

'No, sorry.' Mica shrugged. 'You'd have to ask Ruben.'

Lucy looked over at her. 'How did Ashley seem on Friday?'

Mica sat forward in her seat. 'Sorry, how do you mean?'

'Was there anything troubling him?' Ruth suggested. 'Anything out of the ordinary.'

'No, he was fine. He and Ruben were chatting and laughing at the bar,' Mica explained. 'And then he left.'

Ruth peered at her. 'How would you describe Ruben and Ashley's relationship?'

'Very close,' Mica said without hesitating. 'They do ... sorry, did ... everything together. Played in the same five-a-side team every Wednesday. Went to the gym together. Worked here together.'

'And they never argued?' Lucy asked.

'Of course they did,' Mica replied as if it was a stupid question. 'They were brothers. But it was never about anything serious. And a few minutes later it was forgotten. You know how it is?'

'Had they rowed about anything recently?' Ruth asked. 'At the end of the last week?' She knew that most murders in the UK were committed by people known to the victim, often a family member or close friend.

'No.' Mica shook her head. 'Not that I can remember.'

Ruth looked at her for a few seconds and then asked. 'How did you get on with Ashley, Mica?'

'Fine,' she said, but it was unconvincing. 'I told you that.'

'Did you ever row?'

'No, never,' Mica stated forcefully. 'He said I was like his little sister, so he was very protective of me.'

*Bollocks. Still not buying it. She's hiding something.*

Lucy gave her a dubious look. 'I understand there was an incident where you and Ashley got into a fight and he had to have stitches in his face?'

'Erm, I ...' Mica seemed thrown. She clearly wasn't expecting them to mention the incident. 'I'd had too much to drink one night. Ashley was trying to put me in a cab and I just lashed out.'

'Was that the only time you fought?' Lucy asked.

'Yes,' Mica said indignantly and frowned at them suspiciously. 'Have you been talking to Dion?'

Ruth nodded. 'Yes, we spoke to him earlier today.'

'Don't listen to anything Dion has to say about anything,' Mica snorted as she pulled a face. 'He's a nasty old drunk. Ruben can't stand him. It was only Ashley that ever insisted that he came to family events. Ashley gave him hand-outs so he could get alcohol.' She gave them a perplexed look. 'Why? What did Dion say?'

'He seemed to think that you and Ashley didn't get on and never had.'

'Nah, that ain't true,' Mica huffed as if it was a ridiculous notion. 'Ask Ruben, he'll tell you.'

*Yeah, he's your husband, so he's not exactly a reliable source of information,* Ruth thought.

Lucy turned over the page of her notebook and asked, 'Do you know where Ashley was going on Saturday night?'

Mica took a moment and frowned. 'Didn't you ask Ruben all this last night?'

Mica's tone and body language had gone from polite and helpful to closed off and irritable. She clearly hadn't liked the type of challenging questions they'd been asking her.

'We did,' Ruth said gently. 'But as you said, Ruben's had a shock. There might be something that you remember that he didn't. And sometimes, those little things can really help us catch whoever killed Ashley.'

Mica sat back and peered down at her perfectly manicured nails which were bright scarlet. 'I just assumed that Ashley would be doing what he always did on a Saturday night.'

'And what was that then?'

'Oh, you know. He'd go to various bars and clubs in South London on the pull. One-night stand and then onto the next,' Mica explained in a withering tone. She clearly disapproved of Ashley's lifestyle.

Lucy raised an eyebrow. 'Bit of a ladies' man, was he?'

'You could say that.' Mica gave an ironic snort. 'He had a real knack when it came to women. But he wasn't one for settling down.'

'Did that ever cause any problems?' Ruth asked.

'How do you mean?'

'If Ashley was hitting on women, were there ever any jealous boyfriends or husbands around?' Ruth asked.

Mica thought for a moment and then replied, 'Actually, yes. A man came in looking for him last week. The barman said he seemed really angry. When he found out that Ashley wasn't in, he told our barman to tell Ashley that he was looking for him.'

'Is that barman in?' Ruth asked.

'Felix?' Mica asked. 'Yeah, he's downstairs. In fact, I think he said that the man threatened Ashley.'

Ruth glanced over at Lucy – it sounded like a decent lead.

# CHAPTER 12

Gaughran and Hassan knocked on the door of The Gables, a small cottage about fifteen minutes south of Crawley. The front garden was neat and tidy, and the flower beds were well-tended. An airplane flew low overhead as it made its way over to Gatwick airport.

The door opened and a large, imposing man in his 50s stood there. He had a bushy, greying moustache and Gaughran instantly recognised him as Captain Dennis Hurst. He was wearing a navy sweater with a golf club emblem and cream-coloured slacks.

'Can I help?' Hurst asked with a pleasant, friendly smile.

'Captain Hurst?' Gaughran asked.

'Gosh. I'm afraid it's just Dennis these days,' Hurst replied with a wry smile. 'You look like police officers. Is everything all right?'

Gaughran got out his warrant card. 'DS Gaughran and DC Hassan from Peckham CID. We're investigating the death of Ashley Campbell. We wondered if we could ask you a few routine questions?'

'Yes, of course,' Hurst replied sombrely. 'An old friend of mine rang to tell me what had happened. He seemed to think he was murdered or something?'

Hassan nodded. 'Yes, that's right. Can we come in? It won't take more than a few minutes.'

Hurst nodded, opening the front door for them to come in. 'Yes, of course. Anything I can do to help.'

*He seems very accommodating. That's not the response I was expecting,* Gaughran thought to himself. Carter had painted a very different picture of Hurst.

Hurst showed them into a reception room which was tastefully decorated in pastel shades and soft furnishings. The house smelt of furniture polish and fresh coffee. Classical music was playing quietly on a record player in the corner.

'Please, sit down,' Hurst said, pointing to a large sofa as he went over and turned the music off. 'Can I get you coffee or tea?'

'We're fine, thank you,' Gaughran said.

Hassan took out his notebook and clicked his pen.

'So, how can I help?' Hurst said as he crossed his legs. He wasn't what Gaughran had imagined at all. Hurst had been portrayed as a vicious bully and someone who had been accused of rape. Gaughran was experienced enough to know that the persona projected by someone could be radically different from their true character. However, Gaughran normally had an instinct when a person was hiding something or felt uncomfortable in their own skin. Hurst seemed confident, without being arrogant or false. Either that or he was a sociopath.

'Can we just check where you were on Saturday night?' Hassan asked.

'Golf Club do,' Hurst said. 'Captain's Charity Ball, actually.' It sounded almost as if he had already rehearsed the answer, such was the speed and clarity with which he responded.

'And where was that?' Hassan asked.

'The Cottesmore Golf Club,' Hurst stated. 'And I was there all night.'

*It's almost as if he was expecting us,* Gaughran thought.

'Could you tell us what time you left the Golf Club?'

Hurst pulled an embarrassed face. 'I'm afraid to admit that I was a little worse for wear when I got home. But I think it was after midnight when I got into the taxi.'

*Which gives him a very solid alibi for the time of Ashley's murder*, Gaughran noted.

'I assume there would be plenty of people who could confirm that?' Hassan asked.

Hurst gave a half smile. 'Yes, I'm guessing there would be over a hundred people who saw me that night.'

'The MOD is currently running an internal investigation into events at Cranleigh Barracks, focusing particularly on the suicides of four recruits,' Hassan explained.

'Are they?' Hurst shrugged. 'I keep myself to myself these days. And I've retired so I wouldn't know about that.'

'Ashley Campbell had already given Brigadier Stephen Hastings a preliminary statement. He was due to give more evidence to the inquiry today. We're investigating whether there is any link between Ashley's pending evidence and his death.'

'Gosh, really?' Hurst frowned. 'You think someone killed Ashley Campbell to stop him from giving evidence?'

'It's a possible line of inquiry,' Gaughran informed him. 'We believe that Ashley's evidence concerned events of 16th April 1989. Does that date mean anything to you?'

'Yes, of course,' Hurst replied without hesitation. 'It was the night that Jackie Rosen was raped at Cranleigh Barracks.'

Gaughran was surprised. 'You have a good memory.'

'It's not a night you easily forget. I was in overall command at Cranleigh that night.'

Gaughran narrowed his eyes. 'Did you see what happened to Jackie Rosen that night?'

Hurst shifted uncomfortably in his chair for a few seconds.

There was an uncomfortable silence as Gaughran exchanged a look with Hassan – *that seems to have completely thrown him, doesn't it?*

'Yes,' Hurst sighed very quietly. 'I'm ashamed to say that I did see what happened to her. And I managed to put a stop to it. But I don't think she ever recovered from the attack.'

'No, she didn't.' Gaughran said dryly, 'She committed suicide four months later.'

'Yes.' Hurst nodded slowly. 'And that was a terrible tragedy.'

'No-one was ever convicted of raping Jackie Rosen, were they?' Hassan asked, as he glanced up from his notebook.

'No.' Hurst shook his head. 'No, they weren't.'

Gaughran raised an eyebrow. 'If you stopped Jackie Rosen being raped, then you saw who did it?'

Hurst uncrossed his legs and gave an awkward sigh. 'Yes, I did.'

'Why didn't you tell Surrey Police when they investigated Jackie's suicide?' Hassan asked in a tone of disbelief.

'It's a difficult one to explain, I'm afraid. The British Army has its own laws and codes of conduct,' Hurst said. 'And one of them is a strict code of silence. We deal with things internally, amongst ourselves. We don't air our dirty laundry in public.'

'But the British Army didn't deal with it,' Gaughran snapped. 'No-one was ever charged with Jackie Rosen's rape. And it clearly traumatised her so much that she took her own life.'

'I understand that, but you have to remember that Jackie didn't want to name her attacker,' Hurst said with a sigh.

Hassan frowned. 'I think she was too scared to. My guess is that she was told to shut her mouth and keep quiet.'

'I don't know anything about that,' Hurst replied. 'And the decision not to pursue anyone for her rape was taken above my head. I valued my job, so I kept my mouth shut too. But I do regret that now.'

'Don't you think it's time you told the truth about what happened that night?' Gaughran asked sternly.

For a few seconds, Hurst didn't say anything. He just blinked as his eyes roamed around the room.

'Can you tell us who raped Jackie Rosen?' Gaughran asked.

'Yes. It was Ashley Campbell,' Hurst said eventually.

'What?' Gaughran said in a slightly disbelieving tone as he looked over at Hassan.

'It was Ashley Campbell who raped Jackie that night. She and Ashley had been drinking heavily on guard duty and then he attacked her. I was on patrol when I heard her scream and I pulled him off her,' Hurst explained. 'She was in a terrible state.'

'That doesn't make any sense,' Gaughran said, his brow furrowed. 'He was due to give evidence to the inquiry today.'

'Yes,' Hurst said. 'And I believe he was going to confess to the attack. He nearly admitted to attacking Jackie when Surrey Police were investigating the deaths at Cranleigh. But Ashley was warned by a very high-ranking General not to talk to anyone.'

'How do you know all this?' Hassan asked.

'Ashley and I kept in touch,' Hurst explained.

'Really?' Gaughran couldn't hide his incredulity.

'Strange bedfellows, I know,' Hurst said. 'I think he looked up to me as a father figure when he was at Cranleigh. I'm not trying to interfere in your investigation, but I'd be taking a close look at Jackie Rosen's family. Her father told me at her funeral that no matter how long it took, he would find whoever had attacked his daughter and kill them.'

Ruth and Lucy had been interviewing the barman Felix for about five minutes in *Harvey's*.

'Can you tell us the last time you spoke to Ashley?' Ruth asked.

'The last time I *spoke* to him was Friday afternoon,' Felix explained.

Ruth picked up on Felix's emphasis on the word *spoke* as if it was relevant. 'Friday was the last time you *spoke* to Ashley. Does that mean that you saw him after that?'

'Yeah, I saw him on Saturday morning,' Felix explained. 'But I didn't speak to him or anything.'

'Where was that?' Lucy asked.

'I was driving down Peckham High Street to go and see my mum,' Felix replied. 'Ashley came out the Lloyd's bank and got into his car. I beeped the horn, but he didn't see me.'

'Is there anything else that you can tell us about what you saw?'

'There was someone walking to the car with him,' Felix said.

'Do you know who?'

'Nah.' Felix shook his head. 'I was driving, so I didn't see who it was.'

'Okay,' Ruth said. 'I understand that someone came in here last week and made a threat against Ashley?'

Felix nodded. 'That's right.'

'And this was Tuesday?' Lucy asked.

'Yeah,' Felix stated. 'This man came in, straight up to the bar and pointed at me.'

'What exactly did he say to you?' Lucy asked.

'He asked if Ashley Campbell was around.'

Ruth glanced up from writing in her notebook. 'And you said he seemed angry?'

'Yeah. He was fidgeting, you know, couldn't stand still,' Felix explained. 'He looked like he was going to explode. He told me to tell Ashley that Neil was looking for him and to watch his back.'

'Right,' Ruth said, raising an eyebrow. It sounded as if this man was now a person of interest in their investigation.

'Do you think it's the bloke that attacked Ashley?' Felix asked, looking worried.

Ruth gave him a smile. 'We're not sure.'

'Could you describe this *Neil* for us?' Lucy said.

'Bald, big bloke. He looked hard.' Felix then thought for a few seconds. 'Actually, we've got CCTV in the bar area. Someone should be able to show you.'

A tall Afro-Caribbean woman in her early 20s was heading for the door that led upstairs when Felix glanced over at her.

'Lenora?' he said and then gestured to Ruth and Lucy. 'Have you got time to help these police officers?'

Lenora, who was smartly dressed in a slightly showy way, rolled her eyes as she came over. She clearly wasn't happy at being asked to help them.

'I suppose so,' Lenora shrugged as she looked Ruth and Lucy up and down.

*Wow, what charm school did she go to?*

'This about Ash?' she asked. She sounded thoroughly disinterested.

Ruth exchanged a look with Lucy. Lenora's attitude was grating already.

Felix nodded. 'Remember that bloke who came in last Tuesday. He said he was looking for Ashley and told me his name was Neil.'

'Yeah, you told me,' Lenora nodded, deliberately ignoring Ruth and Lucy. 'You said he was a right mardy twat.'

'Yeah,' Felix gave her a forced smile. 'Could you show them the CCTV from that day, so they can get a look at him?'

Lenora raised an eyebrow and then stared at them. 'You think it was him that killed Ash, do you?'

Ruth shrugged. 'We're not sure yet. But if we could get a look at him on your CCTV, that might help us track him down.'

'Right,' Lenora sighed as she gestured to the back of the bar and said impatiently, 'Come on then.'

Lucy smiled at Ruth and mumbled under her breath, 'She seems nice.'

Getting to the back room, Lenora went over to the stack of VHS tapes and pulled out the one for the Tuesday of the previous week. Putting it into the VHS machine, she sat down and scrolled through the footage from the main bar for the day. As the time-code reached *18.55pm*, she slowed it down.

'This should be it,' Lenora explained as she played the video forward. At *19.03pm*, a thick-set bald man in a leather jacket came into the bar. He had a distinctive tattoo on his neck, which looked like a crucifix. Even from the footage, Ruth could see that he was agitated as he approached Felix at the bar.

'Got you, dickhead!' Lenora said as she paused the video. The man, who they assumed was Neil, was fully visible. 'He looks like a right nutter.'

Lucy pointed. 'Great. We're going to need that tape. In fact, we're going to need the tapes for the whole of last week too.'

'Okay,' Lenora mumbled in a way to signify that she couldn't care less.

'How long have you worked at Harvey's, Lenora?' Ruth asked.

'Since it opened four years ago,' Lenora said. 'Mica is my sister.'

'Oh right,' Ruth said. 'And how well did you know, Ashley?'

Lenora shrugged tetchily, as if this was an irritating question. 'He was my brother-in-law, wasn't he?'

Ruth peered at her. 'So, you were close?'

'He was family,' Lenora sneered. 'Of course we was close.'

'Ashley was an attractive man,' Lucy said. 'Was there ever anything between you?'

Lenora frowned. 'Ash? Eww, nah, he was like my brother. But the man was like a dog with three dicks. He hit on every woman he met.'

'And when was the last time you saw Ashley?' Lucy asked.

'The last time I saw him was Friday afternoon when he came in here to see Ruben,' Lenora explained.

'And how did he seem?'

Lenora shrugged impatiently. 'I don't know. It was Ash. He didn't give nothing away.'

'Can you think of anyone who would want to harm Ashley? Did he have any enemies or had he fallen out with anyone recently?'

'Nah, everyone liked Ash. He was smooth, you know? A charmer.'

Lucy flicked a strand of hair back from her face and asked, 'What about Mica? Did he get on with her?'

'Not in the old days, no,' Lenora explained. 'But in the past few months, they just stopped arguing. They seemed okay, you know?'

'Do you know why it changed?'

'Nah. No idea,' Lenora said. 'But I know it made Ruben happy.'

'And where were you on Saturday night?' Lucy asked.

'Here,' Lenora sighed with an exasperated shake of the head . 'I'm always *here*.'

# CHAPTER 13

Standing in her kitchen, Lucy peered disappointedly into her fridge. There was nothing that seemed remotely exciting except two bottles of San Miguel, which she took out and put on the side. She opened the freezer drawer. It contained a bottle of raspberry vodka and a pizza.

*Bloody hell!*

Putting them next to the beers, she went over and put on the oven for the pizza and grabbed a small glass for the vodka.

She felt a tiny fleck of water splash on her cheek.

*What was that?* she wondered, slightly startled.

As she closed the freezer door, she felt a drop of water plop onto her scalp ... and then another.

*What the ...?*

Glancing up at the ceiling, she saw that a small patch had appeared and was leaking drips of water.

*Shit! It's coming from the flat above!*

Turning on her heels, she jogged towards the front door just in time for someone to knock at the door.

Peering through the spyhole, she saw that her neighbour, James, was standing on the doorstep.

'James?' she said as she opened the door. 'There's something coming through my ceiling!'

'I know,' he replied. 'It's my fault.'

He was standing in a long navy bathrobe, jogging trousers, and had a white towel resting over his shoulder.

'Really sorry...I...left the bath running,' he babbled in his middle-class accent. 'I've ... cleared it up now. Sorry.'

'Come in, it's freezing out there,' she gestured, interrupting him.

James pulled a face as he came in. 'I forgot about it...

'I saw the patch appearing on my ceiling.'

'Oh God,' he sighed. 'I'm such a bloody idiot. I was miles away. I'll pay for any damage, but I think I caught most of it. I've put some towels down now so I really hope it's not too bad.'

Lucy smiled at him. 'Please don't worry.'

'Can I have a look?' he asked awkwardly.

'Yes, come through,' Lucy said as she led the way to the kitchen. She glanced up, and the patch seemed to have stopped expanding and dripping. 'Yeah, it does look like it's stopped coming through now.'

'Thank God,' he said and then looked at her. 'And thank you for being so nice about it. Some neighbours would have gone mad and threatened all sorts of things.'

'Yeah, I'm a copper, remember?' she joked. 'I don't normally go around threatening anyone.'

'No, I don't suppose you do,' James said with a laugh. 'God, just when I thought today couldn't get any worse.'

'Well, don't worry about it.'

As he turned to go, he spotted the contents of Lucy's fridge and freezer on the counter. 'Ah, the old beer, vodka, and frozen pizza combo. Looks like you've been having one of those days too?'

'Hey, I'm always having one of those days,' she admitted as she picked up one of the bottles. She saw him looking at it. 'Fancy a beer before you go?'

'Erm, no, it's fine.'

'Go on. If you've had a shit day?'

He hesitated for a moment and then smiled. 'Yeah, why not.'

Opening both beers, she gestured to the living room. 'Come on, you can have a beer and tell me about your shitty day.'

James laughed again as he went in and sat himself carefully down on the sofa. Lucy put on The Verve's *Urban Hymns* and went and sat down in the big armchair.

'Cheers,' she said as she raised the bottle and took a long swig.

'Yeah, cheers,' James said as he did the same. 'Love this album.'

'Me too ... So, when you say shitty day, do you mean minor fuck up at work, boss is being a twat and the Northern Line wasn't working properly?' Lucy joked. 'Or worse than that.'

'Erm...' James hesitated for a few seconds.

*Oh God, I think I've touched a nerve here, and he's feeling really awkward.*

'Listen, it's fine,' she said. 'Let's talk about something else.'

'Actually, I've just thought of something. I hope you don't think it's weird,' James said. 'I was going to get a curry delivered here from that place, Panahar, down the road?'

'Oh my God, I love Panahar!' Lucy exclaimed. 'The King Prawn Balti is epic!'

'Great!' James smiled.

'Why would I think that's weird?' she asked.

'Well, as a way of saying sorry for ruining your kitchen ceiling, which I'll obviously pay for, why don't I order us both a curry? I mean, I know you've got that lovely frozen pepperoni pizza in there, so you might not be interested.'

'No, I'm definitely interested.'

'Really?'

Lucy grinned. 'That's a brilliant idea.'

*Calm down, Luce. He's got a girlfriend that he lives with. Take it nice and easy.*

'Great,' James said as he swigged his beer. 'I'll go upstairs and phone for it in a minute.'

Lucy laughed and pointed to her phone. 'Probably easier to phone from here.'

'Yes, of course,' James sighed. 'My head's just all over the place, hence the bath.'

'Well, curry and beer normally does the trick.'

There were a few seconds of silence that bordered on awkwardness.

'You see, I think Natalie is having an affair,' James said very quietly.

His comment hung in the room for a second.

'Oh, I'm sorry to hear that,' Lucy said with a concerned frown.

'Sorry, I don't know why I told you that.'

'It's fine ... Are you sure she's having an affair?'

'If I'm honest, yeah,' James admitted.

'What makes you say that?'

'She's gone to this conference thing and her ex-boyfriend is going to be there. And I'm pretty sure she's been meeting him after work and at the weekends behind my back.'

'But you've just moved in together,' Lucy said.

'I know.'

'That doesn't make any sense does it?'

'No, it doesn't,' James said. 'But I'm not easily spooked. And I'm not one of those paranoid boyfriends. I just know that's what's going on. As soon as I spoke to her this afternoon, I knew it. I could tell from her voice.'

'Yeah, I trust my instinct implicitly,' Lucy said.

They looked at each other and smiled.

'Sorry, I shouldn't be off-loading all this on you.'

'I'm a good listener.'

'You know what?' James said. 'If you don't mind, I'm going to go upstairs and get dressed, because wearing this is making me feel awkward. Then I'm going to order us that curry, grab the six beers in my fridge and come back down here. If you're okay spending time with a sad loser?'

Lucy smiled at him. 'Yeah. That sounds really nice.'

# CHAPTER 14

Ruth walked up the road with two heavy shopping bags in her hands. The plastic was actually cutting into her skin. Ella was having a sleepover at her new best friend's, Tabitha. *And* Tabitha's Mum, Nicola, was taking them both to nursery in the morning. *Bliss.*

As she reached the gate to her home, Ruth saw that someone was sitting on her doorstep.

It was Kara.

*Jesus Christ! What's she doing here? Stalker alert!*

Stopping in her tracks, and putting the shopping down on the path, Ruth peered at her. 'What are you doing, Kara?' she asked in a withering tone.

'I texted you twice today,' Kara said, getting up. 'And you didn't get back to me, so I was worried. I thought I'd wait here to make sure you're okay.'

'I am okay, Kara,' Ruth sighed. 'And I didn't get back to you because I was very busy today and I only saw you last night.'

'Sorry,' Kara shrugged. 'I can't help worrying about you.'

'Jesus, Kara. I don't want you worrying about me,' Ruth snapped as she got out her keys and went to the front door. 'Come on, you can help me in with the shopping. But then you'll have to go.'

Opening the door, Ruth grabbed one of the shopping bags and headed down the hallway to the kitchen and living area. Kara followed her with the other shopping bag.

'Do you want me to help you unpack the shopping?' Kara asked.

'No,' Ruth said as she looked at Kara for a second.

'Sorry,' Kara said quietly. 'You seem really angry with me. And after last night, that's a bit confusing.'

*God, I'm being a real bitch, aren't I? Am I leading her on?*

'I'm really sorry, Kara,' Ruth said, going to her. 'My head's a bit all over the place at the moment. Listen, do you want a glass of wine?'

Kara nodded. 'Yes. That would be nice.'

'Good,' Ruth said with a smile. Kara had done nothing wrong except for being a little needy and unsure of herself.

Pouring two large glasses of wine, Ruth went and handed it to her. They both took a large swig and smiled at each other.

Kara gave a nervous little laugh.

*God, she really is beautiful,* Ruth thought to herself. *If I ask her to stay when I don't think we have a future, am I leading her on? Does that make me a terrible person? Fuck it. I don't want to spend the evening here alone, feeling sorry for myself.*

Ruth approached Kara, took the wine glass from her hand, leaned in and gave her a gentle kiss. Putting her hand to her face, Ruth kissed her more passionately.

'I'm taking you to bed,' Ruth said, looking at her and taking her by the hand.

'Oh, okay,' Kara replied in a virtual whisper.


Sitting in his car, Gaughran was listening to BBC 5Live radio. He had been peering into the darkness of the street in East Dulwich for nearly half an hour. He couldn't believe what he was hearing on the radio. Chelsea Football Club had sacked their Dutch manager, Ruud Gullit. It made no sense as Gullit was their most successful manager for over twenty-five years. They had won the FA Cup for the first time in decades back in May. Gullit's brand of slick passing had been branded *sexy football* by the British press. And with his dreadlocks and loafers with no socks, he was by far the 'coolest' football manager in the history of British football. The man had found chart success with his own reggae band for God's sake! Gaughran was crest-fallen. When he grew up, Chelsea had yo-yoed between the old first and second divisions. Being a Chelsea fan was often an embarrassment. An old music-hall joke. Gullit had changed all that and now they'd bloody got rid of him!

The noise of heels on the pavement broke his train of thought. Checking his rear-view mirror, Gaughran saw his father's *girlfriend* walking up the road towards her flat. He had done some digging around and soon found out that her name was Angela Franklin. She was a secretary in the City of London and was known to her friends as Angie.

*Right, let's have this out!*

Opening the car door, Gaughran got out and stared at her as she approached.

'Oh my God!' Angela exclaimed as she stopped in her tracks. 'You scared the bloody life out of me!'

'I think that me and you need to have a little chat, don't you?' Gaughran said.

'Erm, do you want to come in?' Angela asked, pointing to the front door. She was clearly anxious.

Gaughran raised an eyebrow in disdain. 'No thanks. What I've got to say to you can be said out here.'

'Hang on. How do you know where I live?' she asked, now sounding annoyed.

'I want you to stop seeing my dad,' Gaughran said.

'Don't you think you should have this conversation with him, not me?' she snapped.

'Don't worry,' Gaughran said. 'I fully intend to.'

'You're not allowed to find out where people live for personal reasons,' she sneered. 'I'm not stupid, you know?'

'Why don't you report me then?' Gaughran growled. 'My mum and dad have been married for thirty years. And I won't let anything upset my mum or ruin her life. So, this is a warning. Stay away from my dad.'

'You're a copper,' she said. 'You can't threaten me. I know my rights.'

'My suggestion is that you find someone your own age, who's divorced or single,' Gaughran said. 'I don't want to come and talk to you again.'

'How dare you come here and frighten me!' Angie said as she stormed away over to her front door. 'I'm going to report this to your superiors.'

Gaughran watched as she disappeared inside.


Lucy went over to the CD player and turned up the volume. The Verve had been replaced by James' *Ministry of Sound* album and dance music was banging away.

'At least the neighbours can't complain,' Lucy laughed, pointing up to the ceiling.

Having eaten the curry and drunk all the beer, Lucy and James had now progressed to having shots of frozen raspberry vodka.

And they were now dancing around the living room together to *It's All Right, I Feel it* by *Masters at Work*. The uplifting vocals had a slightly gospel feel to them and Lucy spun around the room with her hands in the air.

'I love this!' she said with a grin.

'God, I'm really drunk,' James laughed as he took Lucy's hands in his as they danced and laughed.

'So am I,' Lucy chortled. 'And it's a bloody school night!'

Feeling a little dizzy, Lucy went over to the sofa and slumped down.

'You okay?' James asked.

'Just a bit hot and a bit drunk,' she laughed.

James smiled at her. 'You're more than a *bit hot* from where I'm standing.'

She smiled back at him. 'Watch it, buster. You've got a girl-friend!'

James shrugged, rolled his eyes, and went over to the CD player. He had brought some of his music from upstairs. 'Feels like we need to bring it down a bit now.'

'Yeah, definitely. I need to get my breath back.'

Erykah Badu's latest album played. The track was *On and On*. It was a slow, sultry RnB song.

'Is this better?' James asked.

She looked at him from the sofa, and their eyes locked for a few seconds. 'Definitely.'

James came over, reached out his hands to take hers. 'Come on. Last dance of the night.'

'No, it's all right.'

'Come on. Then I'll go.'

Lucy laughed as she got up, and they danced. He twirled her around and she giggled.

'You know what?' Lucy said as she smiled at him. She knew that her words were now slurring. 'If I didn't know better, I would think that you were trying to seduce me.'

James gave a look of mock indignation. 'Who? Me?'

'Yes, you.'

'What's that line from *The Graduate?*' he said. 'Dustin Hoffman says to Ann Bancroft, *I feel like you're trying to seduce me, Mrs Robinson.*'

Lucy grinned. '*Do you want me to seduce you, Benjamin?*'

They laughed as they looked at each other.

James put his arm around her waist, pulling her towards him very gently. He leaned in slowly and kissed her gently.

*Oh, okay, is this a good idea?*

Lucy responded as she kissed him back and put her hands around his back.

# CHAPTER 15

The doors to CID opened and Ferguson strolled in. He had folders in one hand and a cup of tea in the other. He walked tall with a straight back, and Ruth wondered if he had originally been in the military.

'Thanks for the head's up about the tea from the canteen, guys!' he joked as he made his way to the front of the CID office.

'Does it not meet with your a-*brew*-val, guv?' Gaughran joked.

There were several groans at his terrible joke.

'Jesus, Tim! Please don't give up your day job,' Ferguson laughed. 'Tell me we've got a kettle and teapot in here somewhere? I can't drink this every day.'

Hassan pointed to the far corner. 'Over there, guv.'

'Thank God,' Ferguson sighed as he dropped the cardboard cup into the bin. He walked over to the scene board, which was now full of photos, maps, and information. 'Right, guys, first things first. I want us to do a press conference this morning to see if we can flush out any more witnesses who might have seen Ashley on Saturday. Tim, you're my most experienced DS, so are you okay to do that?'

Gaughran nodded. 'Yes, guv.' He didn't look pleased about the prospect. Brooks had always run the press conferences when he was head of Peckham CID. Clearly Ferguson was less hands on when it came to the media.

'What else have we got?', Ferguson asked. 'Anything on the gun we found in Ashley's boot?'

Hassan looked over. 'I spoke to ballistics. The serial number has been removed so there's no way of tracing it, guv.'

'And what about the false plates or the VIN number?'

'Still waiting for the DVLA to get back to us,' Hassan explained.

'Thanks Syed,' Ferguson said. 'Lucy and Ruth, you interviewed this Jermaine Daniels, didn't you?'

'Yes, guv,' Ruth replied. 'Daniels tried to use Ashley's bank card on several occasions. He was identified by officers in Brixton. Daniels is known to them as he's part of the Brixton Hill Boys gang. There was a dawn raid on Daniels' home yesterday and Ashley's wallet and phone were found. SOCO also removed a pair of orange blood stained trainers.'

'So, we've got him bang to rights?' Gaughran said.

'Daniels claimed he saw Ashley being stabbed and robbed him while he was dying on the pavement,' Lucy explained.

'Jesus!' Hassan muttered as he shook his head.

Gaughran shrugged. 'Well, he would say that. He stabbed him, took his stuff and his defence is that he saw someone else doing it.'

Ferguson took a few seconds to think and then glanced over. 'You and Lucy don't seem convinced?'

Ruth frowned. 'We get lots of stabbings in Peckham. They're nearly all drug and gang related.'

'And Daniels is in a gang!' Gaughran scoffed.

'Yeah, but it doesn't feel right,' Ruth said. 'Ashley's wallet and phone were in his pocket. I've never worked a case where someone has been stabbed to death and then robbed. Every street robbery or mugging I've ever worked, the victim has been threatened with a knife or a gun to hand over valuables. Not stabbed to death and then robbed.'

'Bloody hell,' Gaughran groaned. 'You're splitting hairs, aren't you?'

'Maybe Ashley put up a fight, so Daniels stabbed him?' Hassan suggested.

'There aren't any defence wounds,' Lucy said, shaking her head. 'Ashley is ex-army, so he could handle himself. Whoever attacked him came up quietly and stabbed him in the back before he had time to react. Then they stabbed him in the stomach. The motive for the attack was to kill Ashley, not to take a wallet or phone from a stranger.'

'You don't know that,' Gaughran said.

'Actually, I agree with Lucy. I worked on dozens of muggings in Edinburgh and this doesn't feel right. My instinct is that Ashley was targeted rather than this being a street robbery gone wrong,' Ferguson said.

Gaughran wasn't buying it and rolled his eyes.

'You clearly don't agree, Tim?' Ferguson asked in a tone that left Gaughran in no doubt who was in charge.

'I don't,' Gaughran said. 'Aren't we just over-complicating this? Maybe a bloke just got stabbed outside a club in Peckham and had his wallet and phone stolen.'

'Ashley had false plates, a gun and twenty grand in cash in the boot of his car,' Ruth said. 'He was up to something very dodgy. If we find out what he was involved with, then I think we get his killer.'

'I appreciate what you're saying, Tim,' Ferguson said in a serious tone. 'But I'm going to put that theory on the back-burner. I think the evidence is telling us that Ashley was deliberately targeted and I'd like that to be our line of enquiry at the moment.'

Ruth spotted Gaughran surreptitiously shaking his head at Hassan. She then caught Lucy's half smile. It was always nice to see Gaughran taken down a peg or two.

Ferguson loosened his tie and undid the top button of his shirt. 'Ruth, you and Lucy went to talk to Ashley's father, didn't you?'

'Yes, guv,' Ruth replied. 'Dion Campbell. He told us that Ashley had bragged about coming into some money in recent weeks.'

'Did Ashley tell him where he was getting the money from?' Ferguson asked.

'No, guv,' Ruth replied. 'The only thing of interest that he gave us was that Ashley and his sister-in-law didn't get along. In fact, he claimed that Mica Campbell had physically attacked Ashley at a family gathering.'

'And you've not spoken to Mica Campbell?' Ferguson asked.

Lucy nodded. 'Yes, we did guv. She claims that Dion Campbell was exaggerating and that she'd just had too much to drink one night. She told us that Ashley was like a brother to her. She also said he was a bit of ladies' man.'

'Does the brother Ruben have an alibi?' Ferguson asked.

'Yes, guv,' Ruth replied. 'But Mica Campbell doesn't. She had a headache and Ruben called a cab for her around ten o'clock and she went home.'

'Can anyone vouch for the fact that she went home?' Hassan asked.

'No.'

Ferguson nodded. 'Okay, thank you.'

Ruth got up from her desk and grabbed the image from the CCTV footage from Harvey's and held it up for everyone in CID to see. 'We got something else, guv. This man here came into Harvey's last Tuesday looking for Ashley. The barman said he seemed angry and agitated.'

'Did you find out why he was looking for Ashley?' Ferguson asked.

'No, guv,' Ruth replied as she pinned the image to the scene board. 'But the man told the barman to tell Ashley that *Neil* was looking for him and to watch his back.'

Ferguson raised his eyebrow. 'Right. If this man, Neil, made a threat against Ashley four days before he was murdered, he is definitely a person of interest. Can we check CCTV around there and see if he parked nearby? If we get a plate, then we can track him down.'

'Yes, boss,' Ruth replied as she went back to her desk.

'Anything else from today?' Ferguson asked.

Lucy looked over and said, 'We also met Mica Campbell's sister, Lenora. She works at Harvey's and claims she was there on Saturday night.'

Ruth nodded. 'She described him as being like *a dog with three dicks*.'

There was some stifled laughter from the assembled detectives.

'Right, I think we get the picture,' Ferguson said with a wry smile.

'We also spoke to a barman Felix who claims to have seen Ashley coming out of the Lloyds Bank on Peckham High Street on Saturday morning,' Ruth explained.

'That would be the last sighting of Ashley that we've got until he gets to The Yard?' Ferguson said.

'Yes, guv,' Ruth replied. 'He's pretty sure there was someone walking back to the car with him too, but he didn't see who.'

'I'm guessing there's a decent amount of CCTV coverage on Peckham High Street. And let's go into Lloyds and find out what he was doing in there on Saturday morning,' Ferguson said. He then peered across the CID office. 'Tim and Syed, what have you got for us?'

Gaughran glanced up from where he was sitting. 'Syed and I interviewed a Brigadier Stephen Hastings at Cranleigh Barracks. He's in charge of the MOD's internal inquiry into the deaths of the four recruits in the early 90s. He won't give us a copy of Ashley Campbell's initial statement without a court order. He seemed to imply it was MOD policy, which isn't a surprise.'

'And I'm surprised the local police weren't called in,' Ferguson said.

'They were,' Hassan explained. 'We then went to speak to a DCI Carter at Surrey Police in Guildford. He told us they had looked at all the deaths and they didn't believe that any of them were suspicious. However, he had concerns over an alleged rape of a female recruit called Jackie Rosen, who was one of the recruits that took their own life.'

Ferguson rubbed his chin and asked, 'When was this?'

'Jackie Rosen was raped on the 16th April 1989. She took her own life, four months later,' Gaughran explained.

'And Surrey police investigated the allegation of rape?' Lucy asked.

'They tried to. They reckoned there was just a wall of silence,' Gaughran explained. 'The whole thing was covered up. Recruits were told not to talk to anyone about it or there would be serious repercussions.'

Ruth frowned. 'And Jackie Rosen didn't report it herself?'

'No. Apparently, she was too scared to name her attacker,' Hassan said. 'But we think Ashley did witness the attack.'

Gaughran continued. 'DCI Carter implied that a Captain Dennis Hurst was somehow involved in Jackie's rape and that Ashley was about to tell the inquiry what had happened that night.'

'Have you interviewed this Captain Hurst?' Ferguson asked.

Gaughran pulled a face. 'Yes, guv. Hurst claims it was Ashley Campbell who raped Jackie Rosen in 1989. He managed to stop Ashley and pull him off her. Hurst alleged Ashley was so wracked with guilt that he was going to confess to the attack when Surrey Police came in to investigate events at Cranleigh in 1992.'

'So, why didn't he?' Ruth asked.

'Some General made it very clear to Ashley that he should keep silent or else,' Hassan said.

Ferguson nodded. 'Okay. Did Hurst think Ashley was going to come clean about what he had done to this inquiry?'

Gaughran nodded. 'Yes, guv. But we have no proof of that. Only what Hurst told us and he could be lying.'

'What did you think?' Ferguson asked.

'My instinct was that he was telling us the truth,' Gaughran stated, as he looked over at Hassan.

'Yeah, I thought the same, guv,' Hassan confirmed.

'So, we're going to need a court order to get Ashley's initial statement,' Ferguson said, thinking out loud.

Ruth frowned. 'If Ashley intended to confess to the rape of Jackie Rosen, then the only person he was implicating was himself?'

'Unless he was intending to expose everyone who had covered up the rape?' Lucy suggested. 'Hurst might have been worried that it was all going to come out?'

'My guess is that Hurst was just following orders,' Ferguson said. 'It doesn't feel like a strong motive for murder, does it?'

'No, guv,' Ruth replied.

'Hurst told us that Jackie Rosen's father swore at her funeral that he would track down and kill whoever was responsible for this daughter's attack.'

'So, if he had discovered Ashley had raped his daughter, that would be a motive for attacking him,' Ruth said.

'Yeah, but the only way they could know that is if Jackie had told them who had raped her,' Lucy said. 'And they would have that information since 1989. So, why wait eight years to take any revenge?'

'Either way, Tim and Syed, I want you to track down Jackie Rosen's parents and see what they know.'

# CHAPTER 16

The press conference was due to start, and the room bustled with local and national journalists from newspapers, radio, and television. Gaughran could feel the nerves in his stomach. He had run about half a dozen press conferences in his career, but he never felt comfortable doing them. Hassan sat down next to him and pulled his chair in.

'You okay, Sarge?' Hassan asked under his breath.

'Never better,' Gaughran said sardonically. 'Let's get this bloody thing out of the way so we can do some proper police work, eh?'

Behind them was a photo of Ashley Campbell on the wall, a large image of the Metropolitan Police badge and a map of South London with various locations marked with red plastic pins.

On the table in front of Gaughran were some glasses, a jug of water, and several small tape recorders and microphones that journalists had placed there.

'Good morning, I'm Detective Sergeant Tim Gaughran from Peckham CID. Beside me is my colleague Detective Constable Syed Hassan. This press conference is to update you on the case and to appeal to the public for any information regarding the murder of Ashley Campbell outside The Yard nightclub in Peckham, last Saturday night, just before midnight. This is a dreadful tragedy and the Campbell family are devastated by this loss.

'At this stage in our investigation, we know that Mr Campbell was waiting outside The Yard Nightclub on Macey Road just before midnight, when he was attacked. The club was very busy that night and my appeal is that if you were there that evening and you saw anything out of the ordinary, however insignificant you think it might be, you contact us as soon as you can so we can come and talk to you.'

Gaughran spent the next fifteen minutes fielding questions about the investigation. Despite his own misgivings, he had clarified that Peckham CID felt it likely that someone had targeted Ashley. The attack was not random, and there was no immediate danger to the local community. He reiterated their need for information about anything suspicious that had been seen that night in the immediate vicinity of the club.

An hour later, Gaughran and Hassan pulled up outside a small block of flats off Streatham High Street. It was cold, and the sky was a uniform gun metal grey. The entire area seemed rundown and dilapidated. A long wall stretched across the other side of the road. It was covered in graffiti and razor wire ran along its top to stop anyone climbing over. A car went slowly past with blacked-out windows and a thudding bass that felt like it shook the road.

Gaughran watched it, staring through the windows to try to see inside.

'Dickheads,' he muttered.

'This is it,' Hassan said, pointing to the five-storey block that had been built in the 1930s.

It was the address they had found for Terry and Lisa Rosen, Jackie's parents.

Gaughran pointed over towards the High Street. 'Used to come up here to go to The Studio nightclub in the late 80s. Had a right laugh. They had phones on the tables so you could ring other tables.'

'Oh yeah,' Hassan nodded. 'Used to be the Cat's Whiskers, I think. My dad always reckoned he'd seen The Rolling Stones play there in the early 60s before they were really famous.'

'Bloody hell,' Gaughran snorted. 'Can't remember the last time I went to a nightclub. It was all silky shirts buttoned up to the top, Chris Waddle haircuts and Shalamar the last time I went.'

Hassan smiled. 'Getting old, Sarge.'

Gaughran pointed to the buzzer. 'Yeah, never mind about that. I'm only three years older than you.'

'Four,' Hassan corrected him with a grin.

'Ring the bell, would you?'

Hassan rang the buzzer and a few moments later, a thin, wiry man in his 60s appeared from a ground-floor flat door and approached the communal door.

'Hello?' he said with a curious frown as he opened the door.

'Mr Rosen?' Gaughran said as he fished out his warrant card.

'Yes?'

'DS Gaughran and DC Hassan from Peckham CID,' Gaughran explained. 'We're investigating the death of an Ashley Campbell. We believe he was at Cranleigh Barracks with your daughter, Jackie. We're wondering if you could answer some routine questions for us?'

'It's Terry ... I'm not sure how I can help,' he said. He didn't look like he was going to let them in.

'Can we come in? It'll only take a minute?' Hassan asked gently.

'I suppose so,' Terry sighed as he turned and they followed him back down the hallway and into the flat. He was wearing a t-shirt and jeans, which seemed to hang on his thin, bony body. He didn't look well.

The flat was cluttered and untidy. It smelt of cigarette smoke and stewed tea. They came into the living room, and Terry pointed to a long sofa. 'Do you wanna sit down then?'

'Thanks,' Hassan said, with an appreciative nod.

Gaughran spotted a row of photos on the mantelpiece. Nearly all of them featured pictures of Jackie. A couple of them showed her smiling in her army uniform.

'That one at the end was taken four weeks before she died,' Terry explained sadly, as he scratched his head.

'It must have been very difficult for you,' Gaughran said with genuine compassion as he went over and sat beside Hassan.

'Yeah. It still is. You never get over the death of a child,' Terry said with a sigh.

'No. I can't imagine how difficult that is,' Gaughran said gently. 'We're investigating the murder of Ashley Campbell. He was at Cranleigh Barracks as a recruit with Jackie? I wonder if you remember him or if Jackie talked about him?'

'Yeah, black lad.' Terry jutted out his chin a little with a nod. 'She called him Ash. He came from down the road, so I think that's why they were friends. You know, South Londoners away from home?'

'Did she ever say anything else about him?' Gaughran asked.

Terry shrugged. 'Only that he looked out for her. She said he was like a big brother to her in that place.'

'We understand Jackie was attacked at Cranleigh Barracks in April 1989?' Hassan asked gently as he opened his notebook.

'Yeah,' Terry said, as his face fell. 'She was raped.'

There were a few seconds of silence and then Terry reached for a packet of Silk Cut cigarettes and took one. His hands were shaking as he lit it.

'Did she ever talk about what had happened that night?' Gaughran asked.

'Not really.' Terry shook his head slowly as he took a long drag on the cigarette. 'She spoke to her mum, more than me.'

'Is your wife around for us to talk to?' Hassan asked.

Terry shook his head again. 'She died last year, cancer. But she was never the same after Jackie died. She just stopped living life.'

'I'm sorry to hear that,' Gaughran said.

Hassan glanced up from writing in his notebook. 'I understand that both the British Army and Surrey Police looked into the attack on Jackie and her subsequent death?'

'Oh yeah,' Terry snorted sarcastically. 'What a load of bollocks that was. They had no fucking intention of finding out who attacked Jackie or the circumstances around her death. It was a bloody cover up. It wasn't until we went to our MP that anyone did anything. And even then it was a bloody farce.'

'Did Jackie ever tell you who had attacked her?' Gaughran asked.

'No.' Terry shook his head. 'She said her life wouldn't be worth living if she reported who had attacked her.'

'Did she explain what she meant by that?'

Terry frowned. 'She didn't need to. Everyone knew that the instructors at Cranleigh were bullies. Fucking horrible bastards. They were always trying it on with the female recruits. We spoke to some of Jackie's female friends from Cranleigh at her funeral. They told us all sorts of stories. One officer said he was going to recommend one girl to be discharged from the army unless she came to his room every night and gave him a blow job.'

'Did anyone ever give any names of the men who had done this?' Gaughran asked.

'No, they were all too scared,' Terry explained. 'That's why we didn't think that Jackie had killed herself.'

Hassan raised an eyebrow. 'How do you mean?'

'I always thought that Jackie was about to report her attacker to the police,' Terry explained. 'But before she could, someone shot her dead and made it look like a suicide.'

'You think she was murdered?' Gaughran asked.

'I know my daughter,' Terry said, his voice now trembling with emotion. 'There is no way she would have put a rifle to her head and shot herself. And I know she was very down after she had been attacked, but I know what Jackie was like. Someone was scared that she was going to blow the whistle on them – and they killed her.'

'And you never heard any names mentioned?' Gaughran asked.

'Only one name,' Terry said. 'I heard Jackie and her mum rowing upstairs when she came home on leave after she had been attacked. And Jackie was talking about one officer at Cranleigh. She said he was evil scum, and she wanted him dead. And then I heard her say the name *Hurst*.'

Gaughran and Hassan looked at each other. 'Hurst?'

'Yeah, Hurst,' Terry said with a nod. 'I never forgot it. You know, like Geoff Hurst, who scored a hat-trick in the World Cup Final. I told the inquiry, and I told Surrey Police but they did nothing about it.'

Ruth was hard at work in the CID office at Peckham nick. She got up from her desk and stretched out her back, considering yet another coffee. It was certainly tempting. She couldn't get going and her brain felt like glue. She reached over and pulled over a pile of dispatches over related to the emergency call to the scene of Ashley's death, and the emergency response that followed. She had read the 999 call summaries. Whoever had called in the attack on Ashley had withheld their name so they couldn't be traced as a witness. Glancing over at Lucy, she noticed she was yawning and drinking another coffee.

'Keeping you up, sleepyhead?' she asked as she swivelled round her chair.

'Yeah.' Lucy smiled. 'Not a lot of sleep in this week.'

Something about the way Lucy had said it led Ruth to suspect that there was more to what she was saying than just insomnia.

Ruth looked over at her and just raised her eyebrow.

'What?' Lucy said defensively.

Sounding like a scolding mother, Ruth said, 'Tell me.'

'I don't know what you're talking about,' Lucy protested and went back to her work.

*Right, I'm going to call her bluff this time.*

'Okay,' Ruth said. 'I've just got the CCTV footage from Peckham High Street on Saturday morning, but I can't make out who it is walking beside Ashley. Do you want to take a look?'

Lucy gave her a furtive glance. Ruth knew she was dying to tell her something, but she wasn't used to her not playing her little game.

Lucy pulled a face as if to say, *I'm about to confess to something I'm not very proud of.* 'Can I tell you something?'

'Ha,' Ruth said triumphantly. 'I knew it!'

'What?'

'I knew there was something! And you were dying for me to ask you,' Ruth laughed. 'So, I ignored you.'

'That's very mature,' Lucy said.

'Okay, I need to tell you something, but you can't go mad or judge me,' Lucy sighed.

'Yeah, I can't actually promise that,' Ruth said, giving her a wry smile. 'If you've stolen your neighbour's delivery of wine because she's a stuck-up bitch again, then I can't condone that.'

'Oh my God, that was about five years ago and you said it was funny!'

'Okay. But today would be good,' Ruth said, teasing her.

'I slept with the gorgeous bloke from upstairs called James,' Lucy blurted out and pulled a face to prepare for Ruth's onslaught.

*You did what?*

'Erm, you mean James, the guy who just moved in upstairs with his girlfriend?' Ruth asked in a stern tone.

'Yeah, maybe,' Lucy shrugged. 'I'm not proud of myself.'

'Did his girlfriend not notice him slipping downstairs and then slipping you one?' Ruth quipped with a laugh.

'Ruth!' Lucy exclaimed. 'No. She's at a conference where she's meeting her ex, who she is having an affair with.'

'And James told you that?' Ruth sighed.

'Yeah. He's not lying,' Lucy protested.

Ruth raised an eyebrow dubiously. 'He's not lying about his unfaithful girlfriend to get you into the sack?'

'No. It's not like that.'

'Listen, my advice is to stop it right now before it gets out of hand,' Ruth advised her. 'You do *not* want that to explode on your doorstep, do you?'

'No,' Lucy nodded. 'Yeah, you're right. But he is sooo fit.'

'Lucy?' Ruth snapped.

'Okay, okay.' Lucy shrugged with a grin. 'I hear you.'

Ferguson approached. 'Anything on that CCTV from Saturday?'

Ruth pointed to the CCTV footage on the monitor in front of her. 'This is Ashley coming out of the bank at 10am, guv. And this is the bag with twenty thousand pounds that we found in the boot of his car. I just can't see who it is walking with him across the pavement.'

A phone rang on a nearby desk and Lucy went over and answered it.

Ferguson peered at the image closely. 'It looks like a woman to me.'

Ruth frowned again. 'Why do you say that, guv?'

'Waist and hips,' Ferguson explained. 'They might be wearing a baggy hoodie and baggy jeans, but look at how the waist narrows and then comes out at the hips. That's a girl or a woman.'

As Ruth looked again, she realised he was right. 'Well spotted.'

'What about Lloyds Bank?' Ferguson asked. 'Don't they have CCTV inside?'

'They were having their CCTV upgraded at the weekend, so it wasn't on,' Ruth said, rolling her eyes. 'If you can believe that?'

'Brilliant.' Ferguson gave her a withering look and then asked, 'Have the bank confirmed Ashley withdrew twenty grand from an account on Saturday morning?'

'No, guv,' Ruth said. 'They're looking into it as we speak.'

Putting down the phone, Lucy glanced over at them. 'Right, that was Lloyds Bank. They've gone through their records. Ashley Campbell didn't withdraw any money from an account on Saturday morning.'

Ruth frowned. 'I don't understand.'

'But their records show that a Lenora Garner *did* make a withdrawal for that amount,' Lucy explained.

# CHAPTER 17

Gaughran and Hassan marched down the corridor of King's College Hospital. They'd had a call from A&E telling them that a nurse remembered treating Ashley Campbell for a broken rib and fractured jaw on the 15th January.

Gaughran was still mulling over what they had been told by Terry Rosen. What Hurst had told them was a pack of lies. Gaughran felt annoyed that he'd taken Hurst at face value. He normally trusted his judgement. Maybe his initial thought about Hurst being a sociopath was correct. There was now a suspicion that Hurst had not only attacked and raped Jackie Rosen, he had murdered her to stop her reporting the attack too, while making it look like suicide.

'There must have been some kind of coroner's report into Jackie Rosen's death,' Hassan said, thinking out loud. 'I just don't understand it.'

'Problem is that her death was dealt with by the military,' Gaughran explained. 'And there's no indication that they saw it as suspicious.'

'Or they made sure no-one thought it was suspicious,' Hassan pointed out.

Gaughran raised an eyebrow and nodded. 'True ... And that means no-one would have looked at her body for signs of gunshot residue on her fingers or her forehead. And no-one would have looked to see if it was physically possible for a small woman to hold a heavy rifle, point the barrel at her head and pull the trigger. There aren't even any photographs of her body and how it was found. If the rifle was found next to her, had it fallen to the ground in a way that would be expected if she had taken her own life? It's shambolic.'

'Yeah, and we know it was Hurst who found her dead,' Hassan grumbled. 'I'll bet he wasn't checked for any gunshot residue either.'

Gaughran frowned at Hassan. 'Are we now thinking that Ashley Campbell not only knew who raped Jackie Rosen, but if we go down the theory that she was murdered, did Ashley also know what happened?'

'And if we think Hurst was involved in both crimes,' Hassan said. 'That's a huge motive to kill Ashley to keep him quiet.'

'We need to speak to Cottesmore Golf Club. I've got a strong suspicion that Hurst was lying about his whereabouts on Saturday night too.'

Arriving at the nurses' station in A&E, Gaughran needed to get his head back into the reason they were there. They flashed their warrant cards. 'DS Gaughran and DC Hassan, Peckham CID,' he explained. 'We're investigating the murder of Ashley Campbell and we had a call to say there was a nurse here who remembered treating him here back in January?'

An Asian nurse nodded. 'Yes. That was me.'

Hassan pulled a photo of Ashley from the folder he was carrying and showed her. 'And this is definitely the man who you treated on the 15^{th} January?'

The nurse peered at the photograph. 'Yes, that's definitely him. And I checked the A&E log so we've got his name down there too.'

'Can you tell us what had happened?' Gaughran asked.

'When he arrived, he was covered in blood. We did some x-rays, and he had two cracked ribs and a fractured jaw,' she replied.

'Did he say how he'd received the injuries?' Hassan asked.

'No, he didn't say much,' she explained as she shook her head. 'But I spoke to a uniformed officer who told me there had been a fight outside a pub.'

Gaughran took a moment as he thought of something. 'Any idea what happened to the other man in the fight?'

'How do you mean?' the nurse asked.

'Ashley Campbell was ex-army, and he looked like he could handle himself,' Gaughran explained. 'If someone did that to him, I'd expect the other man to be badly injured too.'

'Let me check for you.' The nurse understood what he was implying and went over to the nurses' station. There was nodding and animated conversation before she returned with a clipboard.

'Jill remembers there was a fight in A&E between this Ashley and another man,' the nurse explained. 'She seemed to think it was a continuation of the fight they'd had outside the pub.'

'Can she remember anything about him?' Hassan asked.

'Not really.' The nurse pointed to the clipboard. 'But she remembered he had a broken nose and a missing front tooth. And we detail injuries against the names in case the police, I mean you, ever need them later.'

'So, you could match the injuries to the name of someone who came into A&E that night?' Hassan asked to clarify.

'It's possible,' the nurse said with a nod. 'It doesn't always work like that as it's sometimes like World War III in here.' She ran her finger down the list of admissions into A&E that evening. 'Yeah, I've got him here. Broken nose, broken teeth, three broken fingers. It says *Neil Jones* here.'

'Ian?' Gaughran asked out loud as he glanced over at Hassan. *Neil* was the name of the man who had come in looking for Ashley the previous Tuesday and told the barman to tell him to watch his back. Was it the same man? It was a huge coincidence if it wasn't.

'That's what it says,' the nurse nodded as she pointed to the list.

'Could you ask your colleague Jill to come over here for a second, please?' Gaughran asked as he put the pieces of evidence together.

'Of course.' The nurse signalled for Jill to come over. She smiled at them and approached.

'Hi Jill,' Gaughran said as she arrived. He pointed to the A&E list. 'We're detectives from Peckham CID. Is there anything else you can remember about this man with the broken nose and missing tooth on the 15th January?'

Jill frowned and then nodded. 'Yeah, he had a big tattoo on his neck.'

'Crucifixion, was it?' Gaughran asked.

Jill raised her eyebrow. 'Yeah, how do you know that?'


Ruth and Lucy arrived at the front door of Lenora's flat in Tulse Hill. They had called *Harvey's* and were told that Lenora wasn't due in until late afternoon and that she should be at home.

Ringing the buzzer, Lucy took two steps back and glanced at Ruth.

'You think there was something going on between Lenora and Ashley?' she asked.

Ruth shrugged. 'She lied to us about the last time she saw Ashley. And that means there's something about the trip to the bank that she doesn't want us to know about.'

'What if they were syphoning off money from the bar and were going to go off together?' Lucy suggested.

'We're going to need to look at Lenora's bank and phone records,' Ruth said.

The door opened and Lenora appeared, dressed in a kimono. She had an orange towel wrapped around her head.

'Hi Lenora. We need to ask you a couple of questions,' Ruth explained moving towards the door.

'Can't it wait?' Lenora growled. 'Jesus, I'm in the middle of getting dressed.'

Ruth and Lucy moved towards her to signal that they were coming in, she liked it or not.

'That's all right, Lenora,' Lucy grinned. 'I once questioned a man who was naked and covered in tomato soup. This won't take long.'

Lenora frowned and gave an audible huff.

The flat was modern and tastefully furnished.

Ruth pointed to the sofa. 'We'll sit down here, shall we?'

Lenora shook her head in irritation, sat on an armchair and glared at them.

'So, what is it?' she snapped.

Lucy pulled out her notebook. 'There are a couple of things in your statement that we need to clarify.'

'What? And you couldn't have done that when I was at work?' Lenora protested.

*She's really getting on my nerves.*

Lucy gave her a sarcastic smile. 'Unfortunately, Lenora, it couldn't wait that long.'

'Really?' Lenora groaned.

'Could you tell us the last time you saw Ashley alive?' Ruth asked.

Lenora narrowed her eyes. 'Are you for real? I told you that. He came into the bar on Friday afternoon to see Ruben.'

Ruth frowned. 'And you're sure about that?'

'Yeah,' Lenora snorted. 'Are you calling me a liar?'

Ruth reached into a folder she was carrying, pulled out a photo, and turned to show her. 'So, this isn't you coming out of Lloyd's bank on Peckham High Street on Saturday morning with Ashley and then getting into his car?'

Lenora peered at the photograph. 'No.'

Ruth pulled out another document. She couldn't believe how brazen Lenora was being in lying to them. 'That's strange, because according to your bank records, you withdrew twenty thousand pounds from Lloyd's Bank on Peckham High Street at 10.12am on Saturday morning.' Ruth then pointed to the photo again. 'And if you look at the timecode on that image from the CCTV, you'll see that it's marked 10.17am on Saturday. Is there anything you'd like to tell us about that?'

Lucy fought the instinct to smirk – they had her bang to rights on that one!

'Must be some mistake,' Lenora babbled, as her eyes darted around the room.

*Not so bloody cocky now, are you?* Lucy thought.

'No. There's no mistake, Lenora.'

'You can't get my bank records!' Lenora snapped. 'They're private.'

'This is a murder investigation,' Ruth stated with a slightly patronising tone. 'So, we can get your bank records, your phone records and anything else we require.'

'So what?' Lenora shrugged. 'I went to the bank with Ash. That's not a crime, is it?'

'No. But lying about it is,' Lucy informed her sternly. 'It's called perverting the course of justice and you could go to prison.'

Lenora pulled a face. 'That's not true. I just forgot, that's all.'

'Come on, Lenora,' Ruth sighed, rolling her eyes. 'You forgot the last time you saw your brother-in-law before he died? That's rubbish, and you know it. You need to tell us what you were doing at the bank with Ashley the morning before he was killed. And you need to tell us why you withdrew twenty thousand pounds in cash, which we later found in the boot of his car.'

'I was lending it to him and I didn't want Mica or Ruben to know,' she explained.

'What did he want it for?'

'He was looking to invest in property,' Lenora explained. 'I thought it was a good idea.'

'But Mica and Ruben didn't?' Ruth asked.

'No. They thought Ash was a chancer. A bit of a wide boy.'

'How were you going to lend Ashley twenty grand without Mica or Ruben knowing?' Lucy asked in a suspicious tone.

'It was my money. And Ash said he was going to make a lot of cash developing properties,' she explained. 'He told me he'd pay me back in six months, with 25% on top.'

'He was going to give you twenty-five thousand back?'

'That's what he said,' Lenora explained with a shrug. 'If that's everything, can I get dressed now?'

# CHAPTER 18

'Do you remember Ashley being attacked back in January?'
Gaughran asked.

Ruben nodded. 'Of course.'

Gaughran and Hassan had been sitting for about five minutes in Ruben's office above *Harvey's*.

'You didn't mention it when you gave officers your statement, though?' Gaughran pointed out.

'Sorry,' Ruben shrugged. 'I didn't think the two were connected.'

'Why's that?'

'He told me it was just a punch up over some girl that he was talking to in a pub in Vauxhall,' Ruben explained.

Hassan's phone rang. He peered at it and got up. 'I'm just going to take this for a minute.' He disappeared outside into the corridor.

Gaughran glanced over at Ruben. 'We think we've identified the man that attacked Ashley on the 15th January as Neil Jones. We think that it's the same man that came into the bar last week asking for Ashley, saying that he was looking for him and to watch his back.'

'Shit!' Ruben shook his head and rubbed his chin. 'I'm sorry. I never thought that this bloke would come looking for him. Jesus.'

'Do you know who Neil Jones is?' Gaughran asked him.

'No, no idea,' Ruben replied.

Hassan appeared at the door, then came and sat down. He looked at Ruben. 'That was Technical Forensics. We've got

Ashley's phone records back and the last person he called on Saturday was a Binita Jones.'

'Jones?' Gaughran said, thinking out loud. 'Same surname as Neil Jones.'

Hassan shrugged. 'It's a pretty common surname, Sarge.'

Gaughran noticed that Ruben was deep in thought.

'Ashley went out with a girl called Binita years ago,' Ruben said. 'She wasn't called Jones though.'

'How long ago?' Gaughran asked.

'Fifteen years ago. They went out at school and then after that for a while,' Ruben explained. 'I thought they were going to get married. And then when Ashley joined the army, they split up.'

'Do you know the last time they saw each other?' Hassan asked.

Ruben shrugged. 'No idea. I thought he hadn't spoken to her in years.'

'But she was the last person he phoned on Saturday,' Gaughran said.

Hassan peered over at Ruben. 'The phone that Binita used was a pay as you go. Have you got an old address for her, by any chance?'

'No, sorry.' Ruben shook his head. 'But I remember her surname. Prasad. It was Benita Prasad. She came from an Indian family.'


Ruth walked into CID holding two cups of coffee from the canteen. She'd received two texts from Kara already and had ignored them until she worked out a plan of action.

'Here you go, home wrecker,' Ruth joked as she put the coffee down in front of Lucy.

'That's not even funny,' Lucy snapped. 'Remember Harry was married when I got together with him. I'm thinking there's something wrong with me. Why can't I just meet attractive single men?'

'Hey, I've got an attractive, single woman, and that's not working, so be careful what you wish for,' Ruth joked.

'Is this the creepy social worker?' Lucy asked.

'I didn't describe her as creepy,' Ruth protested.

'Erm, yes you did,' Lucy corrected her.

'I mean, she's gorgeous,' Ruth explained. 'But her behaviour is just a bit creepy.'

Lucy frowned. 'Explain.'

'I don't know. Way too needy for starters. And because she's not comfortable in her own skin, she seems to take all her social cues from me.'

'Social cues? Get you,' Lucy joked. 'The question is, are you tolerating her weirdness because she is really attractive?'

'Yes,' Ruth answered before she really processed the question.

Lucy shrugged and grinned. 'Well, I think you have your answer. If you continue to sleep with her, then you are a cold, shallow, manipulative bitch.'

'Hang on a second, missy,' Ruth snorted. 'What does that make you?'

Lucy ignored her, gave her the finger and pointed to her cup. 'Thanks for the coffee.'

'Nicely swerved,' Ruth joked.

Lucy pointed to some folders. 'These are Mica and Lenora's immigration files from 1993.'

'They weren't born in the UK?' Ruth asked.

'No, she and her sister were born in Jamaica,' Lucy explained as she continued to turn the pages. 'There are notes on the file. Her father, Marland Cole, owned three hotels in Lucea. In 1992, a gang of robbers held up one of the hotels. Marland tried to intervene and was shot dead. The mother, Jalissa, and her two daughters, Mica and Lenora, came to live in London in 1993.'

'Okay,' Ruth nodded. 'Where's Jalissa Cole now?'

'She died in 1994 from a stroke,' Lucy explained.

'I'm assuming that Marland Cole was a very rich man,' Ruth said, thinking aloud. 'And once Jalissa Cole died, that would make Mica and Lenora very rich young ladies.'

'I guess it would explain why Mica had the money to buy *Harvey's*, and Lenora had twenty grand knocking about to give to Ashley to invest,' Lucy shrugged as she pointed to something in the file. 'I then pulled Lenora's HMRC and tax files. Strange thing is, they all changed their surname legally when they arrived from Cole to Garner. The passport office checked, and they've all got new passports. Mica obviously changed her name and passport again when she married Ruben.'

Ruth raised an eyebrow. 'Sounds like they were worried that someone would track them down over here?'

# CHAPTER 19

Having tracked down Benita, via her tax returns, to a small carpet shop in Camberwell, Gaughran and Hassan pulled up outside. It had just turned 5pm and there was a light sleet in the darkening sky as they walked over to the shop. A bell rang as Gaughran opened the door and a pretty, young Asian woman in her early 30s looked up from behind the counter of the shop.

The woman pulled a face. 'I'm really sorry. We're just about to close. Is there any way you could come back tomorrow?'

Gaughran pulled out his warrant card. 'I'm Detective Sergeant Tim Gaughran from Peckham CID. This is Detective Constable Syed Hassan. We're looking for a Benita Jones.'

The woman's eyes widened in fear. 'Yes, that's me.'

'Is there anywhere we can go to talk?' Gaughran suggested.

Benita seemed flustered. 'Erm, yes. Let me just close up.'

'Of course,' Gaughran said with a kind smile.

He watched as she hurried to the shop door, pushed up the bolt and turned the sign to read *Closed*.

Walking back to them, she signalled to a scruffy door behind the counter. 'There's an office in there where we could go and talk,' she explained nervously.

Gaughran nodded and gestured for her to go in first.

The office was larger than he had expected. There were two untidy desks, a worn sofa, and some wooden chairs. The far wall was covered with rugs and carpet samples and the room smelt of carpet fibres and chemicals.

Gaughran and Hassan sat on the sofa as Benita sat on a chair opposite.

'Oh sorry,' she apologised. 'Would you like tea or anything?'

Gaughran looked at her delicate hands and the array of bangles and jewellery on her wrists.

Hassan shook his head. 'We're fine, thanks.'

'We understand you knew Ashley Campbell?' Gaughran asked.

'Yes.' Benita nodded with a sad expression. 'I saw what happened to him on the news. I couldn't believe it.'

'Were you close?' Hassan asked, looking down at his notebook.

'Once, yes,' she admitted. 'But that was a very long time ago.'

'You were Ashley's girlfriend, is that right?' Gaughran asked.

'Yes,' Benita replied with a troubled expression. 'At school and then after that.'

'What happened?'

'Ash wanted to join the army,' Benita explained. 'He wanted us to get married. But I didn't want that kind of life. You know, being moved all around the world.'

Gaughran looked over at her. He couldn't stop looking at her beautiful, big brown eyes. They were mesmerising. 'So, you broke up?'

She nodded. 'Yes.'

'Can you tell us the last time you saw Ashley?' Hassan asked.

Benita pulled a face. 'Erm, it's a long time ago. A few years. I can't really remember.'

Gaughran rubbed his chin and then asked, 'And you've got married since then, is that right?'

'Yes,' Benita replied cautiously. 'That's right.'

'To a Neil Jones?'

'Yes,' Benita replied.

'Is he here, by any chance?' Hassan asked.

'Erm, no. He's popped out to make a delivery,' Benita explained. 'But he should be back soon.'

'Okay, we might wait if he's not going to be long,' Gaughran said.

'He shouldn't be.'

Gaughran frowned at her. 'To you knowledge, have your husband and Ashley Campbell ever met?'

She immediately pulled a face. 'No. Why would they have met?'

Gaughran was now suspicious. Her answer had been very defensive, and the question seemed to have visibly rattled her.

'It was just a routine question,' Hassan said.

Benita blinked at them – something wasn't right.

'Can you tell us where you were last Saturday night?' Gaughran asked.

Benita pointed upstairs. 'I was here in the flat.'

'All night?' Hassan said.

She nodded. 'Yes.'

Gaughran looked at her. 'Do you know where your husband Neil was last Saturday night?'

Benita thought for a few seconds. 'He was here with me,' she said uncertainly.

Gaughran fixed her with a stare. 'And you're sure about that, are you?'

'Yes,' she said, bristling. 'I'm not a liar.'

Gaughran nodded. 'No. I'm just making sure that you're not covering for Neil because he's your husband or because you're scared of him.'

'No. I'm not.'

Hassan glanced up at her. 'Benita, can you tell us the last time you spoke to Ashley?'

'I don't understand.' She frowned and put her hand to her face nervously. 'I just told you I haven't seen Ash for years. Why are you asking me that again?'

*She's definitely hiding something,* Gaughran thought.

Hassan gave her a benign smile. 'Actually, the first time we asked you when was the last time you *saw* Ashley. And now we're asking when was the last time you *spoke* to him. Sorry, if that's confusing.'

'It would have been the same time.' Benita shrugged. 'I don't understand why you're asking me this?'

Gaughran leant forward. 'We have the records for Ashley's mobile phone. Would it surprise you to know that the last number Ashley called before he died was a mobile phone registered to you?'

Benita visibly swallowed and blinked nervously. 'No, that's not true.'

Hassan pulled a copy of the phone records from the folder he was carrying. 'In fact, according to the mobile phone company, you and Ashley had been talking on the phone regularly for over three months.'

There were a few seconds of awkward silence.

Benita's eyes filled with tears.

'Benita?' Gaughran said in a virtual whisper. 'I need you tell us the truth about Ashley.'

She nodded as she wiped the tears from her eyes and face. 'Yes. I'm really sorry.'

Gaughran gave her an empathetic look. 'It's fine. Don't worry.'

Suddenly, there was the loud noise of banging from outside the shop and shouting.

Benita's face dropped as she glanced at Gaughran. 'That'll be my husband.'

Gaughran looked at her. 'Don't worry. We'll talk to him.'

'Please don't tell him about Ashley.' Benita shook. 'You don't know what he's like.'

'If you think you're in danger,' Hassan explained. '... there are things we can do to protect you.'

Benita nodded, but she seemed terrified.

Going to the office door, Gaughran opened it and looked across the shop at the man who was banging on the glass of the door. He was bald, and he had a tattoo on his neck.

*Neil Jones! Bingo!*

As they approached the door, Jones frowned at them. Then the penny dropped. He turned, ran, and jumped into the battered Ford Escort van he had parked outside the shop.

'Shit!' Hassan muttered as he unbolted the door and opened it.

'Come on!' Gaughran yelled as he sprinted out of the shop and towards where they had parked. He clicked his Tetra radio. 'Control from Delta five-four, over.'

As he and Hassan reached the car, he heard the van engine followed by the screech of tyres.

'Bollocks!' he shouted.

Control then responded on his radio. 'Delta five-four from Control. Go ahead, over.'

'In pursuit of suspect, Neil Jones. Red Ford Escort van, registration Lima Six Two Seven, Foxtrot Tango Alpha. Heading west on A202, Peckham Road, over.'

'Received. Stand by, over.'

They jumped into the car. Gaughran turned the ignition and hit the accelerator, spinning the wheels as they set off in pursuit.

'Let's get this bastard,' said Hassan.

'Get the blues and twos on for us,' Gaughran said, pointing to the dashboard.

Hassan flicked the switch. The siren wailed and the blue lights along the radiator grille flashed.

Traffic moved to the side of the road to clear their path.

'Haven't done this for a while, have we?' Gaughran said, relishing the chance to speed through the South London traffic at high speed.

'No, Sarge,' Hassan mumbled unconvincingly.

*He's such a wimp!*

Once they had passed a waiting bus, Gaughran rapidly built up speed. He was enjoying the feeling of power from driving fast as they hit 50mph.

He glanced over. Hassan gripped the door handle with one hand and the dashboard in front with the other as the car screamed round a bend.

Gaughran sat forwards a little, peering through the windscreen. 'Where are you, you bastard?' He felt the Astra's back tyres losing grip and slipping as they cornered another bend.

Gaughran took a quick look at Hassan. 'You okay, Syed?'

'Brilliant, Sarge. I was just hoping to stay alive today,' he quipped sarcastically.

'Are you criticising my driving?' Gaughran asked with a grin.

'I'd never dream of doing that, Sarge,' Hassan said, as he flinched.

'There he is.'

Gaughran went hammering up Camberwell New Road, and over the lights. A transit van slammed its brakes on to avoid them and then beeped its horn angrily.

'Oops,' Gaughran laughed.

Jones' Escort van was now only about five hundred yards ahead, and they were gaining. Gaughran pulled out to overtake a cement mixer lorry and shot past it at speed.

'Delta-five from Control, over.'

Hassan picked up the radio and clicked the handset, 'Delta-five-four received.'

'We have Unit Tango two-one heading south on the A494 towards your location, over.'

Back-up was on its way if they couldn't stop Jones.

'Received, over,' Hassan replied.

'Sod that. Jones is ours,' Gaughran said with a steely determination, dropping the car into third as they reached the Brixton Road heading south.

'You think Jones murdered Ashley Campbell?' Hassan asked.

'Yeah. I think he found out that his wife was back in touch with her childhood sweetheart, Ashley,' Gaughran said as he pieced together his theory. 'I'm guessing they were having some kind of affair. Jones tracks Ashley down in January. They have a fight and both end up in A&E. But the affair continued.'

Hassan looked over. 'So, last week, Jones goes to *Harvey's* to confront Ashley and maybe attack him. He told the barman to tell Ashley to watch his back.'

'And then Saturday, Jones follows Ashley and waits for him outside The Yard,' Gaughran said. 'And when he's not expecting it, he attacks him from behind and kills him.'

Hassan glanced over at Gaughran and nodded. 'Sounds about right, doesn't it Sarge?'

'I think so,' Gaughran agreed and then gestured to the van. 'But if he's guilty of murder, he's not about to pull over and give up quietly.'

Hassan clicked the Tetra handset again. 'Delta-five-four to control, over.'

'Delta-five-four, received, go ahead.'

'Suspect is heading southbound on the A23 towards Brixton, over,' Hassan said.

A moment later, they screamed past Kennington Park and then screeched round a bend beyond. They were going so fast that Gaughran felt that one wrong move and they could be in a fatal accident.

Just up ahead, a bus pulled out of a stop in front of them. Gaughran steered the car onto the opposite side of the road, missing it by a few feet.

'For fuck's sake!' he bellowed.

Hassan squinted, with his eyes half shut as they careered around another bend.

Jones' Escort van was now only a hundred yards away. It pulled out to overtake another bus, and whizzed past two cars.

However, as Gaughran pulled out to do the same, there was a huge lorry coming the other way. His eyes widened with alarm.

*I'm not sure there's enough space to get through here!*

He dropped into third gear and the Astra roared uncomfortably, but the boost in speed bought them a couple of extra seconds and they made it past with inches to spare.

'Shit!' Gaughran yelled as he stared fiercely ahead at the Escort van, which was now only fifty yards ahead.

'Just don't lose him!'

If they lost Jones now, he might disappear and go into hiding somewhere.

Suddenly, a cyclist pulled slowly out of a road in front of them. Jones' brake lights glared bright red as he slammed on the brakes.

'Fuck!' Gaughran shouted, as he hit his own brakes hard.

The Astra skidded, and as Gaughran glanced ahead he saw Jones had swerved to avoid the cyclist. However, he had clipped the pavement, lost control, and the van flipped over, landing on its roof on the opposite side of the road.

A metallic thud threw them forwards. The scraping of metal against metal, the sound of cracking glass. A glancing blow against a bus had sent the Astra directly on course for the upturned van. Another bang of metal and crunch of glass, with the sensation of spinning. Now they were travelling backwards. After a few more seconds, they came to a stop.

*Jesus Christ!*

Gaughran took a few seconds to get his breath back and clear his head.

'Bloody hell!' Hassan said, looking over at him. 'You okay Sarge?'

'I think so,' he said, looking out towards the upturned van. 'I'm not sure he's going to be.'

'Shit!' Hassan said, opening the car door.

Without speaking, they both ran towards the van. Black smoke was coming from the bonnet.

Gaughran crouched down. Jones was upside down, conscious, but he had blood on his face.

'Help me get him out,' Gaughran said to Hassan as he opened the driver's door. He then looked at Jones, who was blinking – he didn't know what day it was. 'Take off your seatbelt, or we can't get you out, dickhead.'

Jones nodded, reached to his side, and unclipped the seatbelt. As he dropped towards the windscreen, Gaughran grabbed him by the lapels and yanked him roughly out of the van and onto the road.

Gaughran glared at him. 'Neil Jones, you're nicked.'

# CHAPTER 20

Lucy turned on the oven with a blissful smirk. She and James had just had sex on the living room floor. Having stopped at the supermarket on the way home, Lucy had picked up the ingredients for her famous spaghetti carbonara. She had even found diced pancetta, plus a decent block of parmesan cheese. She also planned to stir two eggs into the hot pasta with butter and black pepper. It was going to be immense.

James had been raving about a new CD he had bought by a French band called *Air*. Having put the album on in the living room, he returned to the kitchen and took a long swig from the cold bottle of Amstel lager that she had just opened for him.

'What's the album called again?' Lucy asked as she poured boiling water onto the spaghetti in the pan and threw in a pinch of salt.

'*Moon Safari*,' he told her as he spun her around, took her in his arms, and kissed her.

Lucy looked at him. He was seriously handsome, but Ruth had a point. He lived upstairs with his girlfriend.

He frowned. 'What's wrong?'

'At the risk of spoiling dinner, what exactly are we doing here?' Lucy asked.

He grinned. 'You mean in this kitchen?'

She gave him a playful hit on the arm. 'No. You know exactly what I mean.'

'Do we need to have that conversation?'

'Erm, yes,' Lucy said and nodded. 'I really like you ...'

'I really like you too ...' he said, interrupting her.

'Let me finish, nob-head,' she said with a smile. 'Natalie is coming back in a couple of days. Then what happens?'

James shrugged. 'I run down here to see you every time she goes out?'

'Nice try, buster,' Lucy said as she pulled a face. 'I'm not going to sit down here while you share a bed with your girlfriend every night upstairs, and then jump into bed with you every time she's not around. I know that's what you'd like, but that ain't happening.'

James narrowed his eyes. 'I think that sounds perfect.'

She hit him again playfully. 'I'm being serious. Maybe we can just put this down to experience and we'll go back to being good neighbours.'

James thought for a second. 'Yeah, I don't really want that though.'

'What do you mean?' Lucy asked.

'Being with you for these past few days has clarified a few things,' James admitted.

Before he could continue, there was a knock at the door.

Lucy frowned. She wasn't expecting anyone.

Wandering down the hallway, she opened the front door.

A woman in her late 20s peered at her with a curious expression.

It was Natalie!

*Oh, God! This is not good.*

Lucy's stomach lurched as she took a breath. 'Hi Natalie.'

'Hi,' Natalie smiled at her and frowned. 'I know this is a strange question, but have you seen James anywhere? He left the door unlocked and his phone and wallet are on the table. It's just that I'm a bit worried.'

'Yes, he's in here,' Lucy laughed in her best fake laugh.

With her heart now racing, Lucy focussed on sounding as if everything was completely normal while trying to concoct some cock'n'bull story.

'Is he?' Natalie asked, pulling a face. 'Erm, oh right.'

Lucy gestured to her. 'Come in, come in,' she said in a friendly voice.

Natalie came into the flat hesitantly.

'Hi,' James said, appearing in the hallway. 'You're back early.'

Natalie now seemed incredibly suspicious. 'I'm sorry, but what exactly are you doing here?'

Lucy shared a look with James. Was this the moment they got totally busted?

'I'm such an idiot!' James laughed as he went over, gave Natalie an affectionate kiss and then took her by the hand. 'I left the bath running yesterday and forgot all about it.'

Pulling her gently towards the kitchen, James pointed to the grey patch of damp on the ceiling. 'And so it overflowed and came through to Lucy's ceiling. I just popped down to see what damage I'd done. I said that obviously I'd pay for any damages and get it repaired.'

*Nice save, James. I could kiss you, but it's probably not the right time.*

Lucy laughed. 'I wasn't even in last night so I hadn't even noticed until James turned up.'

Natalie smiled with a look of relief. 'Oh my God, you really are an idiot, James.'

He grinned. 'Memory like a sieve.'

'No harm done,' Lucy reassured them.

*I feel so guilty it's making me squirm.*

'Anyway, Lucy offered me a beer,' James shrugged. 'And she was telling me about her job as a detective.'

'Sounds fascinating,' Natalie said.

'It's really not. Lots of paperwork,' Lucy said, and gave Natalie a beaming smile. 'Now you're here, you'll have to stay for a drink. I've got some white wine in the fridge.'

'Perfect,' Natalie said. 'Thank you. I said to James the other day we should invite you up for a drink to say hello.'

Lucy went to the fridge, took out the wine, poured a glass, and handed it to Natalie.

'Cheers,' Natalie said. 'It's nice to meet you properly, isn't it, James?'

James raised his bottle of beer and smiled at Lucy. 'Definitely.'

The wind was icy and Gaughran's face and ears were numb as he knocked on the door. A few seconds later, his mum, Celia, answered the door and her face lit up when she saw him.

'Tim!' she exclaimed. 'Why didn't you tell me you was gonna pop by you sod?'

Gaughran smiled and shrugged. 'Just a spur-of-the-moment thing.'

They embraced as she ushered him inside. 'Come in, it's bloody freezing out there and you haven't even got a coat on.'

Gaughran was still in his work suit.

'You all right, mum?' he asked as they went down the hall and into the large kitchen. 'You look tired.'

'Oh, I'm fine. You know, I worry about your dad, that's all,' she explained. 'Fancy a cuppa?'

'Lovely, ta,' Gaughran said as he sat down at the kitchen table. It was covered with a checked tablecloth and there were fresh flowers at its centre. 'When is he due home?'

'Tomorrow,' she replied as she clicked on the kettle. 'Early evening.'

'I'll go and get him if you like?' Gaughran said.

'It's all right,' she said, shaking her head. 'Anyway, you've got work.'

'Mum, it's fine. It'll be cold and dark. And you know dad, he's not the best patient. I'll pick him up and I won't take no for an answer.'

'I've been to Sainsbury's and got all his favourite stuff,' she said with a loving smile. 'Couple of sirloin steaks, those little French beers he likes and a massive sherry trifle.'

Gaughran looked at her. It broke his heart to see her so intent on pleasing his father when he was cheating on her with another woman. He wanted to sit her down and explain to her what was actually going on. But he wasn't sure she would ever recover. She hadn't worked for thirty years and his father sorted out all the finances and bills. What the hell was she going to do if he left her?

'Don't spoil him too much, eh?' Gaughran said.

'He's got cancer, Tim,' Celia said, raising an eyebrow. 'I know it's not serious, but it's not like he's got an ingrowing toenail is it?'

She turned and poured boiling water into the two mugs and went to the fridge to get the milk.

'Yeah, well he's lucky they caught it early,' Gaughran said. 'A DCI over at Camberwell that I used to work with got prostate cancer. But he'd left it too late, and he was dead within six months.'

'Don't say that, Tim!' Celia exclaimed as she brought over his mug of tea. She clearly couldn't cope with hearing about anyone dying from prostate cancer.

'That's what I'm saying, Mum,' Gaughran sighed. 'He's gonna be fine because they got it really early.'

She sat down opposite him at the table. 'Yeah, it was me that sent him to Dr Thomas. You know what a bloody fool your dad is. He'd wait for his bloody leg to be hanging off before he'd go the doctors. But he was up every night, peeing for bloody Britain every hour or two, so I rang up and booked him in.'

'You probably saved his life,' Gaughran said. 'I hope he's grateful.'

'Grateful? Chance would be a fine thing,' Celia snorted ironically. 'When I booked him the doctor's appointment, he called me an interfering cow.'

'Charming,' Gaughran said as he sipped his tea. 'That is the best cup of tea I've had in weeks, mum.'

Her face beamed. 'Is it? You know, I've switched to Yorkshire tea recently after I read something in the paper about Michael Parkinson. He said he wouldn't drink anything else.'

'Yeah? I approve,' Gaughran laughed. 'So, I'll give the hospital a ring, see what time dad's being discharged and go and get him. I might even point out that he needs to thank you for making him go to the doctor's, eh?'

Celia rolled her eyes. 'Oh God, don't do that. You know what he's like if you tell him off or tell him to do something. He's like a big baby.'

# CHAPTER 21

It was just before 9am when Ferguson walked over to the scene boards at the far end of the CID office. The room smelt of bacon sandwiches, coffee and the double electric bar heater that glowed orange in the corner and gave off a slightly musty, burnt odour all day.

Ferguson sipped from his tea and looked over at Lucy. 'Thanks Luce,' he sighed. 'Now that is a proper brew.'

Gaughran coughed and muttered under his breath, 'Teacher's pet!'

Ruth and Lucy exchanged a look and rolled their eyes.

'You okay, Tim?' Ruth asked sarcastically. 'Sounds like you've got a nasty cough there. I wouldn't want you to get ill and die suddenly.'

Lucy laughed as Gaughran gave her a sardonic grin and the finger.

'Tim, Syed, I understand you had an accident yesterday while chasing Neil Jones? You okay?'

Gaughran nodded. 'Yeah, guv. Jones flipped his van onto his roof. He's lucky to have got out of there with just a couple of scratches. Doctor gave him the once over and he spent the night in a holding cell.'

'What have we got on Jones so far?' Ferguson asked as he perched on the end of a table - which was now his usual place during briefing.

Gaughran sat up in his seat and looked over. 'We looked at Ashley's mobile phone records. His last call was to a pay as you go mobile phone owned by a woman called Binita Jones.

Closer examination showed that Ashley had been in close contact with Binita Jones for the past three months. We went to A&E at King's College Hospital where we discovered Ashley had been treated for broken ribs and a fractured jaw on the night of the 15$^{th}$ January. According to a nurse who worked that night, Ashley had a fight in A&E with another man and she assumed it was a continuation of the fight from earlier in the evening. We used the A&E log to identify the man as Neil Jones. And Neil Jones has a distinctive tattoo on his neck.'

Ruth frowned. 'This is the guy that came into Harvey's last week and told the barman to tell Ashley to watch his back?'

'Exactly,' Gaughran nodded. 'It turns out that Neil Jones is married to Binita. She was Ashley's girlfriend at school and after that, for a few years. They were inseparable, but when he decided to join the army, she didn't want to go with him.'

Lucy glanced over. 'But they're in contact again now?'

Hassan nodded. 'Yeah. We think they've been having an affair. And if Neil Jones discovered that, it explains why he attacked Ashley on the 15$^{th}$ January and then came into the bar last week to threaten him.'

Ferguson scratched his chin. 'And it makes him our prime suspect for stabbing and killing Ashley on Saturday, doesn't it?'

'Does he own a Range Rover?' Ruth asked. 'Jermaine Daniels claimed to have seen the attacker getting into an SUV, like a Range Rover, and driving away.'

Gaughran shook his head. 'No. Syed and I are going to interview Jones in a minute. We've also got a SOCO team going to the shop and flat above this morning to look for forensics.'

Ferguson nodded. 'Let's see if he's got an alibi. Re-interview the wife and see if we can pick holes in his story.'

'I got the feeling that she's scared of him,' Gaughran explained. 'If I can persuade her we can protect her, then maybe she'll tell us what she knows.'

'Good,' Ferguson said. 'And what about our friend Captain Hurst?'

Hassan read his notebook. 'Hurst claims he was at a golf dinner at the Cottesmore Golf Club. We need to see if that checks out.'

'Ruth, Lucy,' Ferguson said. 'You went to see Lenora Campbell yesterday, didn't you?'

'Yes, guv,' Ruth replied. 'We'd discovered that Lenora Campbell had withdrawn twenty thousand from the Lloyds Bank on Peckham High Street on Saturday morning. She went to the bank with Ashley and the money she withdrew is the money we found in the boot of Ashley's car.'

Gaughran frowned. 'How did she explain that?'

Lucy looked over. 'She claimed she was lending the money to Ashley to invest in property with a 25% return on her money. She didn't want Mica or Ruben to know because she said they would disapprove. Apparently, Mica thought Ashley was a bit of a wide boy.'

'Where did she get twenty grand from?' Hassan asked.

Lucy turned the page of her notebook and said, 'Turns out that Mica and her sister Lenora came to the UK with their mother, Jalissa, in 1993. Their father, Marland Cole, owned three hotels in Lucea. In 1992, a gang of robbers held up one of the hotels. Marland tried to intervene and was shot dead. Jalissa died from a stroke in 1994. Which means that Mica and Lenora inherited their father's fortune.'

'Any idea how much that was?' Ferguson asked.

Ruth shrugged. 'I guess it was enough to not worry about lending her brother-in-law twenty thousand.'

'Do we think there was any bad feeling between Mica and Ashley?' Ferguson asked. 'If she found out that Lenora was lending her brother-in-law money behind her back, it might have really pissed her off?'

'Doesn't sound like a motive for murder though,' Gaughran pointed out.

Hassan, who had just answered a phone call, peered across the room at Ferguson. 'Guv, message from the SOCOs. They reckon they've found something significant in Neil and Benita Jones' flat.'

Neil Jones' face was drawn, and he had a long scratch across his temple from the accident. He was dressed in a grey tracksuit, as his clothes had been taken away for forensic examination. The Duty Solicitor, a tall woman in her 40s, sat next to him, looking through the case files.

Gaughran pulled his chair close to the table, reached over and pressed the red button on the tape machine. There was a long electronic beep.

'Interview with Neil Jones, Interview Room 2, Peckham Police Station, 10am. Present are Neil Jones, Duty Solicitor Fiona Bright, Detective Constable Syed Hassan and Detective Sergeant Tim Gaughran,' he said. 'Neil, do you understand you are still under caution and that anything you say here this morning can be used as evidence in a court of law?'

Jones nodded slowly. 'Yeah.'

Hassan opened his notebook and clicked his pen. 'Can you tell us where you were last Saturday night?'

Jones gave an audible sigh and shifted awkwardly in his chair. 'At home.'

'You were at home in your flat, which is above the carpet shop you own on the Peckham Road?' Hassan asked to clarify. 'Is that correct?'

'Yeah,' he mumbled as he stared down at his feet.

'Is there anyone who can vouch for your whereabouts on Saturday night, Neil?' Gaughran asked.

Jones shrugged. 'My wife, Benita. She was with me all night.'

'Okay,' Gaughran said with a tone of incredulity. He wanted Jones to know that he didn't believe him. 'Can I take you back to last Tuesday, Neil? Can you tell us where you were at around 7pm?'

Jones snorted and raised an eyebrow. 'You know where I was.'

'Humour me, Neil,' Gaughran said. 'If you could tell us, please.'

'I went to a bar called Harvey's,' he explained.

'That's Harvey's bar on Venn Street in Clapham, is it?'

'That's right,' Jones said with a sarcastic smile.

Hassan turned the page of his notebook. 'We understand you spoke to a barman called Felix when you went in?'

Jones shrugged. 'I don't know. I can't remember.'

Gaughran smiled as he reached into a folder and pulled a photo. 'Well, as chance would have it, Harvey's has a CCTV camera. And if you take a look at this image, you can clearly see that you were talking to this barman. Can you see that?'

Jones gave Gaughran a withering look and peered at the photo. 'I suppose so.'

'Can you tell us what you said to him?' Hassan asked.

'No,' Jones said with a shrug. 'I can't remember.'

'Well, Neil, luckily Felix has a very good memory,' Gaughran said sarcastically. 'And he can remember exactly what you said.'

'Can he?' Jones sneered.

'Yeah. You asked if Ashley Campbell was around,' Hassan said pointing to his notebook. 'And Felix told you he wasn't. And then you said, *Tell him that Neil was here and tell him to watch his back.*'

Gaughran fixed Jones with a stare across the table and waited for the tension to build.

'Do you remember saying that, Neil?' Gaughran asked.

'No,' he mumbled.

'The barman Felix has no reason to lie about what you said to him when you came in,' Gaughran explained. 'But it sounds like a threat, doesn't it?'

Jones sat back in his chair and gave a withering sigh. 'Does it?'

'It also means that you've got a huge problem, Neil,' Gaughran said. 'Because Ashley Campbell was stabbed and killed four days after that on Saturday night.'

'I told you I was in on Saturday night,' Jones snapped.

'*If* your wife gives you an alibi that you were sitting at home with her watching the telly all night,' Gaughran said with a hint of a smirk, '...then no-one is going to believe you. I've seen it before. The prosecution will run rings round that as an alibi.'

'Yeah,' Hassan agreed. 'Jurys don't tend to believe alibis given by spouses.'

'No, they don't,' Gaughran said. 'Now, let me take you back to the night of the 15$^{th}$ January. Can you remember what you did that night?'

Jones narrowed his eyes aggressively. 'No.'

'I'll just remind you,' Gaughran smiled. 'You fractured Ashley Campbell's jaw and broke two of his ribs. Can you tell us why you did that?'

'We got into a fight,' Jones said.

'A fight about what?' Hassan asked.

'Nothing really.'

'You got into a fight about *nothing* in which you both ended up in A&E?' Gaughran snorted. 'Come on, Neil. What were you fighting about?'

'I can't remember.'

'Bollocks!' Gaughran said loudly. 'Ashley was shagging your wife, and you wanted to get revenge!'

'No,' Jones said. 'That's bollocks.'

'You wanted to get revenge. You went to find him last Tuesday, but he wasn't around. You tracked him down on Saturday night, found him at The Yard nightclub where you stabbed and killed him, didn't you?' Gaughran thundered.

'No!' Jones snapped.

The Duty Solicitor glared over at Gaughran. 'Sergeant, if you continue with this aggressive tone of questioning, then I will instruct my client not to co-operate with this investigation.'

*Oh, fuck off!* Gaughran thought. He didn't care. He had got to Jones, who couldn't hide the fact that he was rattled.

Hassan gave Jones a polite smile. 'Neil, did you know that your wife, Benita, was having a relationship with Ashley Campbell?'

Jones was staring at the floor, and his foot was jigging nervously.

'It's all right, Neil,' Gaughran now adopting a calm, friendly tone. 'You found out your missus had gone back to her old boyfriend. Maybe you confronted her and she denied it. You were angry. No-one is going to blame you for that. I'd be angry if I found that out. So, you went to have it out with Ashley Campbell. You followed him to a pub in Vauxhall in January. You tried to warn him off. Is that what happened?'

Jones nodded but said nothing.

'For the purposes of the tape, the suspect has nodded to give a positive reply to my question,' Gaughran said. 'Maybe after you'd put him in A&E, you thought he'd back off. But he didn't. So, eventually you tracked him down to his brother's bar. You go in but he's not around. You tell the barman to give Ashley a warning. By Saturday, you can't take it any more. You followed Ashley to The Yard club, waited outside and then spotted him waiting outside on his own. And then you stabbed him, didn't you?'

'No,' he whispered.

Hassan looked over at him. 'We know that's what happened, Neil. There's no point lying to us anymore.'

Jones shook his head and mumbled, 'No, that's not what happened.'

There was a knock at the door. Ferguson poked his head in, looked at Gaughran and asked quietly, 'Borrow you for a second, DS Gaughran?'

Gaughran nodded, got up from his seat and said, 'For the purposes of the tape, DS Gaughran is leaving the room.'

Gaughran went into the corridor with Ferguson. 'What's going on, guv?'

'SOCOs reckon they've found a shirt with bloodstains hidden in Jones' wardrobe,' Ferguson explained.

'We've got him then,' Gaughran said with a smile. 'Can we charge him?'

'I spoke to the CPS. They want to wait for the DNA check on the blood on the shirt to come back before they'll sanction that,' Ferguson explained. 'But I'm hoping we can get an extension on holding Jones from a magistrate.'

'Yeah,' Gaughran said, looking at his watch. 'Otherwise he's going to waltz out of here in just over five hours.'

Ferguson nodded. 'I'll talk to the magistrate now.'


Ruth and Lucy were heading down the back staircase of the Peckham nick as they made their way outside to get the car. Ferguson had asked them to tidy up the loose ends revolving around Hurst and his alibi.

'Do you want to hear something funny?' Lucy said as they headed past the custody suite.

'Always,' Ruth replied.

'Well, James and I had just had some hanky-panky in my flat ...'

Ruth snorted with laughter. 'Hang on a sec! Did you actually use the phrase *hanky-panky*?'

Lucy shrugged. 'Do you want to hear my story or not?'

Ruth pulled a face. 'If it involves any description of you having *hanky-panky*, then *not*.'

Lucy ignored her. 'So, me and James. And then we were in the kitchen...'

Ruth raised an eyebrow. 'Not having *hanky-panky,* I assume?'

'No, I was making spaghetti carbonara, if you must know.'

'Oh, you make a fantastic spaghetti carbonara.'

'I do, don't I?' Lucy smiled. 'So, I'm making the spaghetti carbonara when Natalie knocks on the door. She's only came back from her conference two days early and she's wondering if I'd seen James.'

'Oh, my God.' Ruth's eyes widened. 'How did you explain that away or didn't you?'

'James waffled on about bath's overflowing and damp patches on the ceiling,' Lucy explained.

'Which were easier to explain than the damp patches in your bed,' Ruth joked.

'Eww, do you mind?' Lucy said as they went down the black iron steps that led out into the rear car park at Peckham nick.

As they looked up, two uniformed officers were helping a man out of the back of a patrol car. It was Dion Campbell.

Ruth glanced over at Lucy and asked, 'I wonder what's he been up to?'

'Let's go and find out,' Lucy suggested.

They approached the two male uniformed officers who were leading Dion, who was in handcuffs, away from the car and towards the door to the custody suite.

'Hi Dion,' Lucy said. 'What have you been up to?'

The PC frowned. 'You know this gentleman?'

'Not really,' Lucy admitted. 'What's he done?'

'Stealing rum from a corner shop,' the other PC explained as he rolled his eyes. 'Second time we've picked him up in a week.'

'Second?' Lucy thought for a moment. 'When was the first?'

'Saturday night,' the PC said.

*Dion lied about his whereabouts on Saturday night!*

'Where?' Ruth asked as she shot a look at Lucy.

'Peckham High Street,' the PC informed her.

'What time was this?' Lucy asked.

'Just after midnight,' the PC said. 'He stole some rum and when we tried to arrest him, he did a runner. He was bailed on Sunday morning for theft and resisting arrest.'

'I'm assuming that he was searched thoroughly?' Lucy asked. She was wondering if Dion had something to do with Ashley's death. Why else had he lied to them?

'Of course,' the PC snapped, clearly taking offence at the suggestion that they hadn't done their job properly.

'Sorry,' Lucy said. 'This man's son was murdered close to Peckham High Street just before midnight on Saturday night.'

The PC raised an eyebrow at them. 'That was his son?'

'Yes,' Ruth replied.

'I didn't realise there was any connection,' the PC admitted.

'Neither did we until right now,' Lucy explained. 'But he lied about where he was on Saturday night to us, so when you've processed him, could you pop him into Interview Room 3 for us?'

The PC nodded. 'Of course.'

By the time Ruth and Lucy arrived at Interview Room 3, Dion was looking a little jittery. The Duty Solicitor was sitting next to him. The room smelt of booze and body odour.

'Morning, Dion,' Lucy said as she sat down opposite. 'Do you remember us from yesterday?'

Dion pulled a face and then smiled. 'Of course I do, dear. You're the police officers. You came to talk to me about my Ashley.'

'That's right,' Ruth said, as she looked over at Dion. His eyes were bloodshot and slightly glazed. She assumed he was at the stage of alcoholism where he was just permanently affected by booze.

Lucy pulled out her notebook and turned over a few pages. 'Dion, if you remember, we asked you where you were on Saturday night. You told us you were at home. In fact, you told us you never go out on a Saturday night.'

'Yes,' Dion nodded. 'That's right.'

Ruth glanced at Lucy and frowned. Dion hadn't seemed to register that there was anything wrong with what he told them as an alibi.

'As you know, your son Ashley was attacked and killed on Saturday night, just before midnight,' Ruth said, almost as if talking to a child. 'You remember that?'

'Yes,' Dion said sadly. 'Such a waste of a young man's life, you know?'

Ruth pulled out a piece of paper from the file in front of her. 'Dion, this is the duty log from the custody suite on Saturday night. You were brought into this police station at 12.24am.' She moved the document around so that he could look at it. 'You see here? You had been arrested for theft and attempting to resist arrest just after midnight.'

'Okay, I see,' Dion said, as if the discrepancy made no difference.

*Bloody hell, we're getting nowhere here,* Ruth thought.

'Dion?' Lucy said, trying to get his attention as he peered around the room.

'Yes, dear,' he slurred.

'You told us you were at home on Saturday night, but you weren't,' Lucy explained slowly. 'That means you lied to us.'

Dion smiled and held his hands up. 'I'm sorry. Sorry. My memory wasn't what it was, I'm afraid. I get very confused. If I got it wrong, then I can only apologise.'

Ruth glanced at Lucy again. Dion just didn't understand the severity of giving them a false alibi.

'Dion,' Ruth said. 'Do you understand it looks suspicious that you have lied about where you were the night that Ashley was murdered?'

Dion frowned. 'What are you talking about? I just told you my memory is terrible, dear. And when you get to my age, one day is exactly the same as the next.'

Ruth looked over at him. 'Not only did you lie about where you were the night that Ashley was killed, you were also arrested about five hundred yards from where he was killed and about fifteen minutes after he was attacked.'

Dion frowned as the penny finally dropped, and he understood what was being implied. He seemed horrified as he began to shake a finger at them. 'No, no, no. You think I could kill my own son? You think I could murder my boy Ashley? Oh my God, I can't believe you'd say such a thing.'

Dion's breathing was now rapid as his eyes roamed wildly around the room. He pushed his chair back from the table as he glared over at them. He then frowned angrily at the Duty Solicitor. 'How can you allow them to ask me this?'

'It's all right, Dion. Settle down,' Ruth said gently. 'We want to find out who attacked Ashley. And to do that, we have to talk to everyone who knew him and find out where they were and what they were doing. Does that make sense?'

'This is ridiculous! I'm his father,' Dion growled. 'You should be talking to those bloody sisters Ruben is mixed up with.'

Ruth frowned. 'Why do you say that?'

'They're not what they seem, you know?' he explained. 'The Bible warns of Jezebels. You should ask them how they got all their money.'

# CHAPTER 22

By the time Gaughran and Hassan arrived at the flat and shop where Neil and Benita Jones lived, the SOCO team were packing away. Several officers in full forensic suits were packing evidence bags into the back of the van. The pavement around the shop had been cordoned off with evidence tape and a uniform PC was standing by the door.

Gaughran got out his warrant card as he and Hassan approached the PC. 'Peckham CID. Is the chief SOCO around, Constable?'

The PC pointed to a man with ginger hair and glasses who was standing inside the carpet shop talking to another officer. 'DI Squires is over there, Sarge.'

'Thanks,' Gaughran said as he and Hassan went inside.

Glancing towards the back of the room, Gaughran spotted Benita tidying up behind the counter now that the search was over. She seemed so vulnerable.

'DI Squires?' Gaughran asked as he and Hassan showed their warrant cards.

'Can I help?' Squires asked.

'DS Gaughran and DC Hassan from Peckham CID,' Gaughran explained. 'I understand that you found a shirt with bloodstains?'

'That's right,' Squires said with a nod. 'I've fast-tracked it with the lab.'

'Anything else significant?' Gaughran asked hopefully. He knew it would take up to 24 hours to get the DNA analysis back on the shirt and that would allow Jones to walk out of Peckham nick before he could be charged.

'Hard to say,' Squires admitted. 'Nothing that was obviously incriminating, I'm afraid. We've taken away a few things to be analysed, but that's going to take a few days.'

'We haven't got a few days,' Gaughran moaned.

'Yeah, I heard,' Squires said. 'I'll push forensics as hard as I can.'

'Okay, thanks. This is my card,' Gaughran said, handing over his details. 'You lot look like you've finished here?'

Squires nodded. 'Yeah. We're off, but I'll ring you as soon as we've got anything.'

As Squires went, Gaughran looked at Hassan. 'Got your gloves?'

Hassan patted his pocket to show where his forensic gloves were. 'Yes, Sarge.'

'Do me a favour,' Gaughran said. 'Go upstairs to the flat and give it the once over, just in case. I'm going to talk to Benita Jones.'

'Sarge,' Hassan said, as he turned and headed away.

Benita peered up at Gaughran as he approached. He couldn't help but think how beautiful she was. Her fine cheekbones, long eyelashes and rosebud lips.

'How are you doing?' Gaughran asked.

Benita shrugged. 'Not great.'

'As you know, your husband is under arrest and he's helping us with our inquiries at Peckham Police Station,' Gaughran explained. 'But at the moment, the CPS don't think we have enough evidence to charge him with Ashley Campbell's murder.'

Benita frowned. 'I don't understand what that means.'

'Sorry. The Crown Prosecution Service are the people who decide if we have enough evidence to go to trial,' Gaughran said. 'But at the moment, they don't think we have enough to do that.'

'What?' Benita was scared. 'So, you're just going to let him go?'

'I know that makes little sense to you,' Gaughran admitted. 'But we can only hold him for 24 hours. And when that time runs out, he can go until we re-arrest him.'

Benita blinked as she took in what he was telling her. She was terrified.

'Do you think you're in danger if he's released?' Gaughran asked, picking up on her anxiety.

Benita pulled up the sleeve of her top to reveal large bruises at the top of her arms. 'What do you think?'

Gaughran felt a surge of anger that Jones had hurt her. 'I can arrange for you to go to a refuge, if you want?'

'No.' Benita shook her head. 'I'm not going to some refuge.'

'What about friends or family?'

She shook her head. 'No.'

'How long had you and Ashley Campbell been having an affair?' he asked.

She paused for a few seconds and then looked at him.

'Since the summer,' she said.

'And when did Neil find out about it?'

'At Christmas.'

'What happened?' he asked.

'I left my phone out and Ashley messaged me,' Benita explained. 'Neil found it and read it. He went mad.'

'Did he attack you?' Gaughran asked.

Benita nodded but didn't say anything.

'But you didn't report it?' he asked.

Benita visibly took a breath as her eyes welled with tears. 'No...'

'Has he attacked you before?'

Benita nodded as she wiped the tears from her face. She seemed very shaky.

'Have you ever told anyone about this before?' Gaughran asked.

'No, never,' Benita admitted. 'If I'd told my brothers, they would have killed him.'

'It's all right.' Gaughran put his hand on her arm reassuringly. 'You don't have to stay with him here.'

Benita looked directly at him and smiled. 'It's funny ... Neil always said that coppers were bent or scumbags.'

Gaughran raised his eyebrow. 'I think we know who the scumbag is, eh?'

Benita nodded, and then she stared down at the ground for a moment.

'I think he killed Ashley,' she whispered.

*Gaughran wasn't surprised to hear her say that, but there was the question of the alibi she had given him.*

'Benita?' Gaughran said very quietly.

She looked up and met his eyes.

'Was Neil here at the flat with you on Saturday night?' he asked.

She shook her head slowly. 'No. No, he wasn't.'

'And if we can find somewhere for you to go,' Gaughran said, '...would you stand up in court and testify to that?'

'Yes, yes I would,' she said.

# CHAPTER 23

The sky had darkened to a gunmetal grey by the time Ruth and Lucy pulled into the car park at the Cottesmore Golf Club. Judging by the array of Mercedes, Jaguars and the odd Aston Martin, the members were rich and well-heeled.

'Do you understand golf?' Lucy asked as they parked the car.

'The rules?' Ruth replied, turning off the ignition.

'No. Just the whole idea of hitting a tiny white ball around for hours on end?'

Two men in pastel Pringle jumpers and beige slacks wheeled their golf trolleys past them as they got out.

'And why do you have to dress like a wanker to play?' Lucy joked under her breath.

'Lucy!' Ruth hissed. 'Why don't you say it a bit louder. I think those blokes over there didn't quite hear.'

'Yeah, well places like this make my inferiority complex come out,' Lucy confessed.

'Clearly,' Ruth said, as she opened the large glass doors that led to the impressive reception area.

'I'm not sure that they even let women in here,' Lucy muttered as she pulled out her warrant card as a smartly dressed man peered at them disapprovingly from behind the counter. 'It's all right, mate, don't panic, we're not playing. Peckham CID.'

The young man nodded and Ruth thought he actually seemed to be relieved that he wouldn't have to confront them about what they were wearing or that they just didn't look like members.

'I'm wondering if you know a member of this golf club, Dennis Hurst?' Lucy asked, taking out her notepad.

'Captain Hurst?' The young man nodded emphatically. 'Oh yes, he's here most days. I think he's been a member of this golf club for over twenty years.'

'We're trying to verify his whereabouts on Saturday night,' Lucy explained. 'We believe that there was a function here?'

The young man nodded. 'It was the Captain's Charity Dinner.'

'Captain Hurst claims he left the club in a taxi that he ordered, but he has no idea what time that was,' Lucy said. 'I'm wondering if you keep a record of taxi bookings you make?'

'Yes,' the young man nodded as he went to get a ledger. 'I've got all the taxis that were booked from here on Saturday night.' He ran his finger down the list, frowned, and shook his head. 'No, sorry. His name isn't down as having made a taxi booking.'

'Are you sure?' Ruth asked with a frown.

'I wasn't on duty on Saturday night, so I'll have a quick word with the manager and see if he remembers,' the young man explained as he gestured to an office door and left.

'Bang goes Hurst's alibi,' Lucy said.

'Do we think he could have killed Ashley?' Ruth asked, thinking out loud.

'I think that depends on what Ashley was going to tell the inquiry,' Lucy said. 'If Hurst was telling the truth and Ashley was about to confess to attacking Jackie Rosen, then Hurst has nothing to gain. But if we think Hurst is lying and was responsible for the attack, then that's definite motive. Hurst would go to prison and lose his army pension. I can see why he might think that's worth killing someone.'

The young man came back with a cheery smile. 'I think I've solved it. Captain Hurst went in a taxi with someone who had come as a guest of our Club Captain.'

'And who was that?' Ruth asked.

The young man pulled a face. 'I'm not sure I'm meant to give out information like that.'

Lucy gave him a withering look. 'Yeah, this is a murder enquiry, so unless you want to come back to Peckham Police Station with us right now, you'd better tell us.'

'The taxi was ordered by a Brigadier Hastings,' the young man explained nervously.

Ruth frowned at Lucy. *But Hastings was running the internal inquiry into events at Cranleigh, in which Hurst was implicated.*

'Brigadier Stephen Hastings?' Lucy asked.

'I believe so,' the young man stammered.

'What time was that?' Lucy asked sternly.

'I'm afraid it doesn't say in the log.'

Ruth looked at him. 'We're going to need the name, address and phone number of the taxi company that you use.'


As Gaughran walked into the CID office, he checked his watch. It was 5pm.

*Jones! Shit!*

Turning around, he went out into the corridor and saw Ferguson coming the other way.

'Guv,' Gaughran said urgently. 'Tell me we got an extension on Jones' arrest?'

Ferguson shook his head. 'Sorry, Tim. The CPS still won't go for it until the DNA results come back on that shirt.'

'He lied about his whereabouts on Saturday night!' Gaughran snapped.

'But we have nothing linking him to the crime scene yet,' Ferguson said. 'We've got the motive, the opportunity but not the means ... I applied for the extension anyway, but the magistrate turned us down without confirmation from the CPS.'

'Bollocks!' Gaughran growled.

Ferguson gestured. 'Come on. I've got to sign Jones out of the custody suite now.'

'What if he does a runner?' Gaughran snapped.

'You know how this works, Tim,' Ferguson said, as they reached the back staircase that led down to the custody suite. 'There's nothing we can do.'

'And what if he goes home and beats the crap out of Benita?' Gaughran asked.

'We can't do anything unless she reports him.'

'She showed me what he does to her,' Gaughran protested. 'She's covered in bruises. The only place he doesn't hit her is in the face.'

'Ring round the women's refuges and see if you can get her a space,' Ferguson said. 'We can send a uniform patrol past to keep a check on her.'

'Yeah, she said she doesn't want to go to a refuge,' Gaughran muttered, now wondering what to do next. 'I'm gonna have to warn her that's he's heading home.'

As they rounded the corner, Gaughran could see Jones standing beside the Custody Sergeant. He was looking at the paperwork in front of him.

Jones looked around as Ferguson, and Gaughran arrived. He had a smirk across this face.

The Custody Sergeant pointed to the paperwork. 'You understand that you're being bailed, pending further investigation, according to the Police and Criminal Evidence Act of 1984. Is that clear?'

Jones gave an ironic snort as he signed the paperwork and handed it back. 'Yeah, it's clear.' He then turned and grinned at Ferguson and Gaughran. 'I'll be off then. Cheerio.'

'Yeah, don't get too comfortable in your own bed, eh?' Gaughran sneered.

They watched as Jones sauntered out of the custody suite and through the door that led out to the front car park and the street.

Feeling overcome with rage and anxiety, Gaughran waited for a few seconds and then headed for the door after him.

'Tim?' Ferguson said as a way of warning.

Outside, the air was cold and crisp as Gaughran broke into a jog and caught Jones up.

'Oi, dickhead,' he said as Jones turned to look at him with an ironic frown.

'What the fuck do you want?'

'When you go home, you lay one finger on your wife and I will bury you,' Gaughran warned in a hushed voice.

Jones snorted and then smiled. 'Really? Why, you got a thing for my missus or something?'

Gaughran ignored him, even though he knew there was some truth in it. 'I've met blokes like you before. So, I meant what I said. Lay a finger on her and I'll find you, I'll put you in my car, drive you somewhere and bury you in a hole where no-one will ever find you.'

Jones smiled and then winked. 'See you soon, Detective Dickhead.'

As Jones turned and walked away, Ferguson approached. 'Just leave it, Tim. That's an order.'

It was early evening as Ferguson came through the doors of the CID office. Ruth glanced up from where she and Lucy were working, following various leads.

'Right guys,' Ferguson said loudly as he headed for the scene board. 'The longer this investigation goes on, the more confusing it seems to get. There seem to be more suspects and lines of inquiry than yesterday, so I need everyone to feedback so that we're all up to speed.' He then glanced at his watch. 'And then I want everyone out of here and heading home by nine. You're no good to me if you're too tired to think.' Taking a pen from his shirt pocket, he went over and tapped a photograph. 'Jermaine Daniels. Officers from Brixton discovered Ashley's blood-soaked wallet and phone in his bedroom. They also found his yellow Nike trainers that had blood on the soles. Anything back from Forensics?'

Ruth looked over. 'DNA from the both the trainers and the wallet match our victim's.'

'Okay,' Ferguson nodded. 'So, we know Daniels was around that area when Ashley was killed. Is he a cold-blooded killer or a nasty little opportunist? Ruth, Lucy, you spoke to him, what did you think?'

Lucy sat forward in her seat. 'I don't think he stabbed Ashley, guv. He doesn't have any prior. And as soon as we applied any pressure, he shook and cried.'

Ruth nodded. 'I've been to street muggings that have gone wrong before. I've never seen anyone stab a victim twice with no warning, wait for them to fall to the pavement and then rummage around in their pockets for a wallet and phone.'

Gaughran glanced over. 'And keeping the blood stained wallet, phone and trainers in his bedroom isn't really pointing to him being a career criminal.'

*Tim seems to have changed his tune about it being a simple mugging,* Ruth thought.

'He claims to have seen the killer, doesn't he?' Ferguson asked.

Ruth nodded. 'Yeah. He said he was wearing a hood and mask. He couldn't tell us if he was black or white. He claimed the killer ran off down the road, got into a big 4x4, something like a Range Rover, possibly black, and then drove away, heading for the Cossall Estate.'

'Any CCTV on the estate that we can look at?' Ferguson asked.

Hassan pulled a face. 'It's a rabbit warren once you get into the estate. Half the CCTV cameras have been vandalised.'

'Right. I share your instincts that Daniels is a nasty little opportunist,' Ferguson agreed, and then tapped another photograph. 'Lucy, what about Dion Campbell?'

'Guv, he lied about his alibi, but he's a chronic alcoholic. His memory is shot to pieces and I don't think he can tell one day from the next. But he was found close to where Ashley was murdered and at a similar time.'

'Problem is, he doesn't have a motive, guv,' Ruth explained. 'In fact, Ashley had been bailing his father out with cash for years. It was his brother Ruben who had tried to cut off contact with him. Why would Dion want to kill his son who helped him out?'

'Okay,' Ferguson nodded. 'What's the story with Ruben, Mica and Lenora?'

'Nothing really there, guv,' Lucy said. 'The sisters are very rich. Lenora leant Ashley some money behind her sister's back as an investment. Ruben and Lenora were both at the bar all night, and even though Mica went home early, I can't see a motive.'

'Which brings us to Captain Hurst,' Ferguson said.

'I think we're clutching at straws, guv,' Gaughran said. 'We don't know what Ashley was going to tell the inquest or if he was going to implicate anyone. And Hurst has a watertight alibi.'

'Although we know he shared a taxi with Stephen Hastings,' Ruth pointed out.

Gaughran shrugged. 'It's completely unethical, but it doesn't make him guilty of Ashley's murder, does it?'

'No, it doesn't.' Ferguson then went over to the photograph of Neil Jones. 'As you all know, we arrested Jones yesterday for Ashley's murder. He had discovered that Ashley was having an affair with his wife, Benita, last Christmas. He tracked him down to a pub in Vauxhall in January and attacked him, fracturing Ashley's jaw and breaking his ribs. Last Tuesday, he walked into Harvey's in an angry and agitated state, looking for

Ashley. He told the barman to warn Ashley to watch his back. Jones no longer has an alibi for Saturday night. I believe he followed Ashley to The Yard club, waited outside for him to come out and stabbed him to death. SOCOs discovered a blood-stained shirt at his flat, but we are waiting for a DNA match on that. Unfortunately, we've had to release Jones on bail pending further inquiries. But I believe he is our prime suspect. So, I want you guys to go home, get some rest and when you come in here tomorrow, I want all our efforts to be put into finding more evidence against Neil Jones. Ruth and Lucy, I'd like you to bring Ruben Campbell up to speed with the developments. It only takes one idiot from downstairs to open their mouth in the pub and it'll be on the news – and I don't want him finding out about Jones from the media.'

Ruth nodded, 'Yes, guv.'

'Right', Ferguson said. 'Anyone got anything to add?'

Lucy shrugged. 'As far as we know, Jones doesn't have a 4x4 which contradicts what Daniels told us.'

Ferguson scratched his chin. 'Maybe he borrowed one? Does he have a friend or a relative with a 4x4 that he borrowed on Saturday night? Right, thank you everyone. I'm in my office if anyone needs me.'

Ferguson made his way out of CID as a uniform PC came in and approached Ruth and Lucy.

'Can we help Constable?' Lucy asked as he arrived.

'I'm looking for DC Hunter and DC Henry,' he explained.

Lucy gave him a friendly smile. 'Well, you just found them.'

'Oh, right,' the PC said with a self-effacing smile as he took out his notebook. 'I understand that you're investigating the murder of Ashley Campbell?'

'That's right,' Ruth said.

'It's just that my partner and I were called to a burglary at a flat belonging to a Ruben and Mica Campbell,' the PC said. 'Ruben Campbell is Ashley's brother, isn't he?'

'Yes,' Ruth said, wondering quite where all this was going.

'The weird thing is that when we arrived at their flat, they had tidied up the crime scene, even though the emergency operator told them not to touch anything until we arrived,' the PC explained. 'We took a statement from them, but they insisted that nothing of value had been taken.'

'You think they were acting suspiciously?' Lucy asked.

'Yeah, definitely,' the PC nodded. 'I explained we could pass it onto CID who would come and take fingerprints, but they said they didn't want to waste anyone's time.'

Ruth frowned. 'How come they called 999 in the first place then?'

'That's the thing. They didn't,' the PC said. 'It was the neighbour upstairs who heard the burglars and called it in. Then Ruben and Mica came home.'

'Do you have any idea why they were acting so strangely?' Lucy asked.

'For what it's worth, I thought they didn't want anyone poking around the flat or going through their stuff,' the PC said. 'They just wanted to give us a quick statement and get us out of there.'

'When did you say this was?' Ruth asked.

The phone rang on a nearby desk, and Hassan headed over to answer it.

'Ten days ago,' the PC said, looking at his notebook. 'When I heard about the murder, I thought I should let you know.'

Ruth nodded and smiled. 'Thanks, Constable. That's really useful.'

'That is seriously strange,' Lucy said with a frown. 'I wonder what they were trying to hide.'

Hassan signalled to Gaughran across the office. 'Tim, there's someone at reception who wants to see you. They're saying it's urgent.'

'Who is it?' Gaughran asked.

'Benita Jones,' Hassan said.

# CHAPTER 24

Opening the door to Interview Room 2, Gaughran saw Benita looking up at him from where she was sitting. Her face was a mess. Her left eye was swollen and her lip was split.

'Oh God, Benita,' Gaughran said quietly as he went and sat down next to her. 'I'm so sorry.'

'It's not your fault,' Benita mumbled with the forced smile. She was still very shaky. 'I don't even know your name.'

'Tim,' Gaughran replied. 'It's Tim.'

'Where is he now?' Gaughran growled as his shock turned to anger.

'I don't know. He came back, attacked me, grabbed some clothes and then left,' Benita explained.

Gaughran rubbed his face with his hand. 'Okay. Any ideas where he might have gone?'

'I'm not sure,' Benita said with a shrug. She took a breath.

'It's all right,' Gaughran said, putting a comforting hand on her arm. 'You're safe now.'

'Am I?' Benita asked as tears came into her eyes. 'He'll find me. He knows I told you he wasn't at home on Saturday. He'll kill me if he finds me again.'

'Listen,' Gaughran said gently as he leant forward. 'I'm going to make sure that you're safe. And then we're going to find him and put him in prison. You don't have to see him ever again, okay?'

Benita nodded as she wiped tears from her face. 'Yeah, thank you.'

'Now, can you think of anywhere he might have gone?' Gaughran asked. 'Does he have family?'

Benita shook her head. 'Not really. His mum and dad died a few years ago.'

'Friends?' he asked.

'Not really,' she replied. 'A few blokes he played darts with at the pub. I don't know if they were friends.'

'He's got to be somewhere,' Gaughran said. 'I'm guessing he doesn't have the money to check into a hotel.'

'No,' Benita said, and then she thought of something. 'He's got an uncle in Deptford. Charlie.'

'So, that would be Charlie Jones?' Gaughran asked.

Benita shook her head. 'No, Charlie is on Neil's mum's side.'

'Can you remember her maiden name?'

'Hitchin?' she replied uncertainly. 'No, Hinchcliffe. Yeah, it's Charlie Hinchcliffe.'

'Sure?'

'Yeah, that's definitely it,' she said with a nod.

'And he's in Deptford?'

'Yeah,' Benita replied. 'He runs a garage. You know, fixes cars and does tyres. That sort of place.'

'That's great, Benita,' Gaughran said. 'Now, have you got anywhere to stay tonight?'

Benita shrugged. 'I'll have to stay at the flat.'

'Yeah, you can't do that,' Gaughran said. 'What if your husband comes back?'

She shook her head. 'I don't think he'll do that. He must know that I've gone to the police.'

'It's still a risk,' Gaughran warned her. 'I can see if we can put an officer outside, but I can't promise that. What about relatives?'

'My brothers live in Leeds,' Benita explained.

'Can't you go there for a few days?' Gaughran suggested.

Benita shook her head. 'We don't really speak anymore. They didn't approve of me marrying Neil. They didn't even come to our wedding.'

Gaughran thought for a few seconds. 'I can see if I can get you into a women's refuge.'

Benita looked upset, shook her head, and put her hand on his arm. Their eyes locked for a moment – she was so vulnerable. 'Please, I really don't want to stay in one of those places. Isn't there anything else you can do?'

Gaughran nodded. 'Okay. I'll tell you what I can do. I'll take you back to your flat and you can grab your things. And I'm not in the habit of doing this, but I have a spare bedroom in my house. You don't need to worry, I'm not trying to take advantage of you, but you look like you need a shower, a hot meal and somewhere safe to sleep for the night.'

'Is that allowed?' she asked.

'Not really,' he shrugged. 'But if you don't tell, I won't.'

Benita frowned as tears welled in her eyes. 'Why would you do that for me?'

'You need help.' He smiled at her. 'And I've got a casserole that needs eating, but there's too much even for me to eat. Basically, you'd be doing me a favour.'

'Really?' Benita asked. 'I feel like I'd be imposing.'

'Seriously,' Gaughran said. 'In fact, I won't take no for an answer.'

Benita just looked at him for a few seconds and then whispered, 'Thank you.'

It was gone 8pm when Lucy and Ruth arrived at *Harvey's*. They wanted to ask Ruben and Mica about the burglary and about the article they had seen about the investigation into Marland Cole's murder in Jamaica. Dion's comment about Mica and Lenora had made them wonder about what had actually happened in Jamaica.

Arriving on the first floor of the bar, they saw that the door to Ruben's office was ajar, and that he was sitting at his desk.

Ruth knocked tentatively and peered in. 'Hi Ruben, there have been some developments in the case which we need to bring you up to speed on.'

Ruben gestured to the chairs, 'Of course, come in.'

Ruth and Lucy went over and sat down. Ruben seemed tired – the shock of his brother's death was clearly taking its toll. Ruth noticed a tumbler with a couple of inches of Scotch in it.

Lucy sat forward and said, 'Ruben, we arrested a man yesterday in connection with Ashley's murder.'

Ruben's eyes widened. 'Right ... Can you give me any details?'

'Not really,' Lucy said as she shook her head. 'All we can tell you is that a man has been arrested, and he was released on bail today, pending further inquiries. We can tell you much more if we actually charge him with Ashley's murder.'

'Why can't you charge him now?' Ruben asked.

'It's a decision that is made by the Crown Prosecution Service. They looked at all the evidence that we had against this individual. Unfortunately, at the moment, they don't believe that there is enough evidence to allow us to charge him with murder and go to trial. Does that make sense?'

'Yeah.' Ruben nodded. 'Is there a set time period for bail?'

'No,' Ruth informed him. 'I've known bail to go on for months and sometimes years.'

Ruben was frustrated. 'Really?'

'Look, I know that's not what you want to hear,' Lucy said. 'But please believe me when I tell you that we're doing everything we can to find the person who killed your brother.'

Ruben scratched his chin. 'Do you think you got the right person yesterday?'

'We can't really comment on that,' Lucy said, pulling a face. 'Sorry.'

'Is Benita involved in all this?' Ruben asked.

'Sorry,' Ruth said. 'I don't follow.'

'I told the officers that were here yesterday morning that Benita was an ex-girlfriend of Ash's,' Ruben explained. 'And then you arrested someone for his murder. Is it something to do with her?'

'We're really sorry, but we can't tell you that either,' Lucy said.

Ruben nodded as he took in what they had told him. Taking a long swig of whiskey from his glass, he sat back in his chair and then took a deep breath.

'There are a couple of other things that we'd like to tidy up while we're here,' Ruth stated. 'Just routine stuff.'

Ruben shrugged. 'Fine, no problem.'

'We understand you had a break-in at your flat a few weeks ago?' Ruth asked.

'Yes,' Ruben replied, looking confused. 'I can't see how that's relevant.'

'Bear with us,' Lucy said. 'Sometimes it's the smallest thing that unlocks an investigation. You'd be surprised.'

'I spoke to the officers who came round to your flat,' Ruth said. 'They told us you'd already tidied up by the time they got there.'

'That's Mica for you,' Ruben snorted. 'Total OCD.'

'Oh, it was Mica's idea to clear everything up?' Lucy asked.

'Yes.' Ruben nodded. 'I dropped her off at the flat and then drove around, trying to find a parking space. It's a bloody nightmare around there.'

'Okay,' Ruth said. 'And by the time you got back to the flat, Mica had discovered you had been burgled?'

'Yeah, that's right. Mrs Wright upstairs came down and told her she'd heard something and called the police,' Ruben explained.

'And while you were parking, Mica had cleared up the flat?'

'Yeah. She said she'd checked around and nothing was missing.' Ruben frowned. 'Do you think the burglary had something to do with what happened to Ashley?'

'We don't know,' Lucy said. 'But it is something for us to look into.'

'And you're certain that nothing went missing during the burglary?' Ruth asked.

'Yes,' Ruben said. 'They must have been disturbed because there was cash and jewellery, and they didn't touch it.'

After a few seconds of silence, Ruth peered at Ruben. 'Do you know very much about what happened to Mica and Lenora's father, Marland, back in Jamaica?'

'Not really,' Ruben shrugged. 'They don't like to talk about it very much.'

'No, it must be hard,' Lucy said.

Ruth looked over. 'And it must have been very hard for their mother, Jalissa, wasn't that her name?'

Ruben nodded. 'That's right.'

'Having lost her husband like that. All those years together,' Ruth said. 'And then moving to a new country with two young girls and starting a new life.'

Ruben pulled a face. 'To be honest, I don't think Jalissa was Marland's biggest fan at the time of the robbery.'

Lucy raised an eyebrow. 'Oh, why's that then?'

'There's no reason you would know this,' Ruben explained. 'Marland was in the process of leaving Jalissa for a younger woman. Classic mid-life crisis. Apparently, she was in her 20s and worked at the hotel. They had an affair and Marland broke it to Jalissa that he was leaving and divorcing her.'

'Oh right,' Ruth said with a frown. 'And how long before the robbery was this?'

'A couple of months, I think,' Ruben said.

'I think there was some suspicion that the robbery had been an inside job, if I remember what I read in the paper,' Lucy said.

'Sorry, I don't know.' Ruben shrugged. 'As I said, now that Jalissa's gone, Mica and Lenora don't really like to talk about what happened to their father.'

Ruth smiled at him as she and Lucy got up to go. 'Thank you, Ruben. We'll make sure that we keep you up to date with any developments. And we're sorry that we can't tell you anymore.'

'Just one more thing,' Lucy said.

Ruben raised an eyebrow. 'Yeah?'

'When it came to getting married,' she said, '...did Mica explain why she, Lenora and Jalissa all changed their surname once they'd arrived in the UK? I just wondered if it caused any problems with getting a marriage certificate.'

'What?' Ruben scowled. 'You've got that wrong, I'm afraid. They didn't change their names when they arrived here or Mica would have told me.'

Ruth and Lucy looked at each other. Mica had clearly kept that information from Ruben which was definitely suspicious.

# CHAPTER 25

Gaughran opened the front door and gestured for Benita to come in. Even though he wasn't technically breaking any rules, he wasn't going to tell Ferguson that she was staying at his place until something else could be sorted out. And he had told Hassan to keep quiet too.

'Welcome to paradise,' he said ironically.

'It's nice and warm,' she said awkwardly as she stood in the hallway with her two bags.

'Make yourself at home. Seriously,' Gaughran said as he put on the downstairs' lights.

*This is a little bit uncomfortable*, he thought.

'Right, let's give you the grand tour, eh?' he said with an ironic laugh as he walked up the stairs. He opened the door to the spare room. It was tastefully decorated with a double bed, wardrobe, and a thick rug. 'Spare room, so if you want to chuck your stuff in there.'

'It's lovely,' she said with a smile. 'Did you do all this yourself?'

'You know what, I would love to take credit for all the stuff in the house and the way it's been decorated – and please don't judge me – but my mum might have given me a hand.'

Benita grinned. 'Your mum?'

'Yeah,' Gaughran said. 'I know that's not very cool and you now think I'm some big mummy's boy...'

'No, not at all,' Benita said, looking directly at him. She had a curious expression on her face. 'It's really sweet.'

Gaughran pulled a face. 'Yeah, word of advice. No man wants to be called sweet because his mum helped him decorate and furnish his house.'

Benita laughed.

Gaughran looked at her and her damaged face – all he wanted to do was put his arms around her and take care of her.

'If you were an Indian boy, you'd have no choice,' Benita explained. 'Your mum would have taken over and done everything.'

'Is that what your mum is like then?'

'She was,' Benita said.

Gaughran gave her a quizzical look.

'She died a couple of years ago,' she explained. He could see the emotion of it well inside her for a moment as she took a breath.

'I'm sorry to hear that.'

'Yeah ...' she said quietly. 'Mum and Dad had gone shopping in Manchester for the day. There was fog on the road going back to Leeds and a lorry went into the back of their car. They both died.'

Gaughran gave her an empathetic look. 'God, that's terrible.'

'Sorry,' Benita mumbled, looking embarrassed.

'Don't apologise,' Gaughran said with a kind smile. 'Both my parents are still alive so I can't imagine what it must be like to lose them like that.'

'Yeah, it was difficult,' she explained. 'That's when the stuff with Neil got really bad.'

'I don't understand.'

'I was a bit of a wreck and I was trying to repair some of the bonds with my family,' she said. 'He thought I was neglecting him so he made sure he got my attention ... you know.'

Gaughran shook his head. 'What a self-absorbed prick.'

'Yeah.' She nodded. 'He's a like a toddler.'

'Toddlers don't do that.' Gaughran pointed to her face. 'So, if you don't mind me asking, why did you fall out with your family?'

'I'm a Hindu. They wanted me to marry someone who was Indian,' she explained.

'Oh, I thought it was only Muslims that had arranged marriages?'

'We don't have arranged marriages,' she explained. 'But I was encouraged to have boyfriends from my own culture. Like my mum would say that a certain Indian boy was nice looking, and he wanted to ask me out.'

'And you decided to marry a bald-headed thug with a neck tattoo,' Gaughran said. 'I bet that went down well?'

'Yeah,' she replied with an ironic snort. 'Everyone went mad. I think I was annoyed about the pressure they put me under so I picked a man who was literally their worst nightmare ... And then it turned out to be *my* worst nightmare.'

'Why did you stay with him then?'

Benita shrugged. 'I felt trapped. I was completely ostracised from my family. I was two hundred miles from home with no friends. And I started to believe what he was telling me. That I was useless and pathetic, and that I had nowhere else to go.'

'Jesus,' Gaughran shook his head. 'I've heard that story so many times, you wouldn't believe it.'

'Yeah, I can imagine.'

He smiled at her reassuringly. 'Well, you're safe now.'

For a few seconds, she blinked as her eyes filled with tears. 'Thank you.'

Then her whole body seemed to shake as she wept – it was all too much for her.

Gaughran stepped forward and put his arms around her. He didn't know if he was over-stepping the mark, but she needed consoling and it felt like the right thing to do.

'Hey, it's all right.'

Ruth sat in her living room with a large glass of wine in her hand dressed in a cream-coloured towelling robe. It was 9.30pm. She and Kara had just had sex, and Kara was now taking a shower.

Taking a longer than usual swig of wine, Ruth let out an audible sigh. Her insides were squirming, and she felt very uncomfortable. There was just no connection or spark between her and Kara - so what the hell was she doing? She was leading the poor girl along because she was attractive but it just wasn't sitting right with her. She had allowed herself to be swayed by Lucy's advice that she was in her 20s so what was the problem in having a relationship based on looks and sex. Unfortunately, she had realised it just wasn't her. She needed more, and it was making her feel uneasy.

Mulling over what the problem was, she knew there was a disconnect in virtually everything. Ruth would make a sarcastic comment only for it to fly right over Kara's head as she gazed blankly at her. Or she would make some cultural reference to music or film that would be met with a vacant nod. Kara wasn't stupid – far from it. They just didn't *click* in terms of personality, humour or interests.

*Oh great, I'm going to have to end this when she's dressed, aren't I?* Ruth said to herself with a growing sense of dread.

The thought of it made her feel physically sick. She didn't want to hurt Kara. Was she being horribly arrogant by believing that Kara would be upset if they split up? Maybe Kara would just shrug, put it down to experience and be calmly on her way. That would be perfect, but Ruth's instinct was that it wasn't going to go that way.

'Hiya,' Kara chirped as she wandered back into the room. 'I can't find your hairdryer.'

Ruth's stomach lurched. At least Kara was dressed so she could do it now rather than prolong the agony. *God, is that really selfish?*

'Hi, Kara,' Ruth said as her pulse quickened. 'Can you come and sit down for a minute?'

Kara frowned and then joked, 'Oh, that sounds ominous.'

*Bloody hell. This is horrible.*

'You know I think you're a very attractive, kind and intelligent person, don't you?' Ruth asked.

*Where are you going with this, Ruth?* she asked as her head whirred.

Kara frowned suspiciously. 'Erm, I don't know.'

'And we've had a really lovely time together, haven't we?' Ruth asked.

*You've just used the past tense, you idiot!*

'Are you breaking up with me?' Kara asked.

*'Bloody hell! Let me say my piece first!'*

'No, I mean, yes. But I need you to listen to me ...'

Kara started to cry. 'Why?'

'It's not you, I .. promise,' Ruth stammered. 'I'm looking for someone that I can see myself being with long term ...'

'I don't understand.' Kara frowned at her in anguish. 'I thought we were getting on really well?'

'We are,' Ruth said, grappling for the right thing to say. 'I just feel that I need more.'

'More what?'

Ruth frowned. 'I don't know. Spark. You know ...'

'No, I don't know,' Kara sniffed as she wiped the tears from her face. 'Spark? We've just had sex!'

'I know.'

'Did you know you were going to break up with me when you took me in there?' Kara asked gesturing to the bedroom.'

'No, of course not,' Ruth said, but she knew there was probably part of her that did.

'Don't lie to me!' Kara snapped. 'What kind of person sleeps with someone when they know they're about to finish with them?'

'Sorry, I ...' Ruth was now lost for words.

'You're a cold, selfish bitch, Ruth!' Kara yelled as she got up and left.

*You're probably right. I don't think I could hate myself more at this very moment than I already do.*

# CHAPTER 26

The traffic lights went red, and Gaughran pulled his car to a stop. His father sat beside him in the passenger seat. Having picked him up from the hospital, they had nattered about football and the case Gaughran was working on.

However, Gaughran was seething underneath all the pleasantries and knew that he had to confront his father before they got back home. The thought of it was making him feel sick with anxiety.

*Fuck it, just do it!* he said to himself.

'I went to see Angie a couple of nights ago,' Gaughran said.

*There. I've said it and there's no going back,* he thought to himself. It was a relief to get it out there, no matter what the consequences were.

'What?' Arthur mumbled as his eyes roamed around the car nervously.

'I know you and Angie have been having an affair, Dad,' Gaughran said calmly.

'What the fuck are you talking about, Tim?' Arthur snapped.

Gaughran took a breath and waited for a few seconds. He wanted the tension to mount in the car, just as he would in an Interview Room.

'Are you really going to sit there and just lie to me?' Gaughran asked.

'Seriously,' Arthur said with a frown. 'I don't know what you're talking about. Who's Angie?'

'You can't just sit there and lie!' Gaughran growled. 'What the hell is the matter with you?'

Arthur looked directly at him and shrugged. 'I'm totally confused.'

'Angela Franklin. She works for Salomon Brothers bank as a secretary in the City of London. She's got a nice flat in East Dulwich. She came to see you in the hospital the other night. Just before Christmas, I watched you come out of the golf club, give her a kiss and get into her car!'

Arthur just stared at the windscreen and bristled. 'And what the fuck has that got to do with you?' he sneered in a whisper.

'Oh right, so now you're admitting it?' Gaughran snapped.

'It's none of your fucking business, is it?' Arthur said very quietly.

'Isn't it?' Gaughran shouted angrily. 'And what about Mum? What happens to her is my fucking business.'

Arthur glared at him and rolled his eyes patronisingly. 'She knows, you idiot!'

'What? You've told her, have you?'

'No. I don't need to tell her. She's not daft, your mother. She knows what's what. And we just get on with it,' Arthur explained.

'Have you any idea how out of control your ego is?' Gaughran thundered.

'You're not married, so you wouldn't understand,' Arthur sighed. 'Me and your mother have been together for thirty years. So, you can come and fucking judge me when you've been married for thirty years. Because otherwise, you haven't got a bloody clue.'

Gaughran slammed on the brakes and pulled the car over to the side of the road.

'Yeah, well, you need to get over yourself,' Gaughran yelled. 'Who the hell do you think you are? I sometimes wonder if you've ever had a thought in your head that doesn't revolve around what you want or what you need.'

There was a long silence.

'You driving me home or what?' Arthur asked.

'No,' Gaughran said. 'You can get out and get a cab.'

Arthur shrugged and said calmly, 'Fine. Makes no difference to me.'

Gaughran took a breath as he watched his father get out of the car and walk gingerly onto the pavement.

Putting the car into first gear, he pushed down the accelerator and watched his father standing on the street as he drove away.


Pouring herself a double measure of frozen vodka, Lucy popped two ice cubes into the glass and heard the satisfying sound of the ice cracking. She walked into the lounge and slumped down onto the sofa. Turning to the stereo, she pressed play and a few seconds later the track *Femme D'Argent* by *Air* played. She was confused for a moment as the track itself started with the sound of rain. She thought it was coming from outside. It was actually James' CD, and he'd left it in her flat. But she loved it so much that she was reluctant to pop it back upstairs. Plus, she ran the risk of having to explain why James' CD had been in her stereo.

Taking a swig of the icy vodka, she closed her eyes and listened to the ambient music. Then the conversation with Ruben Campbell popped into her head. How could he have not known that Mica, Lenora and their mother had changed their names legally by deed poll when they arrived from Jamaica? It was a suspicious thing for them to have done unless they felt it was part of the new start? Maybe they didn't want to have their father's surname Cole after they had discovered he was having an affair? If that was the case, why hadn't Mica told Ruben? It felt fishy if there was nothing to hide.

Her train of thought was broken by a knock on the door.

*Who's that at his time?* she wondered.

With her pulse quickening, she instantly thought of Marcus Jankel. Would he be brazen enough to just rock up and knock on her door? Maybe. In fact, she wouldn't put it past him to turn up on her doorstep for a chat – or something darker.

She turned down the music and tip-toed down the hallway. Glancing at the front door, she could see that it was properly locked with the Chubb. Taking a breath, she moved forward and looking through the spyhole.

There was a figure standing on the doorstep.

It was James!

*For fuck's sake!*

Even though there was part of her that was annoyed that he had spooked her, there was also an excitement at seeing him.

Unlocking the door, she opened it and frowned at him. 'What are you doing here?'

James grinned. 'That's not very nice.'

*God, he's attractive. This is not good!*

She spotted that he was holding a gift bag in his hand.

'Yeah, well, after my stalker the other night, I'm a bit jumpy,' she explained. She didn't like to tell him that there was a serial killer out there who had promised to look her up at some point.

'Oh God, sorry.' James pulled a face. 'I wasn't thinking.'

She looked at him quizzically. 'I'm not sure it's a good idea for you to be here.'

James shrugged and lifted the gift bag. 'I got you a present.'

'Does Natalie know you're here?' Lucy asked, pointing up to the flat above.

'Erm, not exactly,' he said with a cheeky smile.

Lucy raised an eyebrow. 'Which I guess means *no*.'

'Don't you want your present?' he asked.

'Yeah, let's just concentrate on the whole girlfriend that you live with thing first,' Lucy said sternly.

James pulled a face. 'She's working late. In fact, she won't be back until gone midnight. The perks of being an accountant.'

'Oh right, so you thought you'd pop down here for a quickie, did you?' she snapped.

'Sorry,' James said. 'I can't stop thinking about you and it's driving me mad.'

'You have a girlfriend, James,' she said.

'Can't we be friends then?' he asked.

'Oh, we're going to just be friends, are we?' she asked dubiously. 'And how exactly is that going to work?'

'Can I come in and give you your present then?' he asked. 'Please? Then I'll go, I promise.'

Lucy gave an audible sigh. 'Oh bloody hell, James. Come on then. But you've got five minutes.'

They went into the hallway, and she closed the front door.

James gestured to the living room. 'You're playing my CD.'

'Yeah, I really love it,' she admitted.

'You'd better keep it then,' he said and then held up the bag. 'I got you this.'

Taking the bag, she pulled out the present which was about 18 inches in diameter and circular. 'Very intriguing,' she said as she ripped off the wrapping paper.

It was a beautiful, stylish wall clock.

'You've got the perfect space on your kitchen wall, just above the fridge. And I looked at it the other day and thought you needed a really nice clock there,' James explained.

Lucy smiled. 'Thank you. Very thoughtful. You're not really like most blokes that I've met, you know that?'

'Oh dear.' James pulled face. 'That doesn't sound good.'

'Oh no. It's the opposite,' she laughed. 'I love the fact that you looked at my wall and thought that what it needed was this wall clock.'

'Oh good,' James sighed.

'However ...' Lucy said in a tone of forewarning.

'Oh dear ...'

'I've got a horrible feeling that you thought that if you turned up on my doorstep with your thoughtful, stylish clock and a cheeky grin, that I would sleep with you?'

James pulled a face of mock indignation. 'No way. The thought never entered my mind.'

'Really?' Lucy laughed.

He shrugged with a cheeky grin. 'I thought it was a possibility.'

Lucy gave him a playful hit on the arm. 'You're such a twat!'

'But I'm serious. I cannot get you out of my head and it's driving me mad,' James explained seriously.

Lucy knew she had thought about James almost constantly since they'd met.

'Bloody hell, James!' Lucy said in frustration. 'What do we do about it?'

James said nothing. Instead, he just looked at her as if he was studying her face. 'All I want to do is kiss you,' he said in a virtual whisper.

Lucy moved towards him. 'Well go on then,' she sighed as she raised an eyebrow seductively.

James took Lucy, pulled her in close and put his hand to her face as he kissed her hard on the mouth.

Gaughran unlocked the front door to his house and stepped inside. Although he was furious with his father, there was also part of him that wondered if he actually had a point? Was it his business to interfere if his father was having an affair? And what if his mum really knew about it and had chosen to ignore it? Maybe they had just found a way of making a thirty-year marriage work? His father had an affair, and she accepted it. What if he went wading in and upset that equilibrium? He could actually make things worse, couldn't he? On the other hand, he couldn't bear to think of his mum at home, cleaning, tidying, or cooking, while his father was off with another woman.

Hanging up his coat, his thoughts turned to Benita. He had told her to help herself to food and drink. Part of him assumed that she would have a bath and go to bed. She seemed exhausted, which was understandable.

He grabbed himself a beer from the fridge and walked into the living room. The television was on quietly and Benita was curled up on the sofa, dressed in pyjamas and fast asleep.

Gaughran sat down slowly in the armchair and watched her. She had her arms wrapped around a cushion that was against her chest. It slowly rose and fell with her breathing. She was so fragile and vulnerable. Despite the swollen eye and lip, her face was symmetrical, with shaped eyebrows and a thin, straight nose. Her jet black hair was still slightly damp from where she had been in the bath, and it curled and fell onto her shoulders.

She stirred slightly and blinked at him. 'Oh hi. Sorry, I must have fallen asleep.'

'Yeah. And obviously I wasn't sitting here watching you sleep, because that would be creepy,' he joked.

She laughed. 'You know what? However hard you tried, I don't think you could ever be creepy.'

'What if I told you I had a couple of pictures of Wham! blue-tacked to my wall when I was a teenager?'

She grinned. 'Yeah, unless that coincided with you being a thirteen-year-old girl, then that is creepy.'

'Hey!' Gaughran laughed.

Sitting up on the sofa, Benita yawned. 'I think I'm going to go upstairs to bed now.'

Gaughran nodded. 'Yeah, I think I'm going to do the same.'

She gave him a smile.

*What the hell did you say that for?*

'Oh, God. Did that sound creepy?' he said, screwing up his face. 'I wasn't ...'

'It's fine. I know what you meant,' she snorted and then smiled. 'I think you worry too much.'

'Yeah, I've been told that before,' he said as he stood up from the chair.

Benita stood up from the sofa and for an awkward few seconds, they stood opposite each other with only two feet between them.

Their eyes met, and they held each other's gaze.

*Whatever you do, do not kiss her, you berk!* he said to himself.

'I need to ask you a favour,' Benita said very quietly.

'Okay,' Gaughran said. 'Anything.'

'I really don't want to be alone tonight,' Benita said. 'So, if you promise not to be creepy, can I sleep next to you?'

*Okay, I'm going to take that at face value.*

'Of course.' Gaughran smiled. 'I mean it's going to be pretty hard for you to keep your hands off me, obviously. But I'll put a row of pillows between us so you're not tempted.'

Benita laughed loudly. 'Tim, you're a real gentleman.'

Gaughran's eyes widened. 'Well, that's the first time anyone has ever said that about me!'

# CHAPTER 27

It was 9.30am by the time Lucy and Ruth parked up on Horsham High Street in Surrey. They had come to Horsham Taxis' central office to speak to the driver who had taken Hurst and Hastings home from the Golf Club on Saturday night. They needed to check what time they had been picked up and if the taxi had dropped Hurst home.

Ruth turned off the ignition, reached inside her jacket for a packet of cigarettes, and pulled one out.

'That's your third ciggie today!' Lucy exclaimed.

Ruth frowned at her. 'What are you, my mum?'

Lucy pulled a face. 'Are you all right? You normally only chain smoke when you're really worried about something.'

Ruth lit her cigarette, wound down the window, took a deep drag, and then blew out a plume of smoke.

'Bloody hell, that's better,' she said with an audible sigh.

'Well, go on then,' Lucy prompted her.

'I finished with Kara,' Ruth explained. Despite drinking a bottle of wine, she had found it difficult to get to sleep the previous night.

'Why?' Lucy asked in a tone of disbelief.

'Because, unlike you, I can't separate sex and emotions,' Ruth explained. 'I can't keep sleeping with someone if I have nothing in common with them. I don't see the point.'

'I think sleeping with an attractive person *is* the point, you doughnut,' Lucy quipped.

'Yeah, and I'm sure the majority of the male population of this country would agree,' Ruth snapped.

'Ruth!' Lucy protested. 'I don't think that's very fair.'

'Sorry.' Ruth knew she had overstepped the mark. 'I'm tired, hungover, and I feel guilty at having led someone on when I knew they were more into me than I was into them. It's shitty behaviour.'

'Fair enough.' Lucy shrugged as she opened the car door. 'We can agree to disagree on the subject.'

As they proceeded from the car towards the taxi office, Ruth glanced over at Lucy. 'Talking of shitty behaviour, I assume you haven't seen your neighbour since the girlfriend popped up on your doorstep?'

'No, of course not,' Lucy said, avoiding eye contact.

*She's such a terrible liar.*

'Please tell me you haven't slept with him again?' Ruth groaned.

'Okay.' Lucy gave an embarrassed laugh. 'I haven't slept with James again.'

'But you have, haven't you?'

'Yes.'

'Bloody hell, Luce!' Ruth exclaimed. 'You do know this is all going to end terribly, don't you?'

'I couldn't help myself,' she explained. 'He bought me this beautiful clock for the kitchen and one thing led to another and ...'

Ruth rolled her eyes. 'You don't have to sleep with everyone who buys you a present.'

Lucy frowned. 'And you don't have to be madly in love with someone to sleep with them.'

They looked at each other for a moment before laughing.

Ruth sighed and pointed to the door of the taxi office. 'Shall we...?'

'Yeah.'

Opening the door, they walked up to the counter where an overweight middle-aged man with terrible comb-over hair sat writing in a ledger.

Ruth flashed her warrant card. 'DC Hunter and DC Henry, Peckham CID.'

'Peckham, eh? You're a long way from home, aren't you?' he asked, as if he'd cracked a hilarious joke.

'We're trying to track down a taxi that was ordered on Saturday night,' Lucy explained.

'I'll just have a look for you,' the man said, wetting his finger with his large tongue and then flicking back through the ledger. He then looked them up and down and grinned. 'Cagney and Lacey, is it?'

Lucy fixed him with her icy stare. 'That's brilliant, because we've never heard that before.'

There were a few awkward seconds as the man went back to the ledger, suitably embarrassed.

'Here we go,' he said, now looking uneasy. 'Saturday night. Where was it from, love?'

*Love? He is such a dickhead.*

Lucy gave a very deliberate sigh. 'What's your name?'

'Sorry?' the man said with an innocent smile.

*Poor bloke,* Ruth thought as she saw Lucy gritting her teeth. *He's not going to know what's hit him.*

'What's your name?' Lucy growled. 'Not a difficult question for a man of your undoubted wit and intelligence.'

He seemed confused. 'Stan.'

'Listen, Stan, it's 1998. Not 1968 or 1978. And I was going to let the whole Cagney and Lacey joke go,' Lucy thundered. 'But my name is Detective Constable or Ms Henry. I'm not *love*. Do you understand?'

Stan winced. 'Sorry, no offence meant.'

'Well consider us both offended,' Lucy snapped. 'So, do not refer to any woman that you don't know as love, sweetheart, darling or treacle. Got it?'

Stan nodded, looking like he wanted the earth to open up and swallow him. 'Got it. Sorry.'

Ruth stared at him and pointed to the ledger. 'Taxi from Cottesmore Golf Club. We think it was ordered by a Brigadier Hastings.'

Stan ran his finger down the list of bookings. 'Yeah, I've got it. The taxi picked him up at 10.50pm. One other passenger it says here.'

'Does it say where it was going?' Lucy asked.

'Cranleigh Barracks,' Stan said.

Ruth thought for a moment. She could see why Brigadier Hastings might be going to Cranleigh Barracks. He might have accommodation there. But Hurst was retired and lived over in Crawley.

'Does it say if the taxi went anywhere else on that journey?' Ruth asked.

'No. The driver reports back to us if there's been a detour on the way,' Stan explained.

Lucy frowned. 'So the taxi definitely didn't drop anyone in the Crawley area?'

'No, no way.' Stan shook his head. 'Crawley's the wrong way. There's no way that taxi went anywhere but straight to Cranleigh Barracks and back here to Horsham.'

Ruth looked at Lucy – what the hell was Hurst doing going to Cranleigh Barracks with Hastings?

Gaughran and Hassan drew up outside Hinchcliffe & Sons garage on the outskirts of Deptford. They were following the lead that Benita had given them as to where Neil Jones might hiding out.

As they got out, Gaughran peered up at the grey, miserable sky, which was filled with drizzle. The garage itself was ramshackle, and the air was filled with the smell of oil, the sounds of metallic banging and a tinny radio playing music.

'This is Bushwhacker country,' Gaughran said as they walked cautiously along the pavement, which was flanked by an eight foot corrugated iron fence covered in graffiti. He was referring to the hooligan firm that was attached to Millwall Football Club, close to Deptford.

'Psychopaths,' Hassan said. 'I remember them invading the pitch at Kenilworth Road and using the seats as frisbees against all those coppers. Nasty bastards.'

Gaughran shrugged. 'Yeah, they're all dockers. Well, they were in the old days.'

Walking through the iron gates, Gaughran saw a couple of cars up on jacks and two large workshops where mechanics were working on a couple of Transit vans.

'The other problem with places like this,' Hassan said. '...is they can spot a copper at a hundred yards. I think it's genetic.'

A thick set man in his late 50s, with a shaved head, sauntered over. He looked at Hassan, shook his head, and tutted. 'That's the problem with the Met these days. They'll let any fucker join up.'

*What a prick!*

Hassan ignored him.

'Charlie Hinchcliffe about?' Gaughran asked, getting out his warrant card.

The man puffed out his chest. He was holding a spanner in his right hand. 'He's not around, sorry.'

'Really?' Gaughran asked dubiously. 'I thought he owned this garage?'

Before the man could answer, Gaughran caught sight of a man walking quickly from an old portacabin and making his way to the far side of the garage site.

It was Neil Jones.

Gaughran glanced at Hassan, gestured, and then looked back at the man. 'That's all right. I think we've found who we're looking for.'

As they turned to follow Jones, the man stood directly in front of them. 'Where the fuck do you think you're going?

'Get out of my way, dickhead,' Gaughran growled.

'You need to search warrant to come in here.'

'No, we don't.'

Suddenly, the man smashed Hassan in the face with his fist, and Hassan crumpled to the floor.

The man squared up to Gaughran and swung the spanner at him. 'Come on then, let's have it!' he yelled.

'Piss off!' Gaughran sneered as he kicked the man hard in the testicles. The man went down onto his knees. Gaughran took a step forward and kicked him as hard as he could in the jaw and knocked him flying.

Hassan groaned and sat up on the ground, nursing a bloody nose.

'You okay, mate?' Gaughran asked.

Hassan nodded and said, 'Yeah, just don't let him get away.'

Gaughran pointed to the unconscious man. 'Cuff that tosser and stay there.'

Hassan gave him a knowing look. 'Be careful and don't do anything stupid. I'll call for backup, so keep your radio on.'

Sprinting away, Gaughran scanned the far end of the garage for Jones. Then he spotted him clambering onto the top of some prefab buildings and climbing over the rear fence.

'Shit!' Gaughran muttered as he stopped in his tracks and calculated it was quicker to run back to the entrance and cut over to the main road.

Running at full pelt, he came out of the garage gates and thundered down a side road to the end. He soon spotted Jones running towards a mini-roundabout. Several pedestrians moved out of his way as he yelled at them.

Setting off in pursuit, Gaughran was trying to work out where Jones was going and how he thought he was going to get away. Maybe he didn't care?

There was the sound of an irate driver pumping their horn as Jones darted through the traffic. Up ahead was an old disused warehouse.

*Oh bollocks, he's going in there.*

Gaughran watched as Jones ran past the boarded up warehouse entrance and then disappeared down the side.

Thirty seconds later, Gaughran arrived at the warehouse and sprinted down the alleyway where he had seen Jones disappear. Sucking in a breath, he stopped running and began to walk. His chest was burning and his shoes were now rubbing his heels.

*Jesus, I'm unfit! I'm not even bloody thirty!*

Half way along the flank wall of the warehouse was a huge loading door, which was partially covered with corrugated iron.

*He must have gone in there,* Gaughran deduced.

As he made his way inside, Gaughran continued trying to get his breath back as he noticed the drop in temperature from the outside. The ground floor of the warehouse was freezing cold and smelled of machine oil and urine.

Walking along slowly, Gaughran gazed up at the low concrete roof and the long line of iron girders that held up the ceiling. The click of his shoes on the concrete floor echoed noisily around the walls.

*Where the bloody hell has he gone?*

Gaughran clicked his Tetra radio as he stepped over a murky puddle. 'Delta five four to Control, over.'

'This is Control, go ahead five four.'

'I'm pursuing suspect Neil Jones. Suspect is now inside a warehouse on Dartford Street, SE8, close to the intersection with Tanner's Hill, but I have lost visual contact. Request backup, over,' he said as his breathing returned to normal.

'Five four, received. Will advise, stand by, over and out.'

Gaughran stopped, listened, and then heard movement over by the door to a flight of stairs. He jogged towards where he had heard the noise and saw that the door that led to a stairwell was open. As he went in, the stench of urine became overwhelming, and there were two syringes on the floor.

*Welcome to Deptford.*

He walked up the stone steps and then heard, from higher up, the sound of someone running.

*Where the hell is he going? And why is he going up to the top floor?*

Picking up the pace, Gaughran grabbed onto the handrail to keep his balance and he sprinted up the stairs.

The sound of movement and of doors opening came echoing from above.

Gaughran yelled – his voice reverberated around the stairwell. 'Oi, stop! Police! You're not gonna get away.'

Gaughran took the steps two at a time, gasping for breath again as he went. The muscles in his thighs began to burn.

The staircase ended, and there was a door out to the roof of the warehouse. As he opened the door, a swirling gust of wind blew against him.

He clicked his radio. 'Five four to Control, I have pursued the suspect to the top floor of the Dartford Street warehouse but still have no visual, over.'

'Control to five four, received. Backup is en route. ETA five minutes.'

Scanning the roof, Gaughran couldn't see Jones anywhere.

*Please don't tell me he's thrown himself off!*


'Can I help?' asked a woman in her 50s, who Ruth and Lucy assumed was Mrs Hurst.

They were following up the lead from the taxi company in Horsham and ahd just arrived at a quaint country cottage just outside Crawley. They wanted to pin Hurst down to his whereabouts at around midnight on Saturday.

'Mrs Hurst?' Ruth asked as she got out her warrant card.

'That's right?' she said, looking worried. Her cheeks were ruddy, and she wore a pastel blue twin set.

'DC Hunter and DC Henry from Peckham CID,' Ruth explained. 'Is your husband around?'

'Dennis? Mrs Hurst asked, sounding utterly confused.

'Yes,' Ruth said as Mrs Hurst showed them inside and then pointed to the door on the right.

'He's in the drawing room, if you'd like to go in,' Mrs Hurst said very formally. 'Can I get you a cup of tea or a coffee?'

Ruth gave her a kind smile. 'We're fine thanks.'

Hurst was sitting in an armchair, reading a *Daily Telegraph* newspaper with his legs crossed. As they went in, he moved the paper and peered at them. 'Did I overhear you telling my wife that you've come all the way here from Peckham?'

Ruth nodded. 'That's right.'

Hurst frowned. 'I'm afraid you ladies have had a wasted journey. I spoke to two detectives from Peckham the other day.'

Lucy pointed to the sofa. 'Okay if we sit down?'

'I suppose so, if you insist that you're staying,' Hurst said in a withering tone.

*What a prick!* Lucy thought to herself as she exchanged a look with Ruth.

Ruth gave Hurst a forced smile. 'It's just a few routine questions to tie up some loose ends.'

Hurst made a show of folding up his paper with an audible sigh.

'Don't worry, it won't take long,' Lucy said as she got out her notebook. 'I can see you're incredibly busy.'

Hurst narrowed his eyes at her for a second. 'I didn't know that sarcasm was allowed when questioning innocent members of the public.'

Lucy fixed him with a stare. 'It's not. But I wasn't being sarcastic.'

As the tension in the room grew, she saw Ruth sit forward. 'We'd like to check your whereabouts on Saturday night.'

Gaughran rolled his eyes. 'Don't you people communicate with one another? I told the others that I was at a charity ball at the Cottesmore Golf Club.'

Lucy raised an eyebrow. 'You were there all night?'

'Yes, all night,' Hurst snapped. 'So, if that's all ...'

'Don't worry, it's not,' Lucy said with a forced smile. 'What time did you leave the golf club?'

'Again, as I told the others, I had a little too much to drink, so I don't quite remember,' Hurst huffed.

Lucy was enjoying the prospect of Hurst telling them a series of provable lies. 'Would it surprise you to know that your taxi picked you up from the golf club at 10.50pm?'

Hurst shook his head in disbelief. 'Maybe I wasn't clear. I don't remember getting in that taxi. But I'm pretty sure it was after midnight.'

'Right, we'll agree that the taxi firm's records are more accurate than your memory,' Lucy said nodding as she scribbled in her notepad. 'Does that mean you won't remember who was in the taxi with you?'

The question seemed to have stopped Hurst in his tracks for a moment. 'I wasn't in the taxi with anyone else.'

Lucy frowned. 'But you've just told me you couldn't remember getting in the taxi.'

'Oh, don't be so bloody facetious, woman!' Hurst growled. 'I meant it was all a bit of a blur, that's all. For God's sake!'

'Okay,' Ruth said with a smile. 'So, you got into the taxi on your own?'

'Yes, of course,' Hurst replied.

Lucy smiled at him. 'Thank you, that's incredibly helpful.'

Hurst frowned. 'Is it? I don't see how.'

Ruth peered over at him. 'As I'm sure you're aware, the MOD is currently running an internal inquiry into events at Cranleigh Barracks from around 1989 to about 1996.'

Hurst visibly took a breath. 'What the bloody hell has that got to do with where I was on Saturday night?'

Ruth ignored him and asked, 'And I assume that you've been helping that inquiry. I mean, you were stationed at Cranleigh as part of the training staff throughout that period, weren't you?'

Hurst gritted his teeth. 'I think you should leave.'

Lucy smiled at him deliberately. 'Yeah, we're not going anywhere.'

Ruth glanced at Lucy. 'What's the name of the officer in charge of the MOD internal inquiry, DC Henry?'

Lucy frowned. 'I believe it's a Brigadier Hastings, isn't it?'

Ruth glanced back at Hurst. 'Would it surprise you to know that in your drunken state, you got into a taxi with Brigadier Hastings on Saturday night?'

Hurst shrugged. 'That's not against the law, is it?'

'Where did the taxi take you?'

'Here, of course,' Hurst said with a shrug, although he was now clearly rattled.

'Unfortunately, that's not true,' Ruth said. 'The taxi took you to Cranleigh Barracks, didn't it?'

'Did it?' Hurst said. 'I don't remember.'

'Where did you go from there?'

'I didn't go there,' he protested. He sounded flustered.

'So, if we talk to the taxi driver from Horsham Taxis, he's not going to tell us he dropped you and Brigadier Hastings at Cranleigh Barracks?'

'If that happened, it's not a criminal act, is it?' Hurst thundered angrily. 'Unless you've got anything concrete, I suggest you leave right now.'

'You lied about your whereabouts on Saturday, *Dennis*,' Lucy said with more than a hint of disdain. 'That is a criminal offence. It's obstruction and seeking to pervert the course of justice. And there can be a custodial sentence for anyone found guilty of those offences.'

Hurst's face twisted a little. 'Don't talk rubbish, woman!'

Ruth shrugged. 'I spoke to our DCI just before we got here. He's happy to apply for a search warrant. And then we can bring half a dozen burly uniformed officers who will trample through your house and tear it to pieces.'

'You wouldn't dare!' Hurst growled.

'Try me,' Ruth said calmly. 'Or you can continue to answer our questions because I'm not sure how your wife is going to feel with all those officers swarming over this lovely home that's she made for the two of you.'

Lucy gave him her best sarcastic smile. 'It's up to you, Dennis.'

# CHAPTER 28

Gaughran stood by the edge of the roof and peered down at the pavement below. It had to be nearly 70ft to the ground – but there was no sign of Jones.

There was a sudden noise from the far side of the roof.

Gaughran could see Jones climbing up onto the narrow perimeter wall from where he had been hiding behind the entrance to the far stairwell.

*Oh shit!*

'Oi! Stop there. I want to talk to you!' he yelled.

Jones glanced back at him and continued traversing along the wall.

*Where the hell does he think he's going?*

Gaughran ran towards him and could feel the wind charging boisterously around the rooftop. It howled and groaned as it swirled around him.

Jones glared at Gaughran as he approached. 'Leave me alone!' he shouted as he balanced precariously on top of the wall.

Gaughran yelled at him over the noise of the wind, 'Whatever you're thinking of doing, don't do it.'

Gaughran wanted Jones to stand trial for Ashley Campbell's murder and for assaulting Benita. He wanted Ashley's family to get justice for what had happened to him. He didn't want Jones splattered all over the pavement.

Moving closer, Gaughran could now see the road below.

'Stay there!' Jones shouted as he put out his arms to keep his balance.

Gaughran slowed his approach. 'Come on, Neil. You don't need to do anything stupid. What about your family?'

Jones shook his head. 'They don't care about me.'

'This isn't the answer to anything, is it?'

'Do you really think I want to sit in a court with all those faces looking at me? And then sit for twenty years in prison for something I didn't do,' Jones shouted over at him.

Gaughran moved closer. 'Don't you think now would be the time to admit that you killed Ashley?'

Jones' voice was filled with anger and resentment. 'Why would I? So you can wrap up your case nice and neatly. I don't think so.'

Gaughran approached him cautiously and reached out. 'Come on, Neil. Just come down, eh?'

Jones shook his head. 'No chance.'

'Come on. We'll go back to Peckham nick, I'll make you a nice cup of tea and you can sit and tell me what actually happened.'

'Oh yeah? Is that before or after you bounce me around the interview room?' Jones sneered at him. 'How's Benita?'

Gaughran bristled. What he really wanted to do was to pull Jones from the wall and kick the living shit out of him – but he needed to keep calm.

'She's okay,' Gaughran said, biting his tongue.

'She deserved that, you know?' Jones snarled. 'Telling your lot that I wasn't with her. Lying fucking bitch.'

'Is that how you get your kicks, is it?' Gaughran snapped. He couldn't help himself.

'It is actually,' Jones smirked. 'She deserves everything I give her. Pathetic little slag.'

Gaughran took a breath and glared at him. 'I tell you what, big man. Why don't you step down from that wall and then you can show me how fucking brave you are.'

Jones laughed. 'Oh, I see.'

Gaughran frowned. 'What do you see?'

'You got a bit of a soft spot for her, have you? Poor little Benita,' Jones scoffed in a mocking tone. 'So, you're the big, brave copper who's going to save her?' Is that it?'

'No idea what you're talking about,' Gaughran said through gritted teeth as he tried to remain calm. 'Just come down off that wall.'

'I need to warn you. She's shit in bed,' Jones leered.

'Get down off the wall.'

'But maybe that's not a problem for a needledick like you.'

Gaughran leapt forward, grabbed the front of his jacket and pulled him.

'What the fuck are you doing?' Jones cried out as he struggled with him.

'Come here, you prick,' Gaughran growled.

'Sarge!' Hassan shouted as he got to the rooftop.

With an almighty heave, Gaughran tried to pull Jones off the wall so he could attack him.

Jones shoved Gaughran backwards and then lost his balance. Jones thrust out his hand and Gaughran grabbed it, taking his full weight.

He now literally had Jones' life in his hands.

*Yeah, now that I've actually thought about it, I don't think I can let Benita see your grinning face in court.*

Gaughran uncurled his fingers and pulled his hand away as he stared directly at Jones, whose eyes were widening in terror.

Jones then fell backwards and dropped out of sight.

As Hassan raced over, they heard a piercing scream from the ground.

They both gazed down at the ground below.

Jones' body lay in an awkward angle on the pavement as passers-by stared in horror.

Lucy waited for a few seconds, allowing the tension to ramp up a little.

'Where did you go when you got to Cranleigh Barracks?' Lucy asked.

Hurst glared at them both, but he was now worried. 'I went for a nightcap at Brigadier Hastings' living quarters, not that it's any of your business.'

'Did anyone see you?' Lucy asked.

'No,' Hurst said.

'Shame,' Lucy said. 'Would you say that there was any conflict of interest in you having a drink with Brigadier Hastings in his living quarters at Cranleigh Barracks?'

'I don't know what you're talking about,' Hurst mumbled.

'Let's not beat about the bush here, Dennis,' Lucy said. 'You had a reputation for bullying, racism and sexually inappropriate behaviour while you were an instructor in charge of recruits at Cranleigh.'

'You can't prove that!' Hurst snapped.

'Jackie Rosen's parents are convinced that you were involved in their daughter's rape,' Ruth said. 'They also believe that their daughter was about to report that rape to the authorities in the British Army when she was found shot. And they believe she was murdered to keep you from facing trial for her rape.'

'Where's their proof?' Hurst asked.

'We are also convinced that Ashley Campbell saw you rape Jackie Rosen that night,' Ruth continued. 'But you warned him to keep his mouth shut or there would be severe consequences. When the inquest opened up a few months ago, Ashley went to Brigadier Hastings in an attempt to tell the truth about what he saw that night. He was due to give a full account of those events two days ago. But by some coincidence, he was stabbed and killed.'

'You think I did that?' Hurst said, shaking his head.

'You were drinking with the officer who was leading the inquiry into your behaviour at Cranleigh an hour before Ashley was murdered!' Lucy growled. 'Hastings told you what Ashley was going to tell the full inquiry. You would have faced prison, loss of your army pension and disgrace. So, you and Hastings went from Cranleigh to south east London, where you planned to kill Ashley to keep him quiet.'

'Don't be ridiculous!'

'Either way, we've spoken to the MOD this morning. We've told them that Brigadier Hastings' inquiry is completely compromised. We've been promised that a new inquiry will take place and I'm guessing it won't be an old friend of yours running it this time.'

The blood visibly drained from Hurst's face. 'You still don't have any proof. Jackie Rosen and Ashley Campbell are both dead.'

Ruth leaned forward on the sofa. 'Unfortunately for you, we discovered a diary in Ashley Campbell's flat. He'd been keeping it for a few years. And in there is a detailed account of the night you raped Jackie Rosen.'

*That's a complete lie,* Lucy thought. *Unethical, but it might just be enough to tip Hurst into confessing.*

Lucy peered over at him. 'Is there anything you want to tell us before we go, Dennis?'

'No,' he said, shaking his head, but he now seemed broken.

'Unfortunately, Ashley's diary alone probably won't get you convicted of Jackie's rape. However, I'm sure the new MOD inquiry will find it fascinating reading,' Ruth said, and then she pointed over to his newspaper. 'And you never know, if an extract accidentally fell into the hands of an investigative journalist, you might end up reading about yourself in your newspaper.'

'You can't do that,' Hurst said with a weak frown.

Ruth and Lucy got up.

Lucy took a card and put it down on the table. 'I'm going to leave my card here in case you think of anything you want to tell us.'

Ruth pointed to the door. 'Don't worry. We'll see ourselves out.'

# CHAPTER 29

Gaughran and Hassan had followed the ambulance to King's College Hospital. They were now waiting in the corridor at A&E to get the latest update on Jones' condition.

Having seen Jones fall, Gaughran had assumed that he had died when he hit the pavement. However, the paramedics had found him breathing and with a pulse. Gaughran kept playing those last seconds back in his head. Reaching out to grab Jones' hand – and then the split decision just to let it go. Was he going to fall anyway? Gaughran didn't know. He just knew what he was going to put in his report. He had tried to save a murder suspect on top of a warehouse, but the suspect had jumped or fallen.

Even though he didn't like to admit it, Gaughran had hoped that Jones had died in the fall. It was a terrible thing to acknowledge. Jones was a nasty piece of work who almost certainly stabbed and killed Ashley Campbell out of sheer hate. The world was a better place without him. And Gaughran didn't want Jones to survive for various reasons. He didn't want Jones regaining consciousness and claiming that he had been deliberately dropped. And he didn't want Benita to have to appear at Jones' trial and face the man who had terrified her for years.

'You know they'll call in the PCA?' Hassan said under his breath. He was talking about the Police Complaints Authority, which was effectively the Met's Internal Affairs unit.

Gaughran shrugged. 'I've got nothing to hide.'

Hassan frowned at him. 'You sure about that?'

Gaughran frowned. 'Are you actually asking me that?'

'I'm just checking before we have to give our official statements, that's all, Sarge,' Hassan said.

'Jones was standing on the edge, threatening to jump. Either he lost his balance or he went to jump. I reached out to grab his hand, but it was too late and he fell,' Gaughran explained. 'That's what happened, and that's all there is to it.'

'Okay. I'm just checking,' Syed shrugged.

'And that's what you saw, isn't it?' Gaughran asked, looking at him.

Hassan blinked for a few seconds and then nodded slowly. 'Yes, Sarge. That's what I saw.'

'Good,' Gaughran said. 'That's not going to be a problem, is it?'

Hassan shook his head. 'Jones was going to face a murder charge. He was trapped, so he jumped.'

'That's right,' Gaughran said.

A young doctor came over. 'Are you the police officers who came in with Neil Jones?'

'Yes,' Gaughran stated. 'How's he doing?'

'Not good,' the doctor said. 'Massive internal bleeding and head trauma. I think his next of kin needs to come down to the hospital. I saw he was wearing a wedding band, so I assume he's married?'

Gaughran nodded. 'I can tell his wife, but I doubt she'll be coming.'

The doctor seemed confused and shrugged. 'Well, if he has family then they need to get here soon.'

'Thank you,' Hassan said. 'We'll let them know.'

As the doctor left, Gaughran saw Ferguson marching up the corridor towards them.

'Oh shit,' Hassan muttered.

Ferguson didn't look pleased when he arrived. 'What the hell happened, Tim?'

'I chased him to the top of the warehouse,' Gaughran explained. 'I tried to talk him down but either he fell or he jumped.'

'Did he say anything?' Ferguson asked.

Gaughran shook his head. 'He was being a prick about his wife. And then he denied that he killed Ashley Campbell.'

Ferguson raised an eyebrow. 'And you saw all this, Syed?'

Syed rubbed his face. 'Not really. I arrived on the roof and saw Tim talking to Jones, guv. A second later, I saw Tim try to reach out to grab Jones' hand as he fell but it was too late.'

'Okay,' Ferguson nodded with a grim expression. 'I really hope that's exactly what happened up there, because we have a problem.'

Gaughran frowned. 'What problem?'

'The DNA on Jones' shirt that the SOCOs found doesn't match Ashley Campbell's,' Ferguson explained. 'But it does match the DNA of Benita Jones.'

'Shit!' Gaughran growled. He had been convinced that the DNA was going to match Ashley's.

Ferguson looked at them. 'I'm just praying something else turns up on Jones. Otherwise, we're going to have to explain why we chased a seemingly innocent man to the top of a warehouse where he jumped off.'

# CHAPTER 30

Ruth and Lucy walked across the car park towards their car. They were going to drive down to Cranleigh Barracks to interview Brigadier Hastings to find out exactly what he and Hurst had been doing around midnight on Saturday.

'Do we actually think that Hurst and Hastings went to Peckham on Saturday night to hunt down and kill Ashley?' Ruth said, thinking out loud.

Lucy shrugged. 'I know it feels far-fetched, but there was a huge amount at stake. Hurst's life would be over if Ashley testified.'

Ruth's phone rang. It was Hassan. 'Syed? Everything okay?'

'Yes. We ran a check on Stephen Hastings with the DVLA two days ago,' he explained. 'Hastings owns a navy Land Rover Discovery. The registered address is Cranleigh Barracks.'

'That's great, Syed,' Ruth said. 'Thanks. We're off to see him now.'

Lucy gave her a quizzical look. 'Everything all right?'

'Hastings owns a navy Land Rover Discovery,' Ruth replied. 'Which he keeps at Cranleigh Barracks.'

Lucy raised an eyebrow as they reached the car. 'Interesting. Dark coloured 4x4. Could be the car that Daniels saw parked up on Saturday night.'

They got into the car, and Lucy turned the ignition. Her phone rang.

'Lucy?' said a voice. It was Ferguson.

'It's DCI Ferguson.'

'Yes, guv.'

'We've had a phone call to the switchboard,' Ferguson explained. 'A waitress in Joe's café on Peckham High Street recognised Ashley from one of the posters. She reckons he was in there on Saturday afternoon.'

'Okay, guv,' Lucy replied. 'We'll go and see her now.'

'Her name's Tracey Dunne,' Ferguson said. 'She's going to be there all day. I'll see you later.'

Ferguson ended the call.

Lucy reversed out of the parking space. 'A waitress served Ashley in Joe's café on Saturday afternoon.'

Putting on her seatbelt, Ruth nodded. 'Was he on his own?'

'The guv didn't say. But we can swing by there and talk to her now before we go to Cranleigh,' Lucy said as she pulled out of the car park.

It was less than a two-minute drive and Ruth didn't even have time to light a cigarette before they were pulling up outside Joe's café.

'I used to come here a lot when I first got to Peckham nick,' Ruth explained as she got out of the car. 'A few of us used to have fish and chips at lunchtime on a Friday.'

'I've only ever been in here for a cup of tea and it was stewed,' Lucy said.

'Yeah, well, a PC told me they'd found rats in the kitchen, so I haven't been back since,' Ruth explained.

'Nice,' Lucy said with a wry smile as they got to the door.

Inside, it was what you would have expected from any London greasy spoon café. Simple tables and chairs. A few daily newspapers scattered around and punters eating fried breakfasts and drinking mugs of tea.

As they approached the till, Ruth got out her warrant card. 'DC Hunter and DC Henry. Is Tracey about?'

A gruff-looking man with a beard nodded. 'You're here about that bloke that got murdered outside The Yard on Saturday aren't you?'

'That's right,' Ruth said.

'You know he was sitting just over there,' the man said, as though they'd had a celebrity visiting the café rather than a murder victim.

'Could we speak to Tracey please?' Ruth asked with a forced smile.

'Yeah, sorry, I'll just go and get her,' the man said as he wiped his hands on his stained overall and shuffled away.

Lucy pulled a face and said under her breath, 'Yeah, I am never going to eat in here. It looks like you could get dysentery just by osmosis.'

Ruth laughed and then put her finger to her mouth. 'You might want to keep that to yourself.'

A few seconds later, a middle-aged woman with bleached blonde hair came over. She was wearing an ill-fitting hairnet and had a tea-towel draped over her shoulder. 'Des says you want to see me? I'm Tracey.'

'Hi Tracey. We're from Peckham CID,' Ruth explained. 'We understand you rang our switchboard today?'

'Yeah, that's right,' Tracey said as she nodded. 'You've put one of them posters up at the bus stop. You know, if you've got information, kind of thing. And I recognised the black fella that was on it.'

'Okay,' Ruth said encouragingly. 'I understand he was in here on Saturday afternoon, is that right?'

'Yeah, he was sitting right over there in the corner,' Tracey replied, pointing over to a table.

'What time would this have been?' Lucy asked.

'About three o'clock, I reckon,' Tracey said. 'We had the radio on in the kitchen with the football on.'

Ruth frowned at her. 'And you took his order?'

'Yeah. I can't remember what he had, if I'm honest,' Tracey said with a shrug.

Lucy smiled. 'That's all right.'

'But I can remember what the bloke he was with had,' Tracey said.

Ruth glanced over at Lucy – he was with someone else!

'Yeah, horrible bloke. He sent his bacon sandwich back. Said there was too much fat on it.'

'Can you give us a description of the man he was with?' Lucy asked.

Tracey frowned. 'He was well dressed, if you know what I mean? Late 50s maybe. He didn't look like he came from around here.'

'Why's that?' Ruth asked.

'I dunno. He was a bit old-fashioned, you know, posh.' Tracey said. 'Oh, and he had a big bushy moustache. Like that bloke from *It Ain't Half Hot Mum*.'

Ruth gave Lucy a meaningful glance – *Hurst!*

'Did it look like they were having a friendly conversation?' Ruth asked.

Tracey snorted. 'No, you're joking, aren't you?'

'Why do you say that?'

'The bloke with the moustache had this big brown envelope. He kept pushing it across the table at the other fella,'

Tracey explained. 'I mean, they were trying to talk quietly but you could hear what they were saying.'

Lucy peered over at her. 'Can you tell us what they were talking about?'

'Well, he kept pushing over this envelope. And he was saying *I want you to take it*. I mean, I assumed it had money in it,' Tracey said. 'And the black fella was getting angry and telling him, *I don't want it.*'

'And then what happened?'

'They started to row. It was getting a bit out of hand,' Tracey explained. 'Then that bloke I saw on the poster stormed out and told the other man to leave him alone.'


Even though it was less than four miles from Peckham nick, it had taken Gaughran and Hassan over twenty minutes to get to the Metropolitan Police Forensic Science Laboratory. Built in the late 60s, the building was a commanding concrete structure with enormous glass windows, external concrete stairways and a fifty-foot concrete ventilator shaft.

Gaughran was desperate for the forensic team to find something that would link Jones to Ashley's murder. He knew he was guilty – they just needed to find that one piece of evidence that would convince the CPS that they had met the threshold to go and charge him. He also knew, deep down, that he had pursued Jones to the top of a warehouse and given him a *helping hand* off the edge. Jones was a scumbag, but it would be a PR disaster for Peckham CID if it turned out that Jones was innocent.

'I still don't know what we're doing here, Sarge,' Hassan said with a frown as they entered the building.

'I told you. We're chasing the forensics on that SOCO search of Jones' flat and shop,' Gaughran snapped.

'Yeah, but we could have done that with a phone call,' Hassan said with a frown.

'Well, I want to make sure the forensic team understands how important it is that they find something linking Jones to Ashley's murder,' Gaughran said. He was losing patience with Hassan's constant questioning. He knew that ever since Jones' *fall*, Hassan had been increasingly distant and disgruntled.

'They're not magicians,' Hassan said. 'They can only examine what they found. They can't find evidence that's not there.'

Gaughran turned and glared at Hassan. 'What the fuck are you talking about, Syed? I'm not asking them to manufacture evidence, am I? I'm putting a bit of pressure on them so that they do a thorough job and do it quickly. If you don't like it, then we can have a chat with DCI Ferguson about it.'

Hassan ignored him as they reached the ground floor forensic laboratory. They showed their warrant cards and were handed forensic masks before entering.

Ted Robinson, the Chief Forensic Officer, who was kitted out in a full white forensic suit, gloves, hat, and mask, approached.

'DS Gaughran?' he asked.

'Yeah, I'm just checking on how the forensic analysis of the stuff the SOCOs found in Neil Jones' flat is going,' Gaughran explained.

'Good timing,' Robinson said, and gestured for them to follow. He came to a white, sterile work surface beside some test tubes and a microscope. A small, 6 inch knife lay on a forensic cloth. 'This was found in Jones' kitchen. It matches the length and diameter of the knife that killed Ashley Campbell. Our initial analysis shows that even though the knife has been washed, there are still traces of blood on the blade and handle.'

*Bingo!*

Gaughran smiled at Hassan. 'Great. That could be what we're looking for.'

Robinson put up his hand. 'A word of caution, Sergeant. You can find this knife in thousands of kitchens. And if it was used recently to cut some kind of raw meat, that would give us a positive test for blood. Until we test for DNA, we can't tell you if this is the murder weapon.'

Gaughran wasn't really listening properly. He knew they'd found the knife that killed Ashley – he was convinced of it.

Ruth and Lucy were hammering down the motorway towards Surrey. They needed to confront Hurst about his failure to mention meeting Ashley a few hours before he was killed. It was incredibly suspicious.

'Sounds like Hurst was trying to pay Ashley off,' Ruth said as they took the exit marked *Crawley.*

'Maybe Hastings warned Hurst that Ashley was going to testify to the fact that he had seen Hurst rape Jackie Rosen,' Lucy speculated. 'So, Hurst meets with Ashley and tries to bribe him to keep quiet.'

Ruth nodded. 'And it sounds like Ashley wasn't willing to take the bribe and left the café.'

'That evening, Hastings and Hurst get drunk at their Charity golf do, and hatch a plan. If Ashley can't be bribed to keep his mouth shut about what he saw, then he had to be killed. So, they get a taxi back to Cranleigh Barracks, take Hastings' car into London and find Ashley.'

'How did they find him?' Ruth asked. 'How did they know he might be standing outside The Yard club just before midnight?'

Lucy shrugged. 'Yeah, that's the bit that doesn't quite add up. It's not as if Hurst and Hastings could go to a few bars in Peckham and ask around to see if anyone knew where Ashley was. They'd stick out like a sore thumb.'

They pulled up outside Hurst's cottage, walked up the garden path, and knocked on the door. A few seconds later, Mrs Hurst appeared at the door. She was flustered and anxious.

'Mrs Hurst,' Ruth said. 'We're police officers. We met earlier.'

Mrs Hurst nodded and ushered them inside. 'Yes, of course. I was going to call someone so I'm so glad you're here.' She sounded frightened.

'Is everything all right?' Lucy asked.

'No, it's Dennis,' she said. 'He's disappeared.'

Ruth gestured to the kitchen. 'Shall we go in there and you can tell us what's happened.'

'Yes,' Mrs Hurst said, blinking nervously. 'I don't know where to start. After you left, he was in a terrible mood and started drinking. He never drinks in the afternoon,' Mrs Hurst said. 'And just after that, some gentlemen came here from the British Army.'

Ruth glanced at Lucy. 'Really? What did they want?'

'I don't really know,' she said, shaking her head. 'They went into Dennis' study. I heard Dennis shouting at them.'

'Any idea what they were discussing?' Lucy asked.

Mrs Hurst frowned. 'An inquiry?'

'An inquiry?' Ruth asked.

'When they had gone, Dennis was ranting about a new inquiry,' Mrs Hurst replied. 'I didn't know what he was talking about. He doesn't really tell me anything.'

'And you said he was missing?' Lucy asked.

'Yes,' Mrs Hurst said as her eyes roamed nervously around the kitchen. 'He said he was going out to the garden to get some fresh air. But he's not there.'

'How long ago was that?' Ruth asked.

Mrs Hurst glanced up at the clock on the wall. 'Nearly two hours ago.'

Lucy looked over at her. 'Are you scared that he might have harmed himself?'

'I just don't know,' Mrs Hurst said, her eyes now welling with tears. 'I've never seen him that agitated before. And he'd been drinking in his study, because his eyes were bloodshot.'

'Is there anywhere else he could have gone?'

'No. And the garage doors are closed, so he hasn't taken the car anywhere,' Mrs Hurst said.

Ruth pointed down to the study. She was getting an uneasy feeling. 'Okay if we have a look?'

Mrs Hurst nodded as Ruth and Lucy got up, walked down the hallway, and entered the study.

'I'm starting to get a horrible feeling about this,' Lucy said under her breath.

'So am I,' Ruth said as she scoured the study, wondering if there were any clues as to where Hurst had gone or why he had been so distressed.

Going over to his desk, she saw a letter headed piece of paper with a handwritten note in ink. It was addressed to Claudia, whom Ruth assumed was his wife.

As she scanned the writing, she soon realised that what she was reading was a *suicide note.*

She saw the phrase – *I am deeply ashamed of what I did to both Ashley and Jackie and the hurt and pain that I caused both their families.*

'Oh God,' Ruth said, holding up the letter. 'It's Hurst's confession. And he's gone somewhere to kill himself.'

'Shit!' Lucy said with a sense of urgency.

Racing from the study, they glanced at Mrs Hurst.

'Which way did your husband go to the garden?' Ruth asked loudly.

She pointed to the side door.

They had to stop Hurst before he took his own life.

Jogging out into the garden, they peered around the well-tended garden.

*Where the hell is he?*

At the end the garden, there was a low fence. Beyond that, some bracken and then fields. About a mile away was a densely wooded area. The air smelt of the countryside, although it smelt like someone was having a bonfire nearby.

'You think he might have wandered down there?'

Lucy shrugged. 'He wouldn't be the first person we've found hanging in woods, would he?'

'No,' Ruth agreed, taking out her phone and hitting Ferguson's number.

'Ruth? What's going on?' Ferguson asked.

'We're at Hurst's house,' she explained. 'He's left some kind of suicide note. It's vague, but it seems to be a confession to Ashley's murder and the rape of Jackie Rosen.'

'Jesus!' Ferguson said, sounding surprised. 'I really thought that Jones was our man.'

'Yeah, so did I, guv,' Ruth said.

'Where's Hurst?'

'That's the problem, guv,' she said. 'He's been drinking, and he's disappeared. There are woods about a mile south of here and we think he might have headed there.'

'Okay,' Ferguson said. 'Let me talk to Surrey Police and see if we can get units over there now.'

'Yes, guv,' Ruth said. 'Me and Lucy will meet them there.'

'I want him alive,' Ferguson growled. 'I want to know what those bastards like Hastings in the British Army actually knew about Jackie Rosen and if they were involved in Ashley's death as some kind of coverup. Keep me posted, okay?'

Ferguson ended the call.

As Ruth turned to Lucy, something occurred to her.

'I thought someone was having a bonfire,' Ruth said.

Lucy agreed. 'Yeah, there's a funny smell.'

'It's not a bonfire though. It's exhaust fumes, isn't it?'

Lucy nodded.

Glancing around, Ruth spotted a large double garage on the other side of the house.

'Shit!' Lucy said as they broke into a run.

The other common form of suicide was carbon monoxide poisoning, often from a hose attached to a car exhaust with its engine running.

As they jogged towards the garage, Ruth could hear something.

A car engine running.

*This is not good.*

The smell of the exhaust fumes were getting stronger and stronger.

Reaching the side door to the garage, Ruth tried the handle – nothing.

'He's locked himself in,' she said as she yanked at the door.

'Shit,' Lucy said urgently. 'Stand out of the way.'

Lucy kicked the door with everything she had – nothing.

*Bloody hell!*

As Ruth glanced up, she saw a row of narrow windows, which were about eight feet from the ground. Grabbing a rock from a nearby flowerbed, she looked at Lucy. 'Give me a bunk-up.'

Lucy formed a step with her hand. Ruth trod on it and Lucy lifted her up.

Ruth smashed at the glass in the windows with everything she had. Placing her hands on the window frame, she used it to take her weight. There were still fragments of glass left and they dug into her palms. She didn't care. She wanted to get Hurst out of there alive so he could stand trial. It's what Jackie and Ashley's families deserved.

Ducking her head inside the garage, Ruth crawled onto the ledge on the other side of the windows. The fumes from inside were overwhelming as the engine pumped carbon monoxide into the car.

Suddenly, Ruth lost her balance and fell backwards onto a pile of old cardboard boxes. It knocked the wind out of her and as she gasped for breath, she realised that her head was now dizzy. The fumes were thick as she coughed loudly.

*Shit! I'm going to suffocate in here if I'm not careful!*

Jumping to her feet, she squinted through the thick fumes and raced to the car. Hurst was sitting in the driver's seat unconscious – or worse. A hosepipe had been put through the back window, with towels blocking any gaps.

Trying the driver's door, Ruth felt her legs starting to wobble. She pulled her t-shirt up over her mouth and nose.

*Do not pass out in here, whatever you do!*

The driver's door was locked.

She was struggling to breathe.

Searching around frantically, Ruth scoured a workbench and found a spanner. In one swift move, she smashed the window on the driver's door, reached inside and popped open the button.

As she opened the door, Hurst's head dropped to one side. His lips were blue and his face was colourless.

*This is not good.*

She turned off the ignition, put her hands under Hurst's armpits and dragged him from the car. He was incredibly heavy, and it was all she could do to get him to the side door.

Ruth coughed hard. Her throat was red raw and her vision had started to blur.

Dropping Hurst to the floor, she unlocked the side door, and Lucy appeared.

'Help me get him out,' Ruth spluttered.

Together, they pulled Hurst out through the door and onto the patch of lawn beside the garage.

Sitting down on the grass, Ruth quickly sucked in air and coughed violently.

'Jesus!' she groaned. 'I thought I was going to pass out in there.'

Lucy was checking for a pulse and to see if Hurst was still breathing.

A figure appeared.

It was Mrs Hurst. She let out a feeble scream.

'Dennis! Oh my God! What have you done?'

Lucy sat back from the body and peered slowly up at them both. 'I'm really sorry. He's gone.'

# CHAPTER 31

*20 hours later*

Ferguson entered the CID office, which was buzzing with the news of Hurst's confession and suicide. Sitting at her desk, Ruth could still feel the effects of the fumes she had ingested the day before. Her throat was sore and her chest tight. Ferguson had insisted that she get checked out by the Police doctor before she went home the previous evening.

'Morning everyone,' Ferguson said as he came and perched on his usual table. 'Ruth and Lucy, you had quite an afternoon yesterday, didn't you? Ruth, you sure you should be in?'

Ruth nodded. 'I feel like I coughed up a lung, but apart from that I'm fine.'

Ferguson smiled. 'Well, good work. Just so that we're all up to speed with the events of yesterday, Lucy?'

Lucy sat forward in her chair. 'Ruth and I were following up a lead we got from Joe's Café in Peckham. A waitress had seen Hurst arguing with Ashley in there on Saturday afternoon. She also saw Hurst attempt to give Ashley a brown envelope. We believe that Brigadier Hastings had informed Hurst that Ashley Campbell was going to tell the inquiry that he had seen Hurst rape Jackie Rosen in 1989. In an attempt to keep Ashley from talking, Hurst met him and offered him a bribe to keep his mouth shut. Ashley turned him down. Hurst and Hastings met at a Golf charity ball on Saturday night and we think they hatched a plan to kill Ashley. They shared a taxi back to Cranleigh Barracks, took Hastings' car to Peckham, tracked Ashley down and murdered him.'

Ferguson nodded. 'That's our hypothesis at the moment. We still need to gather as much evidence as we can. Hastings has been arrested by Surrey Police this morning and they're bringing him here for questioning.'

Hassan frowned. 'Do we know how they managed to track down Ashley?'

Lucy shook her head. 'Not yet.'

A uniform officer came through the door and signalled that he needed to speak to Ferguson urgently.

Gaughran frowned. 'What about the car that Jermaine Daniels saw?'

'Hastings owns a navy blue Land Rover Discovery,' Ruth replied.

'Daniels only saw one person fleeing the scene of the crime,' Gaughran said.

Lucy shrugged. 'Maybe Hastings was just the driver?'

Ferguson came back from speaking to the PC and went back to where he had been sitting. 'We've had a phone call from King's College Hospital. Neil Jones died about an hour ago from the injuries he sustained in his fall.'

Ruth peered over at Gaughran, who was now deep in thought.

'It gets worse,' Ferguson explained. 'The Forensic lab in Southwark called earlier to tell me that the knife they found in Jones' flat didn't have any DNA that matched Ashley Campbell. They said they were almost certain it wasn't the murder weapon. If we believe what Hurst wrote in his note, then that puts Neil Jones in the clear.'

Gaughran shook his head. 'Which means I chased an innocent man to his death.'

Ferguson nodded. 'Tim and Syed. The PCA is going to need a very detailed account of the events leading up to Jones' fall. And off the record, you need to make sure they match, because if there are any discrepancies, they'll be all over you like a rash.'

# CHAPTER 32

*One week later*

Ferguson had asked Ruth and Lucy to represent the Met at Ashley Campbell's funeral at St Stephen's Church in Peckham. As the coffin was lowered into the ground, Ruth felt an overwhelming sadness that Ashley had been killed by men from the very army he had joined to serve his country. She also knew that had the British Army conducted a full investigation into Jackie Rosen's rape back in 1989, both she and Ashley would now be alive. It was the army's archaic attitudes and tradition of dealing with its problems internally that had led to the tragedies. Its lack of transparency allowed for cover-ups and a code of silence.

Ruben, Mica and Lenora approached, took soil in their hands and sprinkled it into the grave. Ruth saw Benita Jones standing to one side lost in thought.

As they walked away, Ruth noticed that Mica and Lenora were whispering to each other. Mica scowled, looking angry as she stormed away from her sister.

*That's weird.*

'They've been like that all morning,' Ruth said, gesturing subtly over to where Mica and Lenora were standing. They were standing apart and avoiding each other.

'Yeah, I noticed that. They avoided each other in the church too,' Lucy said.

'I would have expected sisters to be comforting each other,' Ruth observed. 'They look like they can't stand to be in each other's presence.'

Lucy shrugged. 'Grief does funny things to people.'

'I still wonder what actually happened in Jamaica,' Ruth said quietly as they turned and began to walk away.

'You mean Marland Cole's murder?' Lucy asked.

Ruth nodded. 'Yeah, there is something very fishy about the whole thing. A very wealthy man is about to get divorced, except he is killed in a robbery at his hotel. The police suspect it's an inside job but nothing is ever proved. The family comes to the UK and changes their name.'

'You think they were involved?' Lucy asked.

Ruth shrugged. 'I don't know. I haven't seen any of the case files. But my instinct is that there's something wrong there.'

'Detectives!' said a voice.

It was Ruben.

'I just wanted to say thank you for coming today,' he said with a sincere expression.

'Of course,' Ruth said. 'If there's anything we can do or if you have any questions, please let me know.'

'I read in the paper that Brigadier Hastings is helping Surrey Police with their inquiries,' Ruben said. 'I wish someone could tell me exactly what happened to Ashley that night.'

Lucy nodded. 'I know that must be difficult for you. I hope that Brigadier Hastings does the right thing and tells us.'

'I can't believe that those two men went and killed Ashley,' Ruben said sadly. 'They were officers in the British Army for God's sake.'

'Have you been assigned a Family Liaison Officer?' Ruth asked.

Ruben nodded. 'Yes. And she's been very helpful.'

'If there are any developments at our end,' Lucy said. 'We will come and let you know.'

'Thank you,' Ruben said.

As they turned to go, Ruth looked at him. 'How are Mica and Lenora doing?'

'Erm, ... they're very upset,' Ruben explained, but the question seemed to have thrown him for second. 'They were both very close to Ashley.'

Ruth gave a benign smile. 'Well, at least they have each other. I know how important family is at times like this.'

Her comment seemed to unsettle Ruben. 'Yeah. Of course. And thanks again.'

Ruth and Lucy turned and walked back to their car.

'What was that about?' Lucy asked.

'He wasn't comfortable talking about Mica and Lenora,' Ruth said. 'He's hiding something.'

'They're sisters. And sisters fall out all the time,' Lucy suggested.

'Maybe,' Ruth said as they reached the car. As they got into the car, Lucy glanced over at her. 'You're still not convinced that Hurst and Hastings are guilty of Ashley's murder are you?'

Ruth turned on the ignition and shrugged. 'There's still a couple of things niggling away at me. Hurst wrote, *I am deeply ashamed of what I did to both Ashley and Jackie.* It's vague, isn't it?'

'Is it?' Lucy asked as they pulled away.

'What if Hurst was ashamed of the pressure and threats he made to Ashley to keep quiet about the attack on Jackie Rosen? What if that's what he actually meant?'

'Bloody hell, Ruth. Just because he didn't detail what he had actually done, doesn't mean that Hurst didn't kill him,' Lucy said.

'How did Hurst and Hastings track down Ashley to a side road in Peckham?' Ruth asked.

'I don't know,' Lucy said, sounding annoyed. 'Hopefully that will come out when Hastings is interviewed.'

'Apparently Hastings is opting for *no comment* in interview so far,' Ruth said.

They turned left and stopped in traffic outside the church-yard. Mourners were leaving the church and several cars were now pulling out from where they had parked.

Lenora came marching out of the church gates, turned right and proceeded along the pavement.

Lucy gestured to her. 'She looks furious.'

For a moment, Ruth and Lucy sat in silence.

Lucy seemed a little irritated. 'Okay then. If Hurst and Hastings didn't murder Ashley, who did?'

Ruth didn't answer. She was watching Lenora as she got to her car and pressed the central locking. The indicators flashed.

'Ruth?' Lucy said. 'Hello?'

'Sorry ... I ...' Ruth replied.

'What are you looking at?' Lucy asked.

Ruth pointed.

Lenora had started her car and was now indicating to pull away from the pavement and into the traffic.

She was driving a *black Range Rover*.

Lucy's eyes widened. 'Shit!'

Having changed back into their work clothes, Ruth and Lucy came marching into the CID office. Gaughran and Hassan glanced up.

'How was the funeral?' Hassan asked.

Lucy shrugged. 'Fine. Except we've just seen Lenora Garner drive away from the church in a black Range Rover.'

'We've got Hurst's confession. Hastings has a dark 4x4. What's the relevance?' Hassan asked.

'I just want to tie up any loose ends. Hastings will get himself a very good defence team and we don't want them finding anything that might cast doubt in a jury's mind,' Ruth replied.

'Fair enough,' Hassan said.

Lucy raised an eyebrow as she glanced over at Gaughran. 'Surprisingly quiet today, Tim? Hungover?'

'No,' Gaughran snapped. 'I've got an interview with those fuckers from the PCA.'

Ruth pulled a face. 'Right. If you just tell the truth about what happened up there, I can't see there'll be a problem.'

'That's what I keep telling him,' Hassan said. 'I've got to speak to them too.'

'Yeah, but I'm the one under the spotlight, aren't I?' Gaughran grumbled.

'Hope it goes well,' Ruth said with a genuine nod. 'I know me and Lucy take the piss out of you, and even though it pains me to say it, you are a decent copper, Tim.'

'I wouldn't go that far,' Lucy joked.

Gaughran gave them a sarcastic smile. 'Thanks.'

Ruth and Lucy headed back to their desks on the far side of the CID office.

'We've still got the CCTV tapes from *Harvey's* haven't we?' Ruth said as she rummaged through the stuff on her desk.

Hassan raised an eyebrow. 'Why are you looking at those again?'

'As I said, just tying up loose ends,' Ruth muttered before she picked up the relevant VHS tape. 'Bingo.'

Marching over to the television and VHS player, Ruth wheeled it over so that it was facing her desk. She slotted in the VHS tape and pressed play.

'What are we watching?' Lucy asked as she turned her chair.

'We've never watched the CCTV from Saturday night,' Ruth explained as she fast forwarded the recording, monitoring the timecode at the bottom right of the screen.

'You've lost me now,' Lucy moaned.

'I'm just wondering about something,' Ruth explained as the pieces of her hypothesis formed in her head.

'Oh well, that's made it crystal clear,' Lucy joked sarcastically.

As the timecode got to 10.37pm, Ruth paused the image. She rewound it and then played it again. A figure clearly comes sweeping through the bar and out of the main door to the street outside.

It was Lenora Garner.

'Okay, so Lenora leaves *Harvey's* at 10.37pm,' Ruth said as she played the footage forward. The time code went past 11am, then 12am, 1am. Nothing. 'And she doesn't come back. She told us she was in *Harvey's* all night.'

'What if she came in the back way?' Lucy suggested.

'There is no back way,' Ruth said. 'There's a tiny space out the back where the bins go, but there's no access to the road from there. And there's the fire exit at the foot of the stairs, but you can't get through that from the street. The only way into *Harvey's* is through the main doors.'

Lucy frowned. 'So Lenora left there and didn't come back.'

Ruth peered at her. 'I think we need to go and talk to her and find out where she was and why she lied to us?'

# CHAPTER 33

As they sped through the South London traffic, Ruth and Lucy made their way towards Clapham.

'Okay, let's say Lenora went to Peckham to kill Ashley,' Lucy said as they overtook a bus at speed. 'What's her motive?'

'We've always assumed that Lenora was telling us the truth about the money that she gave Ashley being for an investment,' Ruth said, thinking out loud. 'And Lenora was insistent that Ruben and Mica couldn't know because they would disapprove?'

'You mean the money she gave him wasn't for a property deal?'

'We only have Lenora's word for that,' Ruth explained. 'What if she was giving him money for a different reason?'

'Like what?'

'Do you remember Ruben had no idea that Jalissa, Mica and Lenora had all changed their surname from Cole to Garner when they arrived in the UK?'

Lucy nodded. 'Yeah, that did strike me as strange.'

'And there is something distinctly suspicious about the circumstances of Marland Cole's death. If he divorced Jalissa and re-married, then he may have then changed his will. Maybe Mica and Lenora worried they were no longer going to the be sole heirs to their father's fortune.'

Lucy frowned. 'So they had him killed?'

'It's possible.' Ruth shrugged. 'The police suspected an inside job but couldn't prove it. They move to the UK, change their name and effectively cut all ties to what happened in Jamaica.'

'That all sounds plausible, Miss Marple, but how does that link to Ashley?'

'Ashley found out about what happened in Jamaica. He discovered they changed their name. Maybe someone back in Jamaica was trying to track them down and Ashley found out?'

Lucy nods. 'And he threatens to reveal everything to Ruben and whoever else might want to know their true identity. Lenora has to pay him off to keep him quiet.'

'We know Lenora is a hot-head,' Ruth said as they pulled up outside *Harvey's*. 'She's not going to let Ashley blackmail her, so she goes and kills him.'

Lucy gestured to the bar. 'Let's go and see what she has to say for herself.'

They got out of the car, marched over to the main doors, and went in. The bar was full of mourners dressed in black who were there for Ashley's wake.

The barman, Felix, who was making a cocktail, glanced at them. 'Hi there. Ruben's upstairs. But if you're looking for Mica, she left about an hour ago. I think it all got too much for her.'

'We're actually looking for Lenora,' Ruth explained.

'Yeah, she's upstairs somewhere,' Felix explained as he continued to make the cocktail. He had some chopped sprigs of mint in his hand.

'You're making a mojito?' Ruth asked.

'Yeah, how do you know?' Felix replied.

'You've just chopped up some mint to put in it,' she explained.

Lucy glanced over at Ruth – she realised the significance of what she had asked.

'Have any of your knives gone missing in the last week?' Ruth asked.

Felix seemed perplexed. 'How do you know that?'

'I take that as a yes?'

Felix nodded, but was thoroughly confused. 'Yeah. In fact, I brought in my own knife. I got it in Majorca last year as a souvenir, but it went missing a couple of days ago.'

'Do I take it that Lenora works behind the bar sometimes?' Ruth asked.

'Oh yeah. She loves it,' Felix said. 'And all the blokes fancy her so she gets loads of free drinks and tips.'

'Thanks,' Ruth said with a smile, as they turned, headed for the stairs and went up.

Lucy raised an eyebrow. 'Now we know where the murder weapon came from.'

'Motive, means and opportunity,' Ruth said as they got to the landing.

The upstairs of the bar was virtually silent.

The door to Ruben's office was closed.

As Ruth approached, she heard a strange noise from inside. A cry as if someone was distressed.

They exchanged a look – *what the hell was that?*

Going to the door, Ruth listened again.

She heard the noise again and braced herself.

Throwing open the door, her jaw dropped.

Lenora, who was dressed only in her underwear, was sitting astride Ruben. They were having sex and there were lines of cocaine on the desk.

*Jesus! I wasn't expecting that!*

# CHAPTER 34

Ruth and Lucy were sitting in Interview Room 3 at Peckham nick. Sitting opposite them was Lenora Garner. She was looking at her nails. Next to her sat the male Duty Solicitor, who was in his 30s.

Ruth opened the folder on the table in front of her. She waited for a moment before making eye contact with Lenora.

'Lenora, you have already been read your rights at the time of your arrest, but I need to remind you that you are still under caution. Do you understand what that means?'

Lenora nodded.

'We're also going to be recording this interview, as it may be used as evidence. So, I'm going to press this button. You'll hear a long beep and then I'll start off by naming everyone who is in the room. Okay?'

Lenora shrugged casually. 'Yeah.'

Ruth pressed the button to record and a five-second electronic beep began. 'Interview commencing at eight pm. For the purposes of the tape, present are Lenora Garner, duty solicitor Colin Mount, Detective Constable Lucy Henry and Detective Constable Ruth Hunter.'

Lucy peered over at her. 'How long have you been having an affair with Ruben Campbell, Lenora?'

Lenora let out a sigh, but didn't say anything.

Ruth let the silence play out and the tension build.

'Can you tell us where you were last Saturday night, Lenora?' Ruth asked.

'I told you!' Lenora snapped. 'I was at the bar all night.'

'We've seen the CCTV footage,' Lucy said. 'You left at 10.27pm and you didn't come back.'

Lenora stared down at the floor. 'I don't know. I know that one night I wasn't well and went home. I'm in there every night. They're all the same. How am I meant to remember?'

'You went home sick on Saturday?'

'Yes. I think so.'

'Except this was the night that your brother-in-law, who you told us you were very close to, was murdered,' Ruth said very calmly. 'So, it wasn't the same as every other night. How could you not remember?'

Leonora huffed. 'I don't know.'

'You drive a brand new Range Rover, don't you, Leonora?' Lucy asked, pulling a document from the file.

'Yeah, so what?'

'We have an eyewitness who saw a black Range Rover only a hundred yards from where Ashley was murdered,' Lucy said. 'They also saw the person who killed Ashley get into that car and drive away.'

Lenora looked up slowly and fixed them with a stare. There was something very cold about her expression that Ruth found unsettling. 'I'm not the only person to have a car like that.'

'It must be nice having a brand new car,' Lucy said casually. 'All the mod-cons. Air conditioning, cruise control. Did you know that new Range Rovers also have something called GPS?'

GPS had only just become standard in executive cars.

Lenora frowned.

'Global Positioning System,' Lucy explained. 'It means that there is a little box in your car that tracks and records every journey that you make. It allows you to buy one of those little

Sat-Navs that they're advertising and link it to your car.' Lucy gave Lenora a wry smile. 'Brilliant what they can do these days, isn't it?'

'Problem is,' Ruth said. 'Your GPS is going to have recorded where you went on Saturday night.'

The blood drained from Lenora's face. 'What?'

'And it's going to show that you drove from *Harvey's* at around 10.30pm to Peckham. And I assume that you spent the next 90 minutes trying to find out where Ashley might be drinking.'

Lenora was completely rattled, and her eyes roamed nervously around the room. 'It's not a crime to drive to Peckham.'

'But you've lied twice to us in a recorded interview about where you were on Saturday night. You told us you were in the bar and then you told us you went home,' Ruth said sternly. 'Instead, you drove and parked about a hundred yards from where your brother-in-law was stabbed to death. We have an eyewitness who saw someone kill Ashley and then get into a car exactly like yours. What do you think a jury is going to think about that?'

There were a few seconds of silence.

Lenora's breathing was getting shallow, and she sat forward.

'We know you took a knife from behind the bar, Lenora,' Lucy said loudly. 'We know Ashley was blackmailing you about something. That's why you gave him twenty thousand pounds.'

Lenora put her head in her hands. She was shaking.

'Did Ashley threaten to tell Mica about your affair?' Ruth asked. 'Or was it to do with what happened in Jamaica?'

'You need to tell us the truth, Lenora,' Lucy said.

Sitting up slowly, Lenora blew out her cheeks and then closed her eyes for a few seconds.

Ruth leant forward and asked gently, 'Tell us what happened? Did you go that night with the intention of killing Ashley?'

Lenora opened her eyes, which were now filled with tears. She shook her head. 'No.'

'Why did you go and find him then?' Ruth asked calmly.

'I just wanted to talk to him,' Lenora whispered as she wiped the tears from her face with her palm.

'Was he blackmailing you?'

Lenora nodded. 'Yeah.'

'About what?'

Lenora shook her head. Her entire world was crumbling around her.

'I can't believe that any of this has happened,' she sobbed. 'It doesn't feel real. It's like a dream and I'm gonna wake up.'

'Why was Ashley blackmailing you, Lenora?' Ruth asked.

'About a year ago, someone from the Immigration Service came into the bar looking for me and Mica,' she explained. 'The Jamaican authorities had contacted them. They wanted to speak to us about my father's murder again. But because we'd changed our name, they were having difficulty tracking down our whereabouts.'

'What did Ashley say?' Ruth asked.

'He covered for us,' Lenora explained. 'He told the bloke he had never heard of us. A few months later, he asked to borrow some money from me. He didn't want Mica or Ruben to know. He promised to pay it back, but when it came to it, he said that it was payment for covering for us with the Immigration Service. He said he might need to borrow some more money in the future.'

'And then what happened?'

'Just after Christmas, he caught me and Ruben in the office,' Lenora said. 'A few days later, he said he wanted twenty grand to keep quiet, or he'd tell Mica.'

'Did Ruben know Ashley had asked you for money?' Ruth asked.

Lenora shook her head. 'No, that was part of the deal. If I told Ruben, he would go straight to Mica and tell her what was going on.'

Lucy peered over at her. 'And this was the money you gave him from Lloyds Bank on Saturday morning?'

'Yeah.' Lenora nodded. 'But when he dropped me back home, he told me it wasn't going to be the last payment.'

'What did you say to that?' Ruth asked.

Lenora shrugged. 'I didn't know what to say. But I decided that evening to go and call his bluff.'

'You mean you were going to tell him you weren't prepared to give him any more money?'

'Yeah,' Lenora said.

'So, what happened?'

'When I eventually found him, I told him straight that I wasn't going to pay him anything else. And if he wanted to tell Mica, then he could do that. But Ruben probably wouldn't speak to him ever again. And then we started to have a row. He threatened me. I thought he was going to attack me so I stabbed him.'

*That's utter bullshit!*

Ruth raised an eyebrow as she and Lucy exchanged a look. There were various things about Lenora's account that didn't add up.

'Why did you take a knife with you from the bar?' Ruth asked.

'I was scared of Ashley and how he was going to react,' Lenora explained.

Ruth peered at her for a few seconds. 'Okay, so you were rowing with Ashley. And he came towards you. You were frightened, so you stabbed him?'

'Yeah.'

'Problem is, Ashley was stabbed in his back first. Then in his stomach. And he had no defensive wounds on his hands or anywhere else,' Ruth said.

'Okay, so what?'

'So, that means you're lying to us,' Ruth said.

Lenora glared at her coldly.

Lucy looked at her. 'The evidence proves that you didn't speak to Ashley on Saturday. You just waited for him outside The Yard. And while he was standing outside, you came up behind him, stabbed him in the back and then in the stomach before he knew what had hit him. And then you left him for dead.'

'Believe what you want,' Lenora sneered.

Lucy gave her a withering look. 'The evidence is overwhelming, Lenora. And you're going to prison for a very long time.'

Ruth sat forward in her seat. 'Lenora Garner, I'm arresting you on suspicion of the murder of Ashley Campbell. You do not have to say anything, but it may harm your defence if you do not mention, when questioned, something that you later rely on in court. Anything you do say may be given in evidence. Do you understand?'

Lenora stared at her but said nothing.

# CHAPTER 35

*24 hours later*

It was 6.30pm on Friday as Gaughran walked away from the local driving range and over to the parked car. Benita was sitting inside. Gaughran had checked and his dad and Les had just arrived and were hitting balls down the range with a couple of woods. By the time they'd done that and had a quick drink in the bar, he estimated his dad would be occupied for the next 2-3 hours.

As Gaughran got in and settled in the driver's seat, Benita frowned as she glanced over at him. 'I still don't know why we stopped here or where we're going.'

He grinned at her. 'Magical mystery tour.'

'I'm sorry to break it to you, but golf's not really my thing.'

Gaughran smiled. 'I suspected that.'

'And I need to start looking for somewhere to live.'

Gaughran frowned. 'You've got somewhere to live.'

'Very funny,' Benita said rolling her eyes. 'I can't stay with you, can I?'

Gaughran ignored her and turned on the radio. *Careless Whisper* was playing by *George Michael.*

'Oh, I love this song,' Gaughran said. 'You know George Michael wrote this when he was only sixteen. Imagine being that talented.'

Benita smiled at him and raised an eyebrow. 'Imagine being a tough London copper and having the cheesiest taste in music on the planet.'

'That is totally uncalled for.' Gaughran pulled a face as if he was offended. 'My mate, Jeremy Cavanagh, snogged my first girlfriend Maggie behind my back when we were fourteen. And I remember listening to the lyrics to this song.'

Benita laughed. 'You do know you have destroyed any image that I had of you as this macho detective.'

Gaughran shrugged. 'Hey, I kicked a spanner wielding nutter in the bollocks two days ago.'

'I'm being serious. I need to find somewhere else to live.'

Gaughran made a show of ignoring her as he turned up the radio and joined in with the song, *Tonight the music seems so loud, I wish that we could lose this crowd...*

'I'm being serious,' Benita chortled as she gave him a playful hit on the arm.

Gaughran looked at her. 'What if I said that I didn't want you to move out.'

'Eh?' Benita frowned. 'You want me to be your housemate?'

'Not really.'

'Then what?' Benita asked.

For a few seconds, their eyes met, and they held each other's gaze.

Then Gaughran leaned over and kissed her.


Lucy grabbed a bottle of wine from the fridge and wandered into the living room where Ruth was sitting. It was Friday night, they'd had a rollercoaster of a week and they were going to get drunk.

Ruth was watching the news on the television, which wasn't really in the spirit of the evening. However, she soon realised why Ruth was watching.

The BBC News anchor looked at the camera, '*The Home Secretary Jack Straw has promised today that there will be a full public inquiry into the deaths of four recruits at the British Army Barracks in Cranleigh between 1989 and 1995. It comes after an article in yesterday's Guardian newspaper claimed that the current MOD internal inquiry was at best shambolic, and at worst, a blatant attempt to cover up a toxic culture of racism, bullying and sexual abuse at the barracks in Surrey between these years. This morning, Brigadier Stephen Hastings, the man leading the internal inquiry, bowed to public demands for him to resign. Former Chief of Staff, Lord Bryant said today in the House of Lords that the army had clearly failed in its duty of care at Cranleigh during that time.*'

Ruth glanced at Lucy as he handed her a large glass of wine. 'You think it will change anything?'

Lucy shrugged. 'I would think that changing the culture of the British Army is virtually impossible.'

'It's terrible isn't it?' Ruth said. 'The three people that really knew what happened to Jackie Rosen in 1989 are all dead. And it's not likely that her family will ever find out.'

There were a few poignant seconds of silence.

Turning off the television, Lucy went over to the stereo and put on the *Air* CD again. She skipped it to her favourite track, *All I Need*.

'Come on, we need to drink a lot of wine and talk about our ridiculous love lives,' Lucy laughed.

Ruth gave her a quizzical look. 'Are you actually listening to *Moon Safari*?'

Lucy shrugged. 'Yes. I love it.'

'There's something very wrong here. You don't have any decent CDs,' Ruth teased her.

'Soundtrack to *Trainspotting*?'

Ruth rolled her eyes. 'I bought you that, you muppet!'

'Did you?'

'Yes,' Ruth said, and then pointed up at the ceiling. 'Did lover boy up there buy it for you?'

'Oh, my God. Do you really have such little faith in my musical taste?'

'Yes.' Ruth raised an eyebrow. 'Did he?'

'No,' Lucy said and then pulled a face. 'He left it here, if you must know. And I'm keeping it.'

'Which is technically theft.'

'Arrest me.'

'Is smoking still banned in here?' Ruth asked.

'Yes,' Lucy said as she walked over to the patio doors and opened them. 'Come on, we'll go out here.'

As they got out onto the patio, Lucy noticed that the doors to the balcony were open and loud music was playing. There was laughter from inside.

She bristled at the thought of James and Natalie up there together.

Ruth raised an eyebrow as she lit her cigarette. 'They seem to be getting on very well?'

'Yeah,' Lucy growled. 'Like nothing ever happened.'

'Probably for the best, isn't it?'

'Probably,' Lucy sighed. 'But it still pisses me off.'

'I would say that's men for you,' Ruth laughed. 'But I'm gay and I've had a shitty week too.'

At that moment, Natalie skipped out onto the balcony. She was drunk and very happy.

'Oh good,' Lucy huffed.

Natalie peered down and gave them a beaming smile. 'Lucy! Hi there. And I don't think I've met your friend...?'

'Ruth.'

'Ruth,' Natalie giggled. 'Me and James are celebrating.' Then she waved her left hand over the balcony to show them she was wearing an engagement ring. 'James asked me to marry him about an hour ago.'

*Are you fucking kidding me?*

'Congratulations,' Ruth said with a forced smile.

'Oh, you two will have to come up here for a drink to celebrate,' Natalie insisted. 'We won't take no for an answer!'

Lucy smiled, but couldn't think of the right thing to say.

Ruth pointed to her cigarette. 'I'll just finish this and we'll be up.'

'Perfect,' Natalie yelled as she skipped back inside.

Lucy glared at her. 'What the hell did you say that for?'

'I don't know. I was stalling for time,' Ruth protested. 'And you weren't saying anything, so it was getting weird.'

'And going up there with James won't be weird?' Lucy snapped as she marched back inside.

'Hey, it'll be something to tell the grandkids,' Ruth suggested lamely as Lucy slammed the patio doors closed.

'Yes. Guess what grandma did when she was younger,' Lucy said, shaking her head. 'I'm not going up there, by the way.'

Ruth frowned. 'What are we going to do then?'

Lucy pointed to the front door. 'We'll go and hide in the pub.'

Ruth nodded. 'Very mature.'

'Have you got a better idea?'

'No ... Come on then.'

They marched into the hallway, grabbed their coats, and went to the door.

'What's this?' Ruth said as she picked up a wrapped box, with a red ribbon around it, that was sitting on the doorstep.

Lucy frowned. 'That wasn't there earlier?'

'Looks like someone's left you a present.'

Undoing the ribbon, Lucy opened the box and saw expensive black silk underwear inside. 'Eh? I don't understand.'

Ruth looked up to the flat above. 'You don't think he still believes he can nip downstairs now he's engaged, do you?'

'He can fuck right off,' Lucy growled as she took out a card and read it – *Lucy, I've been watching you and you've been a very naughty girl. I hope these come in useful. MJ x*

Lucy's stomach turned as she showed the card to Ruth.

'Oh, my God!' Ruth gasped.

# CHAPTER 36

Gaughran and Benita walked up the garden path to his parents' house and he knocked on the door.

'So, this is where you lived as a kid?' Benita asked.

'Yep,' Gaughran said, and he pointed to a garden shed. 'I used to smoke Dunhill cigarettes behind there with my brother.'

'And snog your girlfriends?' she asked with a grin.

'I couldn't possibly tell you that,' Gaughran said and then pointed to some patio furniture. 'Although when I was fifteen, I tried to kiss Sarah White over there.'

'What happened?'

'She'd drunk about two litres of Strongbow cider, so she just projectile vomited all over me.'

'Eww,' Benita giggled and then pulled a face.

The door opened, and Celia peered out. 'Hello Tim.'

'Hi Mum. This is my friend Benita,' he explained. He had called earlier to tell her he might pop over and he was bringing a *friend*.

'Hello, Benita,' Celia beamed and ushered for them to come in. 'I'll put the kettle on, shall I?'

'Great idea, Mum,' Gaughran said as they walked into the kitchen.

'I love your home, Mrs Gaughran,' Benita said as Gaughran pulled out a chair and let her sit down.

'Oh, it's Celia, please,' she laughed. 'The only person who calls me Mrs Gaughran is my doctor, and he's a terrible man.'

Gaughran smiled at Benita and rolled his eyes. 'Mum, you only think he's a terrible man because he votes for the Green Party.'

'Yeah, it's a waste of a decent vote, isn't it?' Celia said as she busied herself getting some mugs from the cupboard. As she turned, she noticed Benita's face. 'Oh God, I didn't see your face. What happened to you, dear?'

'Long story,' Benita said with a kind smile. 'Tim has been showing me all your handiwork at his house. I'm very impressed.'

Celia gave them a look of modesty. 'Oh, I didn't really do anything.'

'Mum, you did everything in that house,' Gaughran said. 'If it was down to me, I'd still have cardboard boxes everywhere.'

Celia looked at Benita. 'Yeah, that's true. How did you two meet?'

Benita frowned. 'Yeah, that's a long story too.'

Celia smiled. 'Why don't you take off your coats. You'll stay for a bit, won't you, Tim?'

Gaughran beamed over at Benita. 'Yeah, we can stay for a bit, Mum.'

Your FREE book is waiting for you now

Get your FREE copy of the prequel to
the DI Ruth Hunter Series NOW
http://www.simonmccleave.com/vip-email-club
and join my VIP Email Club

# Acknowledgements

I will always be indebted to the people who have made this novel possible.

My mum, Pam, and my stronger half, Nicola, whose initial reaction, ideas and notes on my work I trust implicitly. And Dad, for his overwhelming enthusiasm.

Thanks also to Barry Asmus, former South London CID detective, for checking my work and explaining the complicated world of police procedure and investigation. My designer Stuart Bache for yet another incredible cover design. My superb agent, Millie Hoskins at United Agents, and Dave Gaughran and Nick Erick for invaluable support and advice.

Made in the USA
Las Vegas, NV
06 February 2023

66978925R00154